The Pilgrim's Tale

The Pilgrim's Tale

Roger Coombs

Published by www.lulu.com

ISBN 978-0-244-33327-0

Book formatted by www.bookformatting.co.uk.

Contents

Whilst in France researching his next book, an author stumbles on an ancient burial deep in the woods where he is looking for ceps, which leads him to discover the answer to a mystery regarding a long lost and valuable religious relic. He sends teasing clues to his daughter in London, fully expecting to tell her what he has found when he returns home, but then he dies suddenly. The clues have to be followed, leading a group of friends across France. However they are not alone. Unscrupulous crooks are on the same trail. Can the amateurs keep ahead of the professionals?

FOREWORD BY CAROLINE TEBBUTT

Roger Coombs wrote this book when he was in his early eighties. It took him many years. He tried very hard to get it published during his lifetime but whilst interest was shown he did not succeed. He died in 2011 leaving the manuscript, along with one other, for his family to read. His own words stated that we should not bother to try and get it published as it wasn't possible. This was before the days of self-publishing. I am his daughter and I am determined to prove him wrong.

Roger was born in Lewisham in 1924, attended Dulwich College Prep School and then at the age of thirteen, when his family moved to Cranbrook in Kent, he finished his schooling at Cranbrook School. At the age of eighteen he signed up for military service in the Indian Army. On the troopship to Bombay he met his first wife Shirley, who was serving in the First Aid Nursing Yeomanry as a radio operator. When they returned to England in 1947 they married. That year also began another important strand in Roger's life. He and Shirley moved to Cambridge and Roger went to Selwyn College to read Classics. Selwyn remained important to him throughout his life.

In the early 1950s Jonathan and Caroline were born to Roger and Shirley. After that marriage ended in 1963 Roger moved to Ashford and then in 1964 he bought a plot of land and had a house built in Goudhurst in Kent and also set up his own PR business. Soon after he met Anne, remarried and they had their two children, Marcus and Cathy. He lived in Goudhurst for the rest of his life.

His pleasures were many. He loved his home and his village and was an enthusiastic member of the local community, helping to set up the village website, music society and links with the Esterhazy Singers. He was also a regular member of the congregation at St Mary's church in Goudhurst.

Words were his business and his pleasure. He loved writing. His other interests were classical music, good food, wine, gardening, sketching, travelling, especially in France and good times with his family and friends. He was also a man with a deep religious belief and conviction.

My contribution to this book has been proof-reading and correcting obvious errors. It has meant that I have read and re-read it several times and I can feel him talking to me from the written page. The cover is a painting he did of a house where he spent a holiday with his wife Anne and the family. It is in the region of France where The Pilgrim's Tale is set and may even have been the inspiration for the book.

Caroline Tebbutt
July 2017

This book is dedicated to Anne.

1 - LEONARD

Two policemen in overalls and sturdy boots were supervised by the local inspector as they excavated the supposed grave in the woods. Standing next to me and watching their progress in silence was a journalist from the Sud-Ouest and the mayor of the tiny commune of Marcignac.

I had been searching for ceps in the private woodland below my house when I stumbled on two pieces of broken marble. Fitted together they bore an invocation incised in Roman characters: BENEDICTUS QUI VENIT IN N.D. - "Blessed is he who comes in the name of the Lord". Clearing the undergrowth I found a rectangle of white chips trodden into the earth. They seemed to mark the dimensions of a grave. I reported my find to the mairie the same day.

When the diggers had removed the dry earth to shoulder height, a piece of bone was suddenly revealed. The inspector called for his men to put down their picks and continue work with trowels and by hand. Gradually they uncovered a human skeleton, lying supine and seemingly intact. Its length was measured and found to be more than two metres. Male obviously and exceptionally tall, the forearms had been crossed over the man's chest. The cause of death was only too apparent; the skull was split in two by a deep cleft. The blow must have been extremely vicious.

I shivered as I imagined the brutal attack. Was this where it had taken place? The careful positioning of the body and crossed arms belied this, suggesting a ritual burial after the killing; but why here and not in the graveyard by the church a few kilometres away? Perhaps the victim was a man deemed unfit for hallowed ground.

'Nasty,' said the police inspector dryly, fingering the sharp-edged split in the skull. One of his men leaned down and picked up a white object, brushed off shreds of earth and passed it to his chief who examined it carefully before handing it to me. It was a small, intact scallop-shell, a hole bored through the hinge threaded with a thin strip of leather. Famously the shell was the emblem of St James carried by pilgrims to his shrine. We were close to one of the much travelled paths across France to Santiago de Compostela in NW Spain, the so-called Route Saint Jacques.

The inspector gestured towards the victim. 'A sudden conclusion to his pilgrimage, whoever he was. We'll probably never know, but the lab will date the bones. Long before my time, I guess, or there would have been a record. When I've closed the case you might like to have the shell as a souvenir, Monsieur Bray.' I nodded my thanks.

The reporter took several photographs of the skeleton. A brief account, with a picture of me holding the scallop shell, was published in the Sud-Ouest a fortnight later.

Auch, 17 Septembre 2005

GRUESOME DISCOVERY BY FAMOUS WRITER

The distinguished English writer Leonard Bray has come across a hidden grave in woods near the village of Marcignac in the Gers département. While searching for ceps Bray tripped over a piece of marble with a Latin inscription, BENEDICTUS QUI VENIT IN N.D. Clearing the undergrowth he found stones outlining what appeared to be a grave. Excavation by the police uncovered the skeleton of a man with his skull smashed in.

Police inspector Alain Carteret says: "It was a savage attack with a sharp and heavy instrument like an axe. The grave also contained a scallop-shell, the emblem of Saint Jacques. It would seem the victim was a pilgrim on the road to the saint's shrine in Galicia. A piece of his bone has been sent for radio carbon dating."

The police are confident that the killing took place long ago before records were kept. M. Bray, 54, said: "Rather gruesome, but it has given me something to think about. I have been wanting to write about the hazardous life of travellers on The Pilgrims' Road to Spain. There have been millions over the centuries."

A few days later I sent my daughter Julia one of my occasional postcards. It was as brief and teasing as usual when I am working abroad. I wrote:

Routine work, then <u>suddenly</u> the Castres connection has cropped up! Other excitements. A medieval murder and a theft that confounded the thief. If that's not enough, this place is <u>haunted</u>. Home quite soon, I hope. Much love, Dad.

The Castres connection was a reference to French forebears from way back. One member of our family had been a prominent landowner in the town of the same name, another was a priest burnt as a heretic during the French king's crusade against the Albigensian Heresy. Would Julia suppose the Heresy to be the subject of the book I was writing? She knew how much it interested me. It amused me to wonder what she would make of the rest of my deliberately oblique message. A theft couched in the form of a riddle? A haunting? She knew how much I relished riddles, rebuses, cryptograms and conundrums. When she sent me her tentative solutions I would mark them in red ink on a scale from beta-minus (frustratingly, no doubt) to an alpha-plus, but without comment. I never provided the answers before sending her the published book.

Julia is highly perceptive and has an enquiring mind. She wouldn't feel patronised. She valued my regard for her intelligence and had often tried to persuade me to share my work with her; to let her take on some of the tedious research which was her special skill and which is a major part of writing a book, but I'm afraid that all she got from me were paltry scraps and dark clues. I knew this was infuriating, but somehow she loved her doting father. We had always been close friends.

It would be good to be home again. I had been in France since April. The previous year I'd spent months in Parma working on an illustrated monograph of the little known medieval sculptor Benedetto Antelami. Ground research was my summer routine. Most of my new book would be drafted before I left Gascony.

I recalled various homecomings: particularly one Christmas when she was thirteen and I turned up unannounced at her school, whisked her away against all the rules to a slap-up tea in the town and presented her with a beautiful icon I had acquired in Greece - not a fake and therefore an illegal export, but I would much rather she had it than anyone else. For the present, all I'd told her was that I was staying at Le Belvédère in a small bastide called Marcignac near Auch. I assumed she would think this to be a chambre d'hôte of the kind I usually patronised.

A requiem mass for the repose of the pilgrim's soul was said in the little church of St Privat. I am neither a churchgoer nor an observer of social conventions, nevertheless I felt it my duty to be present at the last rites for the man who, as we now knew, had been in the forest since the 13th century and, but for my early morning foraging, would still be there. Who was he, and why had he been given a Christian burial so far from the village? A local plague perhaps?

The dead man's remains were not in the church. They had already been prepared for containment in a sarcophagus to be placed in the crypt. The priest and the mayor both agreed this was a proper resting-place for the man already celebrated as "The Unknown Pilgrim". The sarcophagus, said the mayor, would attract other pilgrims to the village. I took a cynical view of this blatant commercialism, but I had been strangely moved by the sight of the long skeleton in the lonely grave and the brief invocation on the fragments of marble that marked it.

My chance discovery gave a new spark to my work. Thinking about the mysterious pilgrim and his fate lifted me, it was as though a friendly hand had touched me and said 'Snap out of it, Bray! Isn't this what you've been waiting for?' Returning from the forest I sat at my work-table overlooking the woods and worked almost without a break for five days.

Looking round the little church, I surveyed the congregation as they assembled. Many I recognised as clients of the village café where I ate each day. One was my burly neighbour, the farmer Eugène Pontet who had left a basket of figs on my doorstep that morning. The mayor was among the last to arrive. Wearing a blue suit and his tricolour sash, he was accompanied by the inspector of police in uniform and a distinguished-looking, elderly man I knew by sight, Baron Edouard de Marcignac, a hugely rich art collector who owned a splendid château nearby. Next to the baron was a fair-haired, good-looking woman who, I assumed, must be his new English wife. Their surprising marriage was much talked about in the commune.

The Mass proceeded, there was no music. I wished the solemn Latin rite could have been used instead of the vernacular. The trite, modern words seemed out of place as a requiem for a medieval pilgrim. The priest, a young man with a fresh complexion and dark curly hair had prepared a homily for the edification of his distinguished congregation and read it ponderously, spinning out his moment centre stage.

I was almost the first to leave the church at the end of the requiem but my purpose to escape as quickly as possible was frustrated by the approach of the baron, who introduced himself in immaculate English.

'Monsieur Bray, this has been a moving occasion, don't you think?'

Not waiting for an answer, he gestured towards a remarkable looking man beside him who was watching me keenly. 'Do you know Monsieur Malvin?'

'No, I don't.'

We shook hands. I had heard of Malvin in the café-bar. He was said to be a dealer in antiquities and an occasional guest at the château where, they said, he was not well received by Madame de Marcignac. His appearance would have been striking anywhere, let alone among the villagers attending the service. His grey silk suit was beautifully cut, his face long and dark, his lips thin, his black eyes deep-set. The clasp of his hand was firm but the palms were soft and his finger nails fastidiously tapered, but his most striking feature was his head which seemed too large for his body. His speech was precise and his manner ingratiating.

'I have read, monsieur, that it was you who came across the grave.'

'It was just one of those chance discoveries.'

'Extraordinary after so many years.'

'Not really. People don't go into the woods.'

'That's true,' said Marcignac. 'As a boy I was always told it was a place to avoid so of course we went there and got lost. It was not a good experience.'

We were suddenly interrupted by a tall, fair-haired Englishman wearing casual clothes.

'You must be Leonard Bray.'

'I am.'

'Frank Middleton, The Sunday Telegraph. Here on holiday. I've enjoyed your books.' I knew his name but took his offered hand grudgingly.

'About the pilgrim. My newspaper could be interested. What's the story?'

'Just a poor sod who had a nasty accident eight hundred years ago. Head smashed in. End of his pilgrimage, end of story.'

Middleton persisted. 'You live here, Mr Bray?'

'No, in London.'

'I have a camera. Would you mind a picture? Won't take a moment.'

I raised a hand and shook my head. 'Sorry. As I say, there's no story. Please excuse me, I have work to do.'

The man smiled feebly, shrugged and walked away.

Marcignac remarked: 'A rather pushy fellow, don't you think?'

'I can't stand prying journalists.'

'All the same, it is quite an interesting story, even for the London press. Do you intend to write about it?'

'I'm not a crime writer, Monsieur. Anything I wrote about the pilgrim would be fiction, wouldn't it?'

Malvin said: 'You never write fiction? Isn't that what most people buy?'

'I don't write for most people.'

Declining an invitation from Marcignac to the château for some refreshment and, with relief that the ceremony and pleasantries were over, I excused himself and walked briskly to the rented Renault I had parked nearby. Without a backward glance I started the engine and took the road back to Le Belvédère.

The house stood next to a large barn at the bottom of a rutted track lined by pollarded chestnuts, some distance from the village. The land and the house looked neglected, as indeed it had been since the death of the previous owner some four years ago. Typical of the region, the house was sturdily built of limestone with a steep roof and small, shuttered windows. It was getting dark but before unlocking the entrance I went across to the barn where I found one of the two large doors slightly ajar. I was sure I had closed them. Peering inside I called out: 'Etes-vous là? I waited a few moments and repeated the question more loudly. No result. The wrong language? Latin perhaps? I tried 'Quis ibi est?' Several times. Still getting no response (what did I expect?) I backed away, shut the barn door, barred it securely and closed the heavy padlock. Was I getting paranoid about noises in the night?

I went into the house, lit a candle and carried it upstairs. Opening the shutters at one end of my work-room, I stood looking out at the barn and beyond it to the woods where I had found the grave. Turning away from the window, I took from my pocket a postcard of the church at Marcignac and pinned it to the wall next to three other pictures. One was a photo of the statue of St James in the cathedral at Santiago de Compostela, one a postcard of the Abbaye de Flaran, an ancient foundation not far from Marcignac, and the third a photocopy I had made of a page from a barely decipherable Latin manuscript.

The only other picture in the room was a photograph of Julia in a silver frame on my writing table: not a studio portrait but one I had taken myself when we were in Cambridge on a day trip the previous year. We had walked along the Backs and turned into the gates of King's, pausing on the stone bridge across the river for me to take several shots of Julia leaning on the bridge with the Chapel as a background. She hated being photographed but stood still while I tried to make her laugh or even smile, which I managed to do by telling her a clerihew about the Master of Christ's being woken by poltergeists. I failed to catch the brief smile however. The photo that stood opposite me on my work-table was of a dark-haired girl with a rosy Renoir face looking serious, self-contained and carelessly beautiful.

2 - JULIA

I got my father's latest postcard on the day I was to meet Nell Sheridan for a long-promised visit to the Wallace Collection. Though Nell, a professional illustrator, was ten years my senior (pushing thirty-five), we had become close friends. Having met as members of a mixed-voice London choir we soon discovered common interests that drew us together. I envied Nell's talent as an artist and was amused by her vaguely Bohemian lifestyle. For her part Nell had said she admired my capacity to organise and direct my life. Hers certainly needed direction.

Neither of us had a man in our lives; Nell because the latest dud experience had left her numb, while I was content with my celibate state. My work was enough; men were a distraction. I knew Nell thought this a poor excuse and also claimed I was wasting myself on the Civil Service, even in the upper echelons when there were so many more interesting opportunities for my enterprise and expertises.

We met under the portico of Hertford House in Manchester Square. I was there on time, Nell arrived in a taxi twenty minutes late, with profuse apologies. As we climbed the grand staircase to the first floor she said it had to be a short visit, primarily to introduce me to the Collection by means of a few of her favourite pictures. The first of these we came upon immediately in the large top floor gallery: the portrait of Rembrandt's son Titus.

'It shows such affection,' said Nell. 'How could anyone doubt he painted it?'

I was charmed by Reynolds' delectable painting of little Miss Bowles and her dog. This, like the Rembrandt, was heart-warming in a different way and I could see Nell was pleased by my responses.

Then nearby I was suddenly astonished to be confronted by Franz Hals' so-called Laughing Cavalier looking as fresh as if he had been painted yesterday.

'I didn't know *he* was here,' I remarked lamely.

'I told you! The Collection is one of London's best-kept secrets. Shamefully so.'

We lingered over the romantic Watteaus and Fragonards on the floor below and smiled at the well-nourished, marshmallow-pink, Boucher women on the staircase. In the shop by the entrance I bought a postcard of Fragonard's The Swing to send to my father.

We talked about him over lunch in a café-restaurant round the corner from the gallery.

'He hopes to be home soon, whatever that means.'

'What is he working on?'

'I've no idea. He never lets on till he's finished. Superstition, I think.'

'How tantalising!'

I handed over his postcard. Nell read it with raised eyebrows.

'A medieval murder!'

'He's come across something. He wouldn't make it up.'

'And the haunted place. Is that the house where he's living?'

'Could be. Then again perhaps not. He's staying in a chambre d'hôte called Le Belvédère. The whole thing might be another tease. He loves riddles and puzzles. It's a game we play when he's away. Tantalising, as you say.'

Nell turned the card over and studied the picture. 'The Cathedral, Auch. Where's that?'

'Gascony. South-west France. I've often wanted to go there. I've got some leave due. Could you get away? We could fly to Toulouse and hire a car. Give my father a surprise.'

Nell smiled ruefully. 'I wish I could. I hope to get some valuable work in Paris. I need it, Julia.'

We left the restaurant, agreeing to find a date for a concert or the opera.

When I got home there was a worrying message my mother had left on the phone. 'Please call me as soon as you get home. Any time, it doesn't matter.'

She sounded distressed. It was clear something was wrong, but nothing so terrible and unexpected as the news when I called back. My mother could only say it as it was, that my father was dead.

I felt numb and sick. I stumbled onto a chair, one hand covering my mouth. My mother was talking, explaining, but I didn't take it in. It couldn't be true, Dad was never ill, he couldn't afford to be ill. Too much to do he always said. His latest postcard lay on my writing table, waiting to be pinned up with all the others. "Home soon." There would be more postcards, wouldn't there? Something to say it was all a mistake.

As I began to hear what my mother was saying I knew he would never come home. He had died suddenly as a result of a fall from a window. The man I loved so deeply and saw so rarely would never come home. Had he been in great pain? Had he called out for me before he died? His photograph stood on the table by the telephone, the man whose wisdom and integrity I revered and whose rare words of praise I valued more than those of my much respected tutor at King's, even those of the Provost and my chief, the Permanent Secretary.

I needed to be with someone. My mother was still talking. What was she saying? It made no sense. I would go to Nell. Nell would be home by now. No need to telephone first.

I managed to say: 'I'll come and see you in the morning, Mum. Will you be all right till then?'

Later I remembered the irony of that remark.

After soothing my mother and putting down the telephone, I sat for a minute or two with my eyes closed, taking deep breaths. I was still wearing my overcoat. Picking up my handbag, I went down the stairs to the street door, holding the handrail to steady myself.

Though it was well past midnight the street was busy. It always was round here. People leaving dinner parties, people going to clubs. I stood at the kerb for five minutes, looking for a taxi. One approached with its light on. I waved an arm but a couple further down the street had already hailed it. I walked on, looking for a lull in the traffic. A cab appeared on the other side of the street going in the wrong direction. No matter. I raised an arm, yelled 'Taxi!' and stepped into the road. I never saw the cyclist coming up fast by the kerb inside a stationary car.

This is a dream. Extraordinary but not at all frightening. It was like being in a theatre, looking down from an upper box, stage left. I was a casual and solitary spectator, calmly watching with close interest a performance which I knew ought to concern me though I had a feeling of total detachment.

The scene was clear enough. Centre stage a hospital table; around it green-clad figures obscuring my view of the patient's face. Lights focused closely on the supine figure. Soft music playing. A string quartet. Haydn. I knew it well. One of the opus 54 I thought, the adagio. The slow and solemn progression of the music was an analogue of the doctor's almost imperceptible movements and his concentration.

One of the nurses moved slightly to one side so that I caught a glimpse of the patient. This was suddenly and immensely disconcerting. Can you see yourself in dreams? There was an alarm. I watched calmly as the theatre surged from *molto adagio* to *presto ma non troppo*. Too late, I was sure. They were wasting their time; the patient was already dead.

The players were well rehearsed. In seconds a piece of equipment was brought to the table, connections were swiftly made. They were hitting me, as though to make me wake up. It was pointless, futile, I wouldn't wake up. I wished they would stop what they were doing.

A bright light was shining into my eyes, blinding. Everything else became black, except this light in the distance. It was like being in a narrow tunnel and I was travelling through it towards the light. I was unafraid, it was going to be all right. The soft voices said so. Among them I recognised my father's voice. It will be all right, he said. Now I could see him outlined through the dazzling light. His hands were stretched towards me like when I was a little girl and he had just come back from one of his trips abroad. Behind him, more faintly, a figure in a monk's white habit, a worrying figure, with a pleading expression as though asking me to recognise him, then fading. I didn't recognise him. My father too was fading. I couldn't reach him. I don't want to go back, I thought. You must go back now, he called. It will be all right. You cannot come over yet. Not yet. Take care of the jewel. Then all will be well.

A doctor came to see me in the evening. I was pleasantly drowsy. His smooth, round face reminded me of a writer who used to come to dinner now and then when my father was at home.

'Comfortable?' he asked, taking my hand in a gentle grasp.

'Yes, thank you.'

'Everything is fine,' he said reassuringly.

'What happened?'

'You had an accident. A cyclist knocked you down.'

'I don't remember.'

'We were a bit worried for a while, but everything is fine,' he repeated.

Something made me say: 'I saw what was happening. Me on the table, you and two others bending over me. There was a panic, wasn't there? My heart stopped, you revived me. I didn't want you to do it. I was moving away to somewhere good, then you brought me back.'

He was looking at me curiously. Physically weak and obviously sedated, I felt myself near to tears of anger at being disbelieved. The memory of seeing and hearing my father was still so vivid, I was sure it was neither a dream nor an hallucination. I had watched the crash team at work. The doctor didn't deny I had been revived.

Afterwards I wished I'd kept quiet. My physical condition was weak enough without the risk of being thought potty into the bargain. I would say nothing to any of the nurses. I shut my eyes and conjured up the comforting, gentle vision. Dad was in a good place.

My mother came the next day. She sat by the bed and listened patiently as I recounted every detail of what I now recognised as a classic near-death experience.

'I really wanted to go. Dad was waiting for me on the other side. It was beautiful there, golden and he looked so calm. I wish you could have seen him. It wasn't a dream, Mum. Much more vivid than any dream, totally real, but he said I couldn't go to him. Not yet, he kept saying, not yet. And there was this other spectral figure, a monk.'

My mother frowned. 'A monk? Your father was an atheist. He wouldn't have anything to do with monks.'

'I know, but he gave me this extraordinary message. "Take care of the jewel", he said. That was all. I've been worrying about it ever since. We don't have any family jewels to speak of, do we? He couldn't have meant a real jewel. A symbol of something valuable, maybe.'

My mother told me not to worry about it. I had been badly shocked and drugged; I was bound to feel peculiar for a while. I insisted that everything I'd seen was real. 'The monk seemed to be party to the message. He was a bit eerie. And I had this glimpse of the other side - a kind of golden light - and then I had to come back. It was real and it was good.'

There were no complications from my accident, just a few abrasions, severe bruising and concussion. One of the nurses told me there had been a moment of anxiety when my pulse stopped, but all the tests were negative. I was advised to take things easy, maybe go away for a week or two.

I called Nell from the hospital twice but got a recorded message each time. The same happened when I returned home a week later. At last, Nell returned my call, full of apologies. She'd been in Paris, hadn't expected to be away so long and, typically, had left her address book at home. She'd read about my father in Le Figaro and was totally devastated. Was I all right? Was there anything she could do?

We lunched together the following day at Mon Plaisir. Nell was solicitous, I was distracted. I had brought the obituary published in

The Times - half a page with a photograph. Nell read it in silence. 'Quite a man!' she said, clasping my hand as she gave back the press cutting.

'My mother's had hundreds of letters,' I said as I folded it carefully and put it back in my handbag. 'There's to be a memorial service in St Martin's. No date yet.'

Nell was reading the obituary.

'He died after an accident, it says. How tragic. And he was only 54. What happened?'

'He fell from a ladder outside the house. A casual caller found him. He never recovered consciousness.'

I showed Nell a letter from the hospital in Auch informing my mother - with the director's deepest sympathy - of Monsieur Bray's death from severe head injuries as the result of a fall. His personal effects were being sent under separate cover. The director asked what arrangements Madame Bray wished to make for the funeral.

I explained: 'My mother's bringing him home - when she feels able. But I've *seen* him, Nell! He spoke to me. Honest.'

I recounted my near-death experience. 'It wasn't at all frightening. I really wanted to go. He was waiting for me. It was more vivid than any dream, totally real.' I took a deep breath. 'You do believe me? My mother doesn't. I tell you that's exactly what happened.'

Nell frowned. 'I've heard of things like that. Very strange.'

I stared at her challengingly. 'My mother puts it down to concussion. I saw him as clearly as I'm seeing you and there was this other somewhat spectral figure in the habit of a Cistercian monk. No one I've ever seen, I'm sure.'

'A monk? That's strange too.'

'You think I was dreaming?'

'The mind can play peculiar tricks.'

'So I'm going off my rocker.'

'I didn't mean that, Julia. It must have been very upsetting. Seeing your father like that.'

'Not upsetting, uplifting. I know he's all right, somewhere good. You can't imagine. But he had a strange message for me, about taking care of what he called "the jewel". It doesn't mean a thing to me. I asked my mother whether she knew of some kind of a jewel he might have brought back from a visit abroad or something he might regard as a precious jewel.'

'And does she?'

'Nothing. All she knew was that there were books he'd asked her to keep safely. She got a bookseller to look through them. He offered her only a few hundred pounds so she put them in a box in the attic.'

'You ought to have another look, Julia. There might be something there.'

'So you do believe me?'

Nell nodded. 'It all sounds very weird but I believe you saw your father, as you say. What about his books then?'

'I have looked right through them. The bookseller was right. You wouldn't get much for them.'

'A jewel could be concealed in the spine of a book.'

'I don't think he meant a real jewel.'

'What then?'

'There has to be a connection with the monk. Why else was he there?'

'What about your father's papers? He may have left some kind of a clue. Otherwise why just talk of a jewel without a hint of what he meant? From what you say he assumed you would understand.'

'There was no time for explanation. It all happened in a few seconds, and then I had to go back. I thought of his papers, of course. There's a mountain of stuff. He travelled a great deal and never threw anything away. It would take days to go through everything. So far I've found nothing relating to a jewel of any kind.'

A week later I called Nell to say my mother had found what we were looking for. A package had been sent home by my father, addressed to himself. It had been delivered shortly before my mother got news of his death. She had put it in his study at the time and forgotten about it.

We met in the café upstairs in the Sainsbury Wing of the

National Gallery. I handed Nell a postcard. 'This came today in an envelope. My father must have mailed it just before his accident. It warns me to have nothing to do with a man called Malvin. The newspaper says he was the caller who found him after his fall.'

'What was he doing there?'

'Visiting my father, he told the police. He's a dealer in antiquities, not to be trusted, Dad says. He sent me the postcard in a sealed envelope.'

Nell studied the postcard and envelope. 'You don't think....?'

I said: 'I don't know what to think.'

Not looking up, I placed a large envelope on the table between us and proceeded to withdraw its contents piece by piece.

'Exhibit A. A document in French dated 1651. The script is difficult to read, but it is clearly the title to a property, a house in a place called Marcignac in the département of the Gers. At first I thought my father must have found this in some local antiquary's shop. He liked all old things. It's nice enough to be framed and displayed but then I saw the name of the owner of the house, Robert de Castres.'

'The name on his earlier postcard. So it could be a family property?'

'He'd have told me, wouldn't he?'

I produced another document.

'Exhibit B. An agreement for the purchase of a property consisting of a house and 3.25 hectares of land near the village of Marcignac. It was signed on the 16th May 2005 by the notaire, Jacques Ambialet of Auch, the vendor, Madame Sabine Cussac of Condom and the buyer.'

I pointed to the buyer's name which Nell read out aloud.

'Monsieur Leonard Francis James Bray de Londres. Goodness! He never said anything about the house?'

'Not a word. It's called Le Belvédère. That was his address until …' I hesitated for the right words, something neutral. 'Until his accident. I had always assumed it was a pension - the kind of place he usually stayed in.'

I had often tried to picture my father's life there - a reclusive and scholarly English writer working in a remote corner of France; the discipline of solitary hours at his desk; the daily stint of so many hundred words. Did he find interesting people he could talk to when he set his work aside?

'Why the secrecy?' Nell asked. 'Why do you think he bought the house? He could easily have rented somewhere.'

I said nothing, but delved into the envelope again and produced a spiral-bound and typewritten manuscript of more than a hundred numbered pages.

'Exhibit C. Journal d'un Pèlerin by François de Castres. A recent annotated translation from the Latin by a professor at the University of Montpellier. A numbered copy, one of only ten. The original, according to the professor, is a 13th century account of a pilgrimage from Lombardy to the shrine of Saint James in Santiago de Compostela in Spain. They set out in the year 1212. The editor's foreword says that François de Castres was a priest who became a monk of the Cistercian order, but he never reached his goal as he was taken seriously ill at Flaran in France. That's near where my father was living. There's an abbey there, founded in 1151.'

I passed a slip of paper to Nell. 'And I found this next to a footnote by the editor. My father's handwriting. The only note he made in the whole document.'

The neatly pencilled comment consisted of just seven words. *"So what did he do with it?"* The footnote by the editor read: *Le texte original est redigé "Ego tradere offendi Rem Sanctam"*

Nell shrugged apologetically: 'I've forgotten my Latin.'

I gave her what was intended to be a withering look. 'Nell, it means the text is rendered as "I have failed to hand over the holy thing".'

'What holy thing?'

'The professor calls it a joyau. My French dictionary gives that as an artefact of gold. A jewel.'

I passed The Pilgrim's Journal across the table. 'Read it right through, Nell. It's an extraordinary story.'

3 - MALVIN

Sitting alone at the table by the window overlooking the Vieu Port in Bastia I was sure that, over the years, my visits to the café-restaurant on the quai must have aroused curiosity and speculation among the regulars who lunched there. It was a simple place that probably saw few strangers but it was a convenient stop for me before going sailing to La Spezia or Marseille. The food was just about OK. Rather than taking the menu du jour I usually ordered an entrecôte and a carafe of rouge, smoked a cigarillo with my coffee, paid my bill and left without speaking to anyone but the waiter. By my speech he would have marked me down as a native-born Corsican but I discouraged questions. I had noticed one of the regulars as a member of the Customs Service at the port and he would have been to tell the other clients that my passport named me as André Malvin, that I had arrived that day on the morning ferry from Marseille and quickly drove off in the direction of Casamozza.

This day I was not in my usual hurry to leave. I lit a second cigarillo and stared out of the window. At midday there was never much to be seen on the quai or in the alleyways between the tall, crumbling tenements that fringed the old port on three sides, but I was not interested in the view from the window. Glancing frequently at my watch, I was waiting as patiently as I could for the neighbouring table to be vacated so I wouldn't be observed when I checked the package I was carrying in my briefcase.

The lunchtime clients were irritatingly slow to leave. There was little more than an hour before the Corsica Serena would sail from the Nouveau Port. At last, unable to wait any longer, I left my half-empty wine-glass and the carafe on the table and took my briefcase into the toilet.

The heavy parcel was wrapped in brown paper and tied with string secured by wax seals. The seals were untouched. I broke them, untied the string and put on the pair of kid gloves that lay under the package. A yellow silk handkerchief wrapped the book, exactly as I'd arranged it five weeks earlier. No one had touched it. Unfolding the handkerchief and opening the goatskin covers as delicately as I could with my gloved finger-nails, I turned to the second folio and stared again with amazement at the illustration on the reverse, an illustration for which alone among all the others someone would pay a fortune.

The book had been a chance discovery while prospecting in the library of a remote and rather desolate abbey in Liguria. It had been tucked behind a larger volume on a high shelf and as soon as I began to turn the pages I could see why it had been kept out of sight. I looked again at the beautifully ornamented first page. *CANTICUM CANTICORUM*. The Latin had meant nothing to me at the time, but I knew at once that the work was of the finest quality. As for the larger illustrations, these were beyond belief. Chance had led me to something quite extraordinary, for which private collectors would compete avidly.

The librarian was an elderly monk. By careful questioning I discovered that he knew little about the collection of vellum and leather-bound folios and quartos in his care. All he could say were that some were as old as the foundation itself and some possibly even older. The possibility that the Canticum might have gone unnoticed for many years was suggested by the haphazard way in which the library shelves were stocked and the absence (confirmed by the librarian) of a proper catalogue. This, he said with a rueful smile, was a task for which he could devote little time between the many daily offices from Matins to Compline.

I decided to 'borrow' the book and obtain an estimate of its worth. It would be a simple matter later to return it to the shelves, pretend that I had an interested client and enter negotiations for its purchase, or at least to handle the sale on behalf of the brotherhood. I formulated a simple plan such as would appeal to simple men.

20

Noting the need for major repairs to the abbey's crumbling stonework, and most essentially to the roofs of the chapel and refectory, I felt the abbot would find it difficult to reject a generous offer of much needed funds in return for parting with just one book from the library. Though they would have to release the Canticum, they would have the assurance that it would be in Christian hands.

My judgement of the book's potential interest proved sound, embarrassingly so. The Canticum Canticorum, as I now knew, was a very early illuminated manuscript of The Song of Songs. The smart-suited antiquarian bookseller I consulted in Milan was ecstatic. Though it was a love poem, and a very sensual one, he was sure the text had never been illustrated in such an erotic way. He stared in silence at successive folios, occasionally turning back for a second look. His opinion, after a good deal of expressive murmuring, was that the book probably dated from the eleventh century and had been rebound in goatskin covers some two hundred years later.

'You know, I'm sure, signor, that this is a contentious part of Holy Scripture. It is explained away by theologians as an allegory for the bond of love between God and Israel. These illustrations, however, suggest no such thing. Do you read Latin? See this page here: "How beautiful are your breasts, my sister, my bride! Your love is more fragrant than wine, and your perfumes sweeter than any spices." And it goes on. I confess this is a passage that I remember from when I was a young student long ago.'

He continued to turn the pages, murmuring to himself and shaking his head. 'One would like to know more about its provenance, of course, but there is no doubt of the quality or authenticity of these pages. No doubt you have it insured? In my opinion it should be covered for not less than a million dollars.'

I was stunned into silence. The sale of so rare and valuable a book would alert the antiquarian world and the abbot would surely hear of it, even in this remote corner of Italy. The irony of its unexpected value escaped me for the moment.

Half-hoping the expert in Milan was mistaken and that the true worth might be much less, I took the Canticum Canticorum to a well-known dealer in Genoa who, after a close examination and much tutting, declared it to be quite the most extraordinary book he'd ever handled.

'It would be of immense interest to collectors, and to others too, because of the unusual illustrations,' he said, turning the leaves carefully and using a glass to study details.

'And this too is most interesting, isn't it?' the bookseller added, turning to one of the vellum end-papers and pointing with a slim finger. 'No doubt you have seen this? An inscription by another hand at a much later date.' He switched on a powerful reading-light and examined the end-paper for a minute or two. 'Anno Domini MCCXVII, it says, the year 1217. The script is difficult but it appears to be an inventory of sacred objects in the possession of the Abbazia di San Benedetto, wherever that might be. The location of the abbey is not stated. The inventory was prepared, the writer records, in tempore pestilentiae.'

He looked up at me and closed the book with a dramatic gesture. 'The Plague. Whole villages were wiped out. The monks must have known their community risked extinction and evidently made a record of treasures they hoped to save, but doubtless, signor, you've already come to the same conclusion.'

I nodded. The dealer's enthusiasm for the book was not welcome. With as much feigned courtesy as I could manage, I declined the offer of further help 'for the time being', shook hands, was bowed out of the premises and went back to my hotel to ponder the situation.

Security was the immediate problem. Insurance was out of the question, even if it were affordable. I do not trust banks, but a family house in the mountains of Corsica is as safe a stronghold as any. I would leave my find there while I considered what ought to be done. The inscription on the end-paper, if I could unravel it, might yield something of value that I could exploit even if I couldn't persuade the abbot to let me sell the book.

I had no Latin beyond the words of the Mass that had been drilled into me as a boy by the village priest, but the discipline of those days now gave me an idea. Priests knew Latin. Sitting in the

hotel bedroom I made a laborious copy of the text on
writing paper and went out into the city streets to look for

I visited four before finding an elderly priest whose de
when talking with other visitors suggested he might be both friendly
and guileless. The priest listened courteously to my fabricated
account; of how the Latin text had been found on a sheet of paper in
a book bequeathed to me by my father's brother; of how I believed
it might relate to a catalogue my uncle, an art historian, had been
preparing for a museum in Sicily but never completed; of how, for
my aunt's sake, I wished to commission the work anew but first
needed to know whether this document was of any significance.

I spun out my story with elaborations and irrelevancies, hoping
to distract my listener and make him impatient to be getting on with
the work of translation in return for a donation to the church. The
white-haired priest nodded all the while, looking at me over the top
of his spectacles, and eventually took the paper out of my hand with
a murmured: 'Scuse, signore' and began to read.

'It is not difficult, my son. You are correct. It is a catalogue. If
you will come into my room, I will write it down for you in Italian.'

He did this deliberately, in a beautiful hand and with
excruciating slowness. When he had finished, I handed him some
euros which the priest at once declared to be most generous. Too
generous? Hoping to deflect further inquiry by a diversion, I
suggested that, if time could be spared, perhaps we could depart
somewhere for a little light refreshment.

Time could indeed be spared. After several glasses of wine in a
nearby café, and then (as further time could perhaps be spared) a
bottle of rosso to accompany tortelloni, a veal chop, followed by a
granita, coffee and a generous measure of grappa, there were
amicable farewells and further expressions of gratitude by the priest
as he made a slightly unsteady departure. I was sure the old man
would be left with recollections of a pleasant few hours but little
else.

Back in my hotel, I examined the slip of paper with the
translation the priest had made. It was, as the dealer in Genoa had
surmised, an inventory, but an unusual one. It consisted of a list of

23

treasures removed from a certain Abbazia di San Benedetto in 1217. The importance of the chalices, patens, crucifixes, reliquaries and other religious objects was obvious. Against a description of each item was set the name of the religious foundation to which it had been sent for safe-keeping.

Not sure how to make use of this information, but instinctively feeling that it might offer a profitable alternative to my original plan, I decided I first needed to confirm what had happened to each item that was recorded. Back in Marseille, I set my nephew Carlo, a keen young art student, the task of checking whether all the listed treasures were in the hands of the abbeys, priories and churches to which they had been assigned.

Carlo's report, after weeks of research, was at first disappointing. All the religious foundations were Benedictine or Cistercian and still in existence. Most were in Italy, a few in France and all had confirmed to Carlo that the items sent to them at the time of the Plague were either still in their possession or were now in museums, galleries or private collections. However, there was one item Carlo couldn't trace. This was a reredos said to be by the 12th century sculptor Benedetto Antelami. Despite following every possible line of inquiry, he could find no proof of its existence at any time (he stressed the words). Leading authorities on Antelami dismissed the possibility that an unknown work of the 11th century master sculptor might be extant.

The list on the end-paper of the Canticum Canticorum recorded that the Antelami reredos had been sent to the great Abbaye de Cluny in Burgundy. Carlo added a note to say that the abbey had been closed in 1790 and largely demolished after the Revolution. Regretfully he didn't have time to go to Cluny and investigate personally but he felt sure that, if the abbey had ever possessed the reredos, it would have been recorded and in any case widely known. Antelami was a highly regarded and influential sculptor of his period. Carlo's opinion was that the reredos must have been incorrectly attributed.

I thanked and rewarded my nephew. I was well content. I now knew who might be persuaded to pay handsomely for this information; a man, moreover, who could certainly afford to buy the book if it were for sale, and who would reward me fairly for arranging a deal.

The Corsica Serena sailed on time. Sitting at a table in a quiet corner of one of the lounges, I sipped a pastis as I re-read Carlo's report. He had done well. I put the document back in my briefcase, took out the Wall Street Journal I had bought before leaving Italy and looked up the latest bid prices of my investments. Within a few hours I would be in La Spezia. The next day I would drive to the abbey and replace the book in the library. Then I would lay my plans and contact Edouard de Marcignac.

4 - NELL

I couldn't think what to make of Julia's story. I'd read accounts of near-death experiences in magazines. Julia's vision of her father seemed to be so exactly as others had reported after a near-fatal accident that it might have come out of a textbook, but what was I to believe of the coincidence of the spectral monk in Cistercian robes (Julia knows things like that) and the Cistercian author of Le Journal d'un Pèlegrin, with the professor's commentary?

'Read it right through' Julia had instructed me. My French was just about good enough without looking up too many words, so on my first free evening I settled down with a long G&T and opened the first page.

We set out from the Abbazia San Benedetto early in the morning after Easter Sunday Mass in the year of Our Lord 1212, wonderfully fully refreshed from celebrating the glorious Resurrection. Our party numbers fifty-four souls, of whom nine are members of our order. We expect to meet many others within a few days, and in the weeks ahead to join countless numbers from all over Christendom making their pilgrimage to the saint's shrine.

At first it was not an easy read. François de Castres's account of his journey to Santiago de Compostela in Galicia had long introspective passages. He seemed to be a deeply religious man in personal torment for some deeply felt wrong he had done someone. Was this the reason for his pilgrimage? An expiation for a serious sin? Not principally so, as I discovered after a while.

As a record of a remarkable journey across France and Northern Spain the Journal was a disappointment. It conveyed nothing of the perils or privations that would have been faced by medieval travellers in unknown country. There were no descriptions of the regions they passed through, no interest in the people they may have met and no mention of François's fellow pilgrims except for his closest companion, a man he called Magnus, presumably because of his stature. François de Castres seemed to be detached from everything around him, caught up in self-pity. It was not until well into the journey that he let it be known he was on a secret mission. From then on, I was gripped.

The abbot in Lombardy had delegated François to take a "most precious" relic to the shrine of Saint James. This was the "Holy Thing", the res sancta, translated by the editor as le joyau - the jewel. According to a long footnote, the relic was a legendary ring said to have been given to Saint James the Great by a merchant from Ephesus not long after the Crucifixion. James wore the ring as a symbol of 'la promesse et le pouvoir du Dieu vivant' - the promise and power of the Living God.

The editor noted that James was the first of the apostles to be martyred. "After he had been beheaded by Herod Agrippa, the ring is supposed to have been removed from his finger by one of the women disciples and sent to a secret place of safety. No more is recorded of it until centuries later during the Crusades to the Holy Land when a much venerated ring, supposed to have been that of Saint James, was discovered in a remote church and taken by the returning Crusaders to Béziers in the Languedoc. No sooner was it thought to be in safe keeping in a Christian land than it was almost lost again in 1209 during the massacre in Béziers of adherents to the Albigensian Heresy. One of the few survivors is said to have fled to Lombardy, taking the ring with him."

It was an extraordinary story, as Julia had said. I had never heard the legend of St James's ring. François made no further reference to it until near the end of the Journal. After becoming very sick with a fever on the road towards the northern passes of the Pyrenees, he rested at a hostel in Gascony and was taken to the newly founded abbey at Flaran. Too ill to continue the journey, and thought to be near death, he abandoned his pilgrimage. His mission had failed. He said nothing of what had happened to the "Holy

Thing" entrusted to him, only that he had not completed his task.

'He kept it,' Julia said confidently the next day in her flat, handing me a large ice-laden Campari and soda across the kitchen table.

'What makes you say that?'

'He says so himself. "I have failed to hand over The Holy Thing." I read this as a confession of guilt rather than an admission of failure.'

'Okay, he kept it, but it would have been discovered, his abbot would have instituted a search. It was a very important relic.'

'If it had been discovered, whether then or at any time afterwards, someone would have taken it to the shrine, wouldn't they?'

'You're going to tell me it's not there.'

'I've checked. No one's even heard of it. No more than I had.'

'Stolen?'

'By whom and what for? It would have no value without its provenance, the connection with St James. It was just a ring.'

'So where could it be?'

'I believe my father knew.'

'But why would François want to keep it?'

'As some kind of talisman, perhaps. You've read the Journal. He was wracked with guilt for some reason. He keeps calling upon God's mercy. Peccavi. Miserere mei. Over and over again. For some oppressive sin, presumably. Tiresome, I thought, like verbal flagellation. Perhaps he thought the ring had special powers, that it could heal him, that if he parted with it, he would be lost.'

'I suppose it's plausible.'

'I'm sure my father thought so, or something like that. I also think he knew what happened to it.'

'What makes you say that?'

'Intuition. And the message he gave me.'

5 - LOUISE

I had instructed the steward, with Edouard's amused approval, that from the first warm days of April breakfast should be taken on the south-east terrace instead of the Delacroix Room where he used to eat alone before our marriage. The table with its white cloth and polished silverware was set by the footman so I could look across the park to the rolling Gascon landscape where the stone buildings of a hilltop farm glowed in the morning sun.

The move from the dark-panelled breakfast room to the sunny terrace was one of a few modest alterations I had dared to make to the daily routine of the château. By ordering such changes I hoped to establish my authority as the new châtelaine without seeming to challenge the management of the household, which was in every respect beyond criticism. Despite the impeccable behaviour of the servants, I sensed it would take a long time to gain their respect. I was neither French nor, in their eyes, of the right caste for the wife of a French nobleman. What is more, they knew I had been his mistress since becoming the tenant (rent free, it was said) of one of his properties near the château.

Edouard dismissed servants' gossip as being of no account. He was a respected widower of some years, not an errant husband. As for his friends, the French of his class took a pragmatic view of sexual liaisons, legitimate or otherwise. His improbable courtship of me was amusing only in that he had failed to move me into the château until we were wedded. All very right and proper.

My new-found state as the wife of the Baron Edouard de Marcignac seemed quite unreal, as I had written to my old school chum Nell Sheridan.

I still feel a complete impostor. Edouard is so considerate but you cannot imagine what it's like to be nominally in charge of this place. Of course, everyone knows I'm not really in charge. I'm consulted about menus, but the only time I've dared to comment on one of the chef's proposals was to steer him away as tactfully as I could from his suggestion of Le Rosbif avec Le Yorkshire Pudding on the occasion of a dinner for the British ambassador. Edouard handles the guest lists. In any case, I don't know anyone to ask to dinner other than the few of his friends we invite to bridge or tennis, and the social protocol down here is so tricky I'd rather leave it to him.

Don't misunderstand me, Nell. Life is good. I love being properly married, and as well as spoiling me with endless indulgences, Edouard is very loving - not passionately or madly but gently and comfortingly. I thought long and hard before accepting him and it won't be my fault if this marriage is not a success.

Now to the point. I have persuaded Edouard to invite your London choir to take part in our summer arts festival. Pamphlet enclosed. I can billet everyone in local houses. You and Julia must stay here of course. If her father is still working near here that will be specially nice for her. Ring or write soon. Not e-mail please! Lots of love. Lou.

After a moment's thought I added a postscript:

And what about Alastair Hadley? Are you still seeing him? He buys wine for Edouard from time to time. Shall I invite him too?

My husband was an early riser. The long years since the death of his first wife had fixed him in a routine which, to his relief, I insisted he should in no way change on my account. By seven o'clock he was generally exercising one of his hunters across the park in the company of his two English retrievers; by eight he would usually be in his study engaged upon matters relating to the household and his magnificent collection of paintings, drawings and books; but invariably he would leave his writing table by nine to join me at breakfast - he the poised aristocrat of some sixty years, I the middle-class, middle-aged Englishwoman from Sussex wishing I could be a good deal younger.

We had met in Paris three years earlier when, dining alone not far from his apartment in the place des Vosges, he glimpsed me at a nearby table and claimed he was instantly struck by un coup de foudre such as men of his age and urbanity are not supposed to experience, let alone take seriously. I had brought Nell to Paris that morning, planning to introduce her to the French director of the PR firm I worked for in London. For our first dinner in Paris together I had booked a table at Bofinger near the Bastille, sure that the Belle Epoque décor and gaiety would meet with approval.

We were seated in the downstairs room under its canopy of stained glass - "as pretty as a box of jewels", Nell said. The mirrored walls, the fittings of polished brass, the mahogany screens, the huge vases filled with flowers, the white napery on the tables and ankle-length white aprons on the agile waiters who balanced full trays with one hand above their heads would, she remarked, have satisfied any film director recreating the period. The tables set close together along banquettes that flanked the room created a sense of shared intimacy that helped to animate the whole restaurant. I insisted that Nell should sit facing the theatrical scene.

From a nearby table Edouard was observing our obvious enjoyment. I had my back to him. Nell was doing most of the talking, with her hands and eyes as much as with her lips. Her glowing complexion, high cheekbones and chestnut hair cut in a gamine style kept him glancing in her direction. He said he took her to be French until she turned to speak to the waiter and he picked up her voice but he said it was when I glanced over my shoulder in his direction that he claimed to have fallen, recalling another time and another place. Nell caught his eye, smiled and jokingly assured me I had a secret admirer who, judging by the attention given to him by the waiters, was a man of some importance. I dismissed the suggestion with a light laugh and thought nothing more of it at the time.

By chance Edouard saw me the next afternoon in St Germain looking at the window of a small boutique. Later I told him that if he had acted rationally, he would have relished the moment, regretted the passing years and walked on. Having nothing particular to do at that hour and seized by a mad impulse, he followed me into the boutique, sat in an armchair with a magazine and pretended to be waiting for someone.

It was absurd. I indignantly threw that very word at him when, first by flattery and then by charm and guile, he lured me into joining him for an aperitif in the foyer of a nearby hotel. There he apologised disarmingly for being so forward, with the excuse that I was "irresistible", and invited me to dine with him that evening. Bemused and alarmed, I backed away with a string of excuses - that I was a married woman; that I was in Paris with a friend; that I knew nothing about him apart from the imposing name on his calling card, which might or might not be factual, and that he was being impossibly forward.

My fluent put-down, cool indignation and quick departure made him the more determined. He found out from the boutique the name of my hotel and sent me a ticket for the opera - just one ticket with a soft, persuasive note of sincere and deep apology and a promise to meet me in the foyer.

It was at a time when I was all too vulnerable to his suave, gentle but persistent advances. Within only a few days he had broken my resistance and swept me away to Gascony, first to stay a while in perfect respectability in the château as his house-guest and then, while I pondered the state of my marriage to Geoffrey, installed in a small but beautiful villa nearby where his constant attention slowly won me over.

My flight to France was to the astonishment, misapprehension and anxiety of Nell Sheridan who was sure the Baron de Marcignac was not what he pretended to be, that the château in Gascony was as fictitious as his title and that I was behaving like a love-smitten schoolgirl. I denied that I was engaging upon an affair and claimed that my only reasons for accepting his invitation were, in the first place, that it was probably a unique opportunity to try my wings after years of confinement in a disappointing marriage and, secondly, that I would once again see a part of France I had enjoyed on an exchange visit as a girl. My eyes were wide open; I knew exactly what I was doing. Edouard was charming and thoughtful, but he didn't deceive me. Nor did I deceive myself. Nell's silent disbelief made me protest the more that this was simply to be an interesting interlude - a brief voyage of discovery under the protection of a man I liked and felt I could trust.

Nell had been entirely wrong about Edouard, as she had to admit when she visited me some months later. The baron was all he claimed to be, and indecently rich into the bargain. He had inherited from his father the title, the beautiful Château de Marcignac in an estate of thousands of hectares, other properties scattered around France, the major part of an astonishing art collection and a great fortune. The simple life which he claimed to prefer to the social round mostly revolved, according to the season, around life in Gascony, the villa at Antibes, the box at Longchamps and the apartment in the place des Vosges which, to his surprise and delight, I never discouraged him from using on trips to Paris, as was his habit before our marriage.

The expense of all this must have been prodigious. As to the art collection, even in the short time since our marriage I knew he'd bought three important paintings at the cost of some millions of francs. Once when I teased him gently about indulging himself impulsively with an Old Master drawing seen in a dealer's window in London, he simply took me in his arms and said: 'I know, my darling. I am the luckiest man in all the world.'

Now, reading through my letter of invitation, I wondered if I should put Nell and Alastair in the Poussin suite which had two bedrooms as well as a pretty little drawing room. It was where the Princess stayed during her visit when Edouard had insisted I should take the place of his mother who was in America. It was a few days that began with panic at being asked to act as hostess when I was not even married to Edouard and ended with relief at having got through the ordeal safely.

After our wedding my mother-in-law, Sophie de Marcignac, moved out of the château into a nearby gentilhommière on the estate. She was not in the least what I expected - no grande dame, despite being in her eighties, but a woman of enormous energy who seemed to spend more time travelling than at home. At our first meeting she gave me a little lecture in excellent English.

'My dear, I know nothing about you, but since Edouard has chosen you above all the most eligible French ladies we have encouraged him to desire, then I will say no more, except to give you a gentle piece of advice. Because you will feel insecure in your new position you may be inclined to indulge your husband. He will take every advantage of that because he is terribly spoiled. You must be firm. If he truly loves you, he will give way. And you need not fear for your position socially. You will be accepted by Edouard's friends because of who he is, and they will make allowances for you as an Englishwoman.'

Yes, he was spoiled. I discovered how spoiled during that first encounter in Paris which he had cunningly contrived. In answer to my inquiry as to what he did, he had outlined a privileged way of life that seemed to me to be entirely sybaritic if not downright indolent and self-indulgent.

His gentle self-mockery was beguiling and he was impossibly charming. I was not taken in by this. I'd impulsively accepted his invitation to go away with him not because of his charm and the hope of love, nor because of the temptation to see the château and revisit the Gers where I'd spent happy weeks as a girl, but because of the opportunity to test my capacity to be my own person and not just the wife of a successful businessman and the mother of two promising sons.

Did I indulge Edouard? Surely it was the other way round? I had never been so indulged.

6 - EDOUARD

Louise was at the breakfast table when I joined her on the terrace. I had showered and changed from my riding clothes into light trousers and a pale blue cotton shirt with a paisley kerchief. As we exchanged kisses I noticed an envelope beside her plate.

'To Nell Sheridan,' she said. 'Inviting her for the festival.'

'I look forward to meeting her again.'

'I am also inviting Julia Bray, a friend of hers. It was her father, the writer, who discovered the Pilgrim's grave, you'll remember. She has inherited his house and is keen to inspect it.'

I said I'd heard of Julia from Nell Sheridan when she visited us. 'I gather she's something of a scholar. Got a first at Cambridge. I have asked her to do a little research for me in England.'

'Really? What kind of research?'

'A description of a medieval reredos which seems to have vanished some years ago. I've been unable to discover anything about it from my own resources so I've asked Julia to find out what she can.'

The footman poured coffee and handed me a basket of croissants and petits pains. We discussed our plans for the day. I had a meeting in Toulouse, Louise had more letters to write. To James in his last year at Cambridge and to Hugh going up in October. And to Julia Bray. I hoped she would accept Louise's invitation. The lost reredos was a great mystery.

7 - MALVIN

I left the Grand Hotel de l'Opéra in Toulouse with light steps and made for a small restaurant nearby where I could lunch quietly and review my meeting with the baron. I had not been put out by the apparently cool way in which Marcignac had examined the photographs I'd made of pages from the Canticum. He had neither challenged the authenticity of the book nor shown surprise at the price I asked. He had even agreed to pay for it to be insured, a considerable sum, while he borrowed it for a few weeks. I was sure he intended to take the illuminated manuscript to Paris where I was confident any expert would concur with the assessment of the highly reputed booksellers in Italy.

As I relaxed on the faded red banquette of the small bistro sipping a Pernod, I congratulated myself on the book's discovery and the expected reward. Anticipating a good outcome from Marcignac's consultations, I decided to move my plans forward. The abbey was in a remote part of Liguria - a tiring drive from La Spezia. Each visit from Marseille required at least three days. Much time and effort would be saved if I could pay a call upon the abbot on the same day I proposed to borrow the Canticum while the librarian was distracted. I would introduce myself to the abbot as the confidential emissary of a very rich but reclusive nobleman who was also a bibliophile. I would say that my client, who preferred to remain anonymous, was much distressed by the condition of the abbey's fabric and was prepared to make a very large donation towards repairing the roofs and the stonework and so make the building safe. All he required in return were a couple of books for his collection, as a memento. The abbot would surely agree that this was a generous offer - one which would enable the brotherhood to prevent the dilapidation of their ancient heritage.

It was a credible story, I felt, but it would need skilful advocacy. I refined the argument in my mind as I ate my entrecote, adding touches which I felt would make it more persuasive and cogent.

Three days later, after again making the slow journey from the port to Levanto and up into the remote Costa Castagnolasca, I parked my car on the rutted track below the abbey and climbed the rocky path to the gateway. A little out of breath, I rang the bell. The wicket was opened by an elderly monk who listened impassively to my request for an urgent meeting with the abbot on a matter of great importance. The monk nodded and replied curtly that he would convey the message as soon as the office of Nones, which was in progress at that moment, was concluded. He padded away, leaving me to walk impatiently up and down outside.

After some twenty minutes the monk returned, opened the gate and led me through the musty entrance hall, along dark corridors and two sides of a crumbling cloister to the door of the abbot's room. This proved to be a cell of such chilling discomfort and sparseness that I was for the moment unable to voice the greeting I'd prepared but stood in silence until a gesture from the monk who had escorted me indicated that I should sit. There was a single empty chair; this was placed before a plain but well polished table at which was seated a thin-faced man wearing a white habit under a black scapular.

The abbot's gaunt face creased momentarily in what might have been a smile as I took my seat. 'Welcome, my son. Have you come far? Can we offer you some refreshment?'

'You are kind, Father. I will take nothing, thank you. I have indeed come far and I bring you what I hope you will find to be very good news.'

'Good news? The good news is that of the Gospel, my son. What other good news can there be?'

I blinked at this unexpected put down. 'News of a different kind, Father. I am sent to you by a man who wishes to help - financially, that is - with the restoration of the abbey which he has seen to be in a sad and even dangerous condition. He is a man of noble birth and considerable means, and greatly generous towards the causes he favours. When he visited the abbey he saw your library, which he also found to be in a sorry state. He is a great lover of books and a notable collector, and he could not bear to see such neglect. Please forgive the word, Father. My patron, your would-be benefactor, knows neglect is due only to lack of resources. He wishes to remedy that - to make a large donation to the abbey for the work of restoration. In return, all he asks is to be allowed to choose a few books for his own library where they would be very well cared for - certainly better than in a building which has no heating in winter nor air-conditioning in summer. Old books are at peril in such conditions.'

I paused for quite a moment before adding: 'I should say that the sum he has in mind to donate is three hundred thousand euros.'

The abbot sat in silence for some while with eyes lowered as if in thought. Then at last he looked up and said: 'Money means little to us, my son. We do not have dealings with money. We are self-supporting. The brothers look after the buildings and do all the work of repairs themselves. Still, there is work - urgent work perhaps - which is beyond our capability for we are few in numbers. I have known that one day, in my own time probably, parts of the abbey may fall into disuse. This is a poor place. Tourists do not come here and local people are not able to help us. We have accepted this as God's will. There have always been more important things to pray for than a new roof over our heads; we have plenty of roofs to shelter our small community. But perhaps God's will is otherwise and he has therefore sent us this benefactor. May I know his name?'

'My patron wishes to remain anonymous. He is a distinguished scholar but reclusive. He is a benefactor by stealth, you might say. But I can assure you that he is as honourable as he is generous and that this offer is genuine. He has asked me to say that on your verbal acceptance of his offer, the sum I have mentioned will be paid in full within a few weeks.'

Again the abbot sat in silence. His face was expressionless. I wondered if my proposal had been too extravagant. Three hundred thousand euros was a fraction of the price I expected to receive from Marcignac for the manuscript.

I didn't flinch as the older man's eyes seemed to search into my heart. At length the abbot said: 'Your patron's offer is certainly generous. I wish I had met him when he visited us. A book collector, you say. Do you know which books he would like in exchange for this proposed gift of money towards our repairs? We possess some valuable volumes.'

'And of what value will they be to future generations if you continue to keep them in a building that is slowly disintegrating?'

'That is an important question, my son. One I have not considered. We do not give much attention to worldly matters.'

'If I may dare to say so, Father, it is not a worldly matter to safeguard the heritage of Christian scholarship which your library represents.'

The abbot pondered this remark. Feeling I'd made a point, I continued. 'I do not know if my patron has any particular books in mind. Just one or two. They would be simply a token, as I said. A record of your appreciation for his gift to the abbey. I've been asked to put this to you today just as a matter of principle, which is this: would you exchange a few books from the library for a gift of money that would save the abbey's buildings from further deterioration - a threat which you may feel only God can prevent?'

It was a telling thrust. At length the abbot nodded. 'I will need to consult my brethren. How can I communicate with you?'

I was always well prepared for this question. 'I travel a great deal, Father. It would be best if I communicate with you. I shall do so within four weeks. Will that be time enough, would you say?'

The abbot got up from the table and held out his hand. 'That will be time enough. Go in peace, my son. I thank you for your visit.'

The librarian is a fool, I thought. It was pathetically easy to divert his attention by asking his opinion of an old missal I'd bought in the market for next to nothing and, while he was peering at it through flimsy spectacles, to move casually among the shelves to the dark corner where I would find the Canticum Canticorum partly concealed. Turning my back on the librarian, I swiftly removed the book from the shelf and secreted it within the special inner pocket of my waterproof. Earlier, with unnecessary bravado, I'd drawn the librarian's attention to my coat by complaining about the capricious weather in the mountains; the man had simply smiled. He was still examining the missal when I returned to his table. Offered it as a gift, he accepted with fulsome expressions of gratitude. He was a fool. The book was of no value.

So far it had been almost too easy. The next stage would be crucial. Though I didn't doubt that Marcignac's sources in Paris would confirm the book's authenticity, I was sure I would meet resistance on the matter of price. I couldn't afford to bargain. Having stated "my client's" price, I would lose credibility if I showed willingness to negotiate. It would take courage to stand firm, but I was confident that if Marcignac wanted the book he would eventually agree the terms.

A large profit was almost assured. This was an opportunity such as I'd hoped for ever since the day I walked out of the Corsican seminary at the age of seventeen and abandoned the profession my mother had urged upon me for a precarious life of dealing. I recalled my first successful coup: a small, rather grubby oil painting bought in Villefranche and which was later verified as a Vuillard. If only I could have afforded to keep it! The value today would be fifty times higher. Still, I was now about to catch a much bigger fish. Little could go wrong if I kept my head. So many times in years of setting up deals I had been on the verge of a spectacular coup only to see it slip through my hands because of the stupidity of partners. I'd learned that lesson. Now I operated alone, trusting nobody, relying on nobody, confiding in nobody.

Making my way back down the rugged track to my car, with one hand against my side to protect the heavy book from swinging against the saplings that lined the path, I thought with satisfaction of how the Genoese bookseller's sharp eyes had spotted the note on the end-papers, and of the interesting outcome of my nephew's research. Marcignac should not be allowed to see the end-papers. I would remove it with great care. Or rather, I would employ someone with the expertise to do it. Someone who could not read Latin.

Labadie looked at me sideways in that sly way of his and turned the package round and round as though the wrapping would tell him something.

'Why not open it, Bernard? It's a nice little job for you,' I said. 'Just to remove the end-papers from an old book. Maybe an hour's work, but well paid.'

Stripping off the thick paper sealed with wax Labadie placed the Canticum on his table and stared at my preparation of it in puzzlement. To keep its identity secret I had close-wrapped the covers, spine and everything within except the final end-papers in cloth and taped it carefully.

At length, fingering one of them delicately, he said: 'And this is what you want me to remove?'

I nodded. Labadie gestured at the protective covering. 'All this will have to come off.'

'You must manage without doing that, Bernard,' I said. 'That is an essential protection. The book is very old and extremely fragile.'

'Old books are. I have handled thousands.'

'Maybe, but this one is exceptionally delicate, and valuable, of course.'

'Then why would you want to remove the end-papers? That is bound to reduce the value.'

'On the contrary. The end-paper is a much later addition, it doesn't belong. Without it the book will be in its original condition and more valuable. That is expert advice.

The little bookbinder made an impatient gesture. 'Nevertheless, the end-papers cannot be removed without taking off this covering. It is impossible.'

I tried to hide my annoyance. 'All you have to do is to make a neat cut close to the spine.'

Labadie laughed. 'What do you know about books, my friend? If I were to do that all the end-papers would come adrift. The only way is to take off the binding, remove the end-papers as a whole and rebind the book in the old covers, if they are in good condition.'

'They are in excellent condition.'

'Well then, let me do it.'

I hesitated. I'd thought this a simple enough task. Now I was worried. Labadie had been practising his trade for years. He was well respected. A bit bent, for sure, and with a police record but he knew his craft. The precautions I'd taken to prevent him seeing the book appeared to be futile.

I sifted through various possible explanations which would be plausible and serve to deflect Labadie from asking awkward questions. After a moment's silence I looked him in the eye, smiled and said:

'All right, I will tell you about this book. It is an illuminated manuscript recently bequeathed to an English gentleman. He can't afford to insure it so he's decided to sell it in London where he will get the best price. The auctioneers have asked that nothing be made known until they publish the catalogue of the sale in the summer. If you are to see the book I must have your promise of secrecy until then.'

Labadie regarded me coolly. 'All my work is confidential. You know that.'

'You agree? You will say nothing?'

'I am not interested in the book. Only how much you will pay me.'

'How long do you require?'

'I can't say without seeing the binding.'

'It must be done today, while I wait.'

'Then I cannot do it.'

He picked up the package as though to hand it back. I held up my hands, smiled again and thought quickly. 'It has to be done. We can come to an arrangement. You have a safe?'

'Of course.'

'When could you start?'

'Depending upon the price, quite soon.'

'How soon?'

'Perhaps this afternoon or evening.'

'And complete it tomorrow?'

'Perhaps.'

'Not perhaps, Bernard, definitely. No later than tomorrow evening, and you will keep it in your safe when you are not working on it. I will give you six hundred euros because of the urgency. A very fair price for a small job.'

It was the bookbinder's turn to smile. 'Twelve hundred would be fairer. Six hundred now, the rest when I complete the job.'

I hesitated. 'That is a lot of money for a few hours work.'

'Not a lot considering this is a book the owner cannot afford to insure and I must say I find it strange that the London auctioneers are willing for the end-papers to be removed.'

He turned the package over and over thoughtfully. Quietly and without looking up, he said: 'You have an interest in this book, don't you, my friend?'

I knew I was cornered. Without a word I took out my pocket knife and began to cut the tape that bound the cloth. Labadie watched keenly as the wrapping was removed and the covers exposed. He touched it with his finger-tips and remarked 'Goatskin. Typical medieval covers.'

I handed him the newly revealed Canticum Canticorum which he opened with great care, turning the pages slowly and staring in obvious amazement at the illustrations. After a long while he spoke.

'This is beautiful. Worth a fortune, I'd say.'

I said: 'Tomorrow evening. At six. Be sure to have it done.'

I was probably mistaken to suppose that by removing the end-papers the Canticum would be in its original condition. Any expert would see it had been rebound previously, probably in the thirteenth or fourteenth century, as Labadie had said, for the leaves were rather older than the leather-bound boards. So what? No one could know what had been written by a later hand on the end-paper. Except Labadie.

8 - NELL

Alastair Hadley's call took me by surprise. We had met only once, at a lunch in Paris, arranged by his father, a little mischievously I thought. He was like his father, tall and spare, totally English in his light grey suit, cream shirt, gold cufflinks, pale blue tie and highly polished brogues. On the right side of fifty, I guessed, though with his father's genes that could be deceptive. Alastair had the same aquiline profile as Ronnie, the same quiet voice and the same searching look that was at once disturbing and pleasing. He seemed to be interested in me, as I was in him. We talked about books, music and his love of French 19th century art. He told me about a pencil drawing of a girl he'd bought for a song when he was an undergraduate and how a friend thought it could be by Modigliani. 'And was it?' I asked him. 'Of course not! And that was lucky. I loved her and wouldn't have to sell her.'

When we parted I was willing him to suggest we could meet again before he left for a visit St Emilion but was disappointed not to hear from him again. His call now, weeks later and right out of the blue, was to say he had been given two tickets for a concert at St John's, Smith Square that evening. The programme was of string quartets by Haydn and Elgar. He remembered me saying how much I loved Elgar's music. He was apologetic; it was ridiculous, he said, to expect I might be free at such short notice. It *was* ridiculous and equally ridiculous that I was so flustered by his call but yes, I was free as it happened. He was kind to think of me.

We met in the crypt for a drink beforehand. What was it about this man that he had stayed in my mind throughout my time in Paris? Having met Ronnie had something to do with it. Alastair seemed just as solicitous and dependable - the sort of man others would rate a good companion in a tight corner. A man's man, I judged, which meant a man for whom a woman would have to make unusual sacrifices.

During the concert he was noticeably engaged by the music, as of one who knew it well. His quiet comments showed discernment that could have come only from serious knowledge. He compared the performance of the Elgar with one he had on a CD. While we queued for the buffet supper in the buttery I told him about the choir preparing some of Elgar's part songs for our next concert.

'Will you invite me?' he asked.

'It will be somewhere in France.'

'All the better. I go there frequently.'

'Of course, I forgot. Your wine buying trips.'

I enquired about his visit to the Médoc and asked after his father.

'He's fine,' Alastair said. 'Off to a conference of organists in Cambridge.'

I remembered Ronnie's passion and how in Paris I'd disappointed him deeply by not finding time to go with him to St Sulpice to hear the newly restored and much celebrated organ.

As we took seats at an empty table and hoping to enliven the conversation I asked: 'Alastair, do you know anyone who's had a near-death experience?'

He poured the wine and handed me a glass. 'Not personally but I've read about it.'

'What have you read?'

'Someone's had a serious accident and the heart may have stopped beating. They seem to leave their body and watch dispassionately while people try to revive them. Is that right?'

'Go on.'

'And they seem to travel through a tunnel towards a bright light and hear voices of people they know, but they come back when they are revived.'

'They all tell the same story. They see loved ones who've passed over and a beautiful place the other side, but they're told they can't cross over - not yet. That's what happened to my friend Julia after an accident. Her father had died a few days earlier in France where he was working. He's Leonard Bray, the writer.'

He looked at me quizzically. 'Really? I read his obituary in The Times. Sad death, I thought.'

'Julia travelled through this tunnel to the bright light and then she saw him. She insists it was not a dream. Her father spoke to her, he held out his arms to her, but he said she couldn't go to him. "Not yet", he said.'

'A disturbing experience.'

'Disturbing, yes, but elevating. It's lifted her up.'

I took a sip of wine, wondering how much to tell him.

'I haven't finished the story. Her father gave her a message: "Take care of the jewel".'

'What jewel?'

'It made no sense. The family doesn't have any valuable jewels. They searched his possessions in London but found nothing. Julia thinks there may be something in France.'

'Where was he working?'

'In a house he'd bought near Auch. He's left it to Julia but there was something else. With her father she saw the figure of a monk, a Cistercian. She could tell that by his habit.'

'Sounds eerie.'

'Her very word. Am I boring you?'

'Not at all. It's a fascinating story.'

He seemed to mean it. I told him all I knew up to the discovery of the package Leonard Bray had mailed home from France with the ancient title to Le Belvédère, the record of its recent purchase by Bray himself and the anguished Journal d'un Pèlerin by François de Castres. 'And François was a Cistercian monk' I concluded.

Alastair smiled. 'One of many.'

Not so many these days. Another thing. The name de Castres has a family connection, Julia says. She thinks that's why her father bought the document.'

'You've read it?'

'It tells an extraordinary story. François was on a secret mission.

46

He was taking a sacred relic to the shrine of St James in Santiago de Compostela - a ring supposed to have belonged to James himself. François simply calls it The Holy Thing. Res sacra.'

He listened intently as I told him of François's repeated expressions of guilt, the sudden illness that ended his pilgrimage and his admission of failure to hand over The Holy Thing.

'Julia is convinced her father knew what happened to it - that it is there somewhere for her to find. She argues that's why he said *take care* of the jewel rather than *look* for it?'

'An emotional response. Natural, but wishful thinking.'

'Maybe, but she argues her case well. First, her father's inexplicable message and the vision of a Cistercian monk. Then the Journal turns up with an account by a Cistercian monk, of something sacred being taken to St James's shrine. The editor of the Journal recounts the legend of St James's ring and calls it "un joyau" - a jewel. François says he failed to hand over the sacred thing when he abandoned his pilgrimage. So he stole it. Julia's father wrote on his postcard to her about "a theft that confounded the thief". Something went wrong. The thief didn't get what he wanted.'

'Someone else took it from the monk?'

'Possibly.'

'Why would François want to keep the relic, if that's what it was?'

'Who can say?'

Alastair sat in silence. It was quite a while before he spoke. 'What do *you* believe, Nell?'

'I don't know what to believe.'

He changed the subject, inquiring after my work in Paris and if I had seen Louise since her sudden departure to Gascony and her marriage to Edouard. I told him about my visit to Marcignac and how I'd found the château was as real and beautiful as Louise had told me.

Alastair said: 'As it happens I know the place quite well. Edouard asks me to buy wine for him. I've had an invitation to stay, with a three-line whip from Louise. She says you'll be there. A bit obvious, I thought.'

9 - EDOUARD

My feeling that I was being deceived by Malvin made me change my mind about taking the Canticum Canticorum to Paris. There would be time for that later. First I wanted to meet the Milanese bookseller who, according to Malvin, had valued it so highly. When I telephoned to make an appointment I was told that the principal of the firm was away for a few days but one of his colleagues would be honoured to receive me and to be of service. I hesitated. I needed to discover at first-hand what had been said to Malvin during his visit. I promised to call again when the principal returned, rang off and looked up the telephone number of the dealer in Genoa.

The premises of Cardoso e Figlio were in a narrow street near the inner harbour. Having given notice of my visit, I was greeted deferentially by a tall, very slim man who introduced himself as Aldo Cardoso and offered coffee. After courteous preliminaries, I explained that I was considering the purchase of an illuminated manuscript which I believed Signor Cardoso may have seen previously. I was seeking an opinion on it and would of course be willing to pay a fee for this.

The slim bookseller smiled deprecatingly. He knew of me as a much respected collector and would certainly not charge for an opinion. Might the firm's services be of assistance in other respects?

As soon as the Canticum was unwrapped from its protective covering Cardoso raised his hands in a gesture of pleasure. 'Of course, Signor! Naturally I remember. It is a most remarkable volume. It was brought to me by someone I took to be the owner's agent, though he didn't tell me as much. I did some research after he left but there is no record of the Canticum that I can find.'

'It could be a fake, then?'

'I spent some time examining it. In every respect it is typical of the eleventh or twelfth century. The illustrations are astonishing but certainly of that same period. To produce a credible fake would require great skill, the right materials and much time. Who would attempt it, knowing that scientific tests would expose the work as fraudulent?'

He slowly turned the leaves as he spoke, punctuating his remarks with little murmurs of approbation. After many minutes, he closed the book, examined the covers closely, then opened it again and used a magnifying glass to study some of the details.

'No, Signor. I do not doubt its authenticity but what can you tell me of its provenance?'

'Nothing, I'm afraid. That is why I have doubts and why I've brought it to you. I thought a book of this obvious quality must be known in the book world.'

Cardoso shook his head. 'As I've said, it is not known. I can only guess that it has been carefully guarded because of the illustrations which the monks who made them knew were sinful.'

'Sinful?'

'In the teaching of the church. I forget the reference, but didn't St Paul say that to be carnally minded is death? Whether you find this work carnally minded or, as I do, a beautiful expression of a man's desire for a woman, the monks would have wanted to keep it hidden. I am not surprised it is unrecorded, but how was it discovered?'

'I don't know. It was brought to me by someone who has a knack of finding rare works of art.'

Cardoso put down his glass. 'You're a fortunate man, Signor, if you're able to purchase it, but in my opinion it belongs in a great public collection, like one of our national libraries in Rome or Firenze or in the Bibliotheque Nationale or Musée du Louvre in your own country.'

He continued to turn the leaves, exclaiming at each image and commenting until at last he reached the end, whereupon he looked closely at the book with a puzzled expression and then at me.

'Signor, this is most strange. The end-papers are missing.'

'Missing?'

'When I first examined the book I was struck by an inscription on one of the end-papers. They were intact. Now they are not here.'

'How can that be?'

'They must have been removed. It was of great interest. I examined it as best as I could, though the script was difficult to read and I had little time.'

'What made it so interesting?'

'It was inscribed Anno Domini 1217. I noted the date. In my opinion that was at least a hundred years later than the manuscript, possibly even two, and it was evidently a list of important treasures owned by a Benedictine abbey at that time.'

'What kind of treasures?'

'The gentleman who brought me the book was impatient to leave. He was not an Italian. The inscription was in Latin, of course. I had only a few minutes to look at it but I noted crucifixes, chalices, reliquaries, paintings and other such things. As I told my visitor, the list appeared to have been made at the time of a plague, in case the community did not survive.'

I took a sip of coffee and pondered this suggestion.

The bookseller produced a powerful magnifying glass and studied the binding closely. At last he said: 'There is only one explanation. The book must have been taken apart, the end-papers removed and the leaves rebound. It has been expertly done. I would never have known had I not previously seen the inscription.'

He laid down the glass and handed the book to me. 'You must draw your own conclusions, signor.'

I had already done so. I asked: 'Would you be willing to give me a written confirmation of what you saw previously?'

Cardoso hesitated. 'This is a delicate matter. The removal of the end-papers must have been done with the knowledge of the owner and his agent.'

'At least you could tell me the name of the abbey. You remember it, no doubt.'

'Yes, but that now seems to have become private information - the property of the book's owner.'

'I don't agree, signor. The book and everything in it, or anything that was in it, is for sale and must properly be available to anyone interested in its purchase. I have such an interest and have made this known to the owner through his agent.'

Cardoso smiled and touched the book with the tips of his fingers. 'Signor, is not this the property offered to you? A book for which a price has been stated?'

'Certainly.'

'Then if the seller has chosen to retain a part of the property which you have not seen, that is his business. Why he should have done this, I cannot say. I told the gentleman who brought me the book that the inscription added to its interest. Perhaps he believes he can sell the end-papers as an interesting old document.'

'It could have a value on its own?'

'A few thousand dollars maybe.'

On my way home I puzzled over the bookseller's dismissive remarks. The possibility of gaining a few thousand dollars was hardly a reason for taking such trouble and expense to remove the end-papers. I was right in suspecting something fishy in the offer made to me. I knew Malvin was naturally deceitful, but how could I tax him with this deception? It was true, as the bookseller said, that the book without the end-papers was the property exactly as offered. The inscription had not been mentioned. It was only by chance that I knew of its existence. I had been shown the Canticum without the end-papers and inscription and asked if I was interested. Perhaps I should now reply: 'I will buy only if I can deal directly with your client.'

When I put this to Louise she said: 'Malvin won't agree to that, will he? He would lose his commission. And if he doesn't agree, there's nothing you can do.'

She was right. Besides, did the removal of the inscription really matter? The Canticum was extraordinarily beautiful and very desirable as it stood, but why was it not being offered on the open market for auction by one of the big international sale-rooms? The question of the book's provenance and the owner's title to it was critical.

I sat at the writing-desk in the drawing room of our suite and examined it once more, page by page. It was indeed "quite magnificent", as the Genoese dealer had said. Louise had been equally overwhelmed by the beauty of the illuminated text and the eroticism of the imagery. I was surprised and pleased that she hadn't discouraged my interest.

We went together to Milan to an appointment with the other bookseller. Making the excuse that Louise ought not to wander the streets on her own, I took her to the Brera and left her there to look at the Venetian paintings. 'I'll not be long,' I told her, 'and after lunch I'll take you to the Convent of Santa Maria del Grazie to see the city's greatest treasure, Leonardo's painting of The Last Supper.'

The dealer's premises were only a short walk from the gallery. I was received by the principal of the firm with extravagant courtesy and an apology for his earlier absence. Yes, he well remembered having seen the Canticum Canticorum. It was a privilege to have been shown so superb a volume, but no, he had not observed the inscription on the end-papers.

'I hardly had time to look at the book itself, signor. It was a strange meeting. One does not see a volume of this quality more than a few times in one's life. It was not brought by one of my regular clients but by a stranger who seemed to know little about books and nothing at all about this one. So you are the fortunate purchaser, signor?'

'Not yet.'

'The book is still for sale?' He opened it at the title page and shook his head in disbelief as he looked at the painting of young girls in an orchard preparing to robe a naked, dark-skinned bride in a many-coloured gown of exquisite detail.

'I told my visitor that it might be dated as early as the eleventh century. I advised him to insure it for at least a million dollars. This seemed to surprise him. He left almost at once without asking any questions or giving me an opportunity to examine the book further. I'm delighted to see it again. May I enquire how much the owner is asking for it?'

'Nine hundred thousand dollars. I've not yet had the opportunity to get an expert valuation.'

The bookseller said nothing but continued to turn the pages, shaking his head as before and making small noises of appreciation. At last he said: 'This is almost impossible to value. On the right day and in the right place I believe it could achieve two or three times the price I first suggested. I'm frankly amazed, signor, that it is being sold privately. If it were offered to us, we would buy it in at the asking price without hesitation.'

10 - LOUISE

The early morning after our return to Marcignac promised another warm day. A distant clock chimed the hour. Edouard would be out riding by now. I walked across the bedroom in my nightgown, opened the windows and shutters to the balcony and was almost assaulted by the heady scent of lilac. It was one of those golden mornings when you wouldn't want to be anywhere else. The new borders I had planted below the terrace were already a great success. Cool irises, clouds of gypsophila and white poppies were set among roses and peonies that glowed in the Gascon sun. The long wall of honey-coloured stone was draped with the creamy blooms of Alberic Barbier.

In the kitchen garden beyond there would be a harvest of tender broad beans, petit pois, baby turnips, new potatoes and spring onions. The first shoots of asparagus were piercing the dark earth and baskets of Griottes, Coeurs de Pigeon, Burlat and Montmorency had already been gathered and taken to the kitchen for making compôtes and for preserving in Armagnac. It was a time when families and friends gathered throughout the Gers to celebrate the abundance of la belle saison. England was a million miles away.

Edouard had an appointment in Auch and left immediately after breakfast. He returned at midday and asked me to come to his study where he took a letter from his pocket and put on his reading glasses.

'This is from a bookbinder in Marseille named Bernard Labadie. Not someone I know. He writes: "Monsieur, I believe it is possible you may be offered a very fine old manuscript. Recently this was brought to me and I was asked to remove the end-papers from the book and rebind it. If you are considering the purchase of this book (or even if you are not) you may be interested to see a photocopy of one of the end-papers. It has an unusual inscription which I am sure contains information of some value".'

Edouard looked at me over the top of his glasses. 'What do you make of that, chérie?'

'Nothing Malvin does surprises me.'

'As it happens, the bookseller in Genoa had already pointed out that the end-papers were missing. When Malvin took him the book it was intact.'

Louise shrugged. 'Well, he's a crook. I've always said so. What are you going to do about it?'

'Malvin has done nothing illegal, just deceitful. That I cannot stomach. I will tax him with it later. Meanwhile, I shall see what this man Labadie has to offer. From what the bookseller in Milan was willing to tell me the inscription could be very interesting. Malvin obviously thinks so or he wouldn't have taken so much trouble to keep it to himself.'

'Well, be careful! Labadie is probably an accomplice. It sounds like some kind of a scam to me.'

Edouard smiled indulgently. 'You are right to be suspicious. I promise to be most careful.'

11 - MALVIN

In the bedroom of my hotel in Foix-en-Gascogne I poured my a large whisky and sat in an armchair by the window. Putting on my gold-rimmed half-moon spectacles I read and reread the scrawled copy I had hurriedly made of a paper I'd found at Le Belvédère before Bray suddenly appeared on the ladder at the window. It was our angry argument and confrontation that caused him to lose his balance and fall. I dismissed the dramatic moment from my mind as a tragic accident (his fault entirely) and returned to the paper, studying it line by line. It was headed by the figures 383, evidently a page number. The content, beginning at the end of a sentence with the words "it had failed to protect the saint", was extraordinary.

Though such a relic would certainly have been held in awe and greatly treasured, nothing more is heard of it for a thousand years. It vanished as completely as the Holy Grail. Then, I believe, it was rediscovered. Two manuscripts of the 12th century record its existence. One I found in the library of a dilapidated abbey in Liguria, the other I traced to Montpellier. The chance discovery of a modern French translation by a professor at the University of Montpellier has already been explained in Chapter 3.

The Ligurian document records that in 1148 a treasure associated with the apostle St James (S. Jacobus) was deposited in the Abbey by a Templar returning from Jerusalem, and that it was accepted by the abbot as an atonement for sins committed by Christians during the attempt to liberate the Holy Land from the Turks. The abbey's archives listed my ancestor François de Castres as a member of that order at this time, but there is no record of his pilgrimage to Santiago de Compostela. This is not surprising. Many such pilgrimages took place over the years.

Everything I have found in researching this book convinces me that the ring of St James was the "treasure" brought from the Holy Land to the abbey in Liguria and subsequently given to François de Castres to take with him in secret on his ill-fated journey.

The very stuff of fiction, but Bray had denied he wrote fiction. He was widely regarded by critics as a scholarly and original craftsman. I had read a couple of his books. The page I had copied was obviously part of a substantial piece of work. I hardly had time to copy the page before Bray furiously snatched it from me. He accused me of deception and theft and ordered me to leave as though I was a trespasser instead of a respected friend of the baron interested in Bray's work. My deprecating apology was angrily rejected.

There was no cause for such violence. We could have reached an agreement if only Bray had understood the advantage of sharing knowledge. Now the police had locked the house, I would need to make out a very good case for going back. Next time through the front door instead of by the ladder I'd found in the barn.

The inspector had questioned me the day after Bray's death. Did I know what Monsieur Bray was doing up the ladder? Did I see him fall? No? Did I attempt to lift him or move him from where he lay? Did Monsieur Bray speak to me? He was unable to speak, I said. How long was it before I called for the ambulance? The police inspector was polite, even deferential. He apologised for having to observe the necessary routines. It was a sad affair. The English gentleman had been much respected, both as a famous writer and for discovering the Unknown Pilgrim.

I read the page once more. Where was the remainder of the text? The original was written in pencil with no visible corrections. Bray seemed to have no use for a typewriter let alone a word processor. He was of the old-fashioned school. Somewhere there must be at least four hundred more pages of manuscript. If the book was finished it would surely have been sent to his literary agent or publisher, but this was refuted by a report in the Sud-Ouest saying that, although his publishers had confirmed Bray was working on a new book, they had not yet received the manuscript. So where had he hidden it? And why? The tempting answer was that the book contained evidence to support his claim that the so-called ring of St James had been "rediscovered". And by Bray himself, surely! It was a sensational claim. One that Bray must have intended to keep it to himself until the book was launched.

12 - JULIA

Let's go back to the beginning,' I said as Nell and I pored over a map of the Gers. 'I've been looking at all the cards my father sent me from France. The messages are brief and puzzling but they may help. You've already seen this one.'

I handed it to her and Nell looked at the picture again and read my father's enigmatic message.

> *"The long hot summer goes on. Routine work, then <u>suddenly</u> - that's underlined - the Castres connection has cropped up! Other excitements - a medieval murder and a theft that confounded the thief. And if that's not enough, this place is <u>haunted</u> - underlined. Home soon, I hope."*

'We know about the Castres connection and the murder,' I said. 'But what about the theft that confounded the thief? Is he saying that something was stolen from the pilgrim's grave?'

'The jewel?'

'If so, the murdered pilgrim would be François de Castres. That doesn't fit with my father's reference to other excitements, as though to separate the murder from the Castres connection.'

'Is there an earlier postcard referring to the Castres connection?'

'No.'

'That suggests your father hadn't seen the Journal before he discovered the pilgrim's grave.'

'I'm not so sure. I think it was the Journal that took him to Marcignac in the first place. It's on one of the pilgrims' routes. I think he had been puzzling over the Journal for months. Look at this.'

I handed over another postcard with a sentence highlighted in yellow. Nell read it aloud. 'Interesting visit to Montpellier. Fine city but couldn't stay long. All for a scrap of paper.'

I said: 'That was not long after he arrived in France. The professor who translated the Journal was at the University of Montpellier.'

'Your father went to meet him?'

'And came back with what he dismissively calls a scrap of paper. Knowing him, I would say it's more than that but I haven't found anything. Maybe in France.'

I put the postcard to one side and read from another one.

'He says: "Extraordinary abbey at Flaran. Deserted. But not quite. Didn't much like it." Deserted, but not quite? What could that mean? I looked up the history of the abbey. It was a built in the twelfth century, deconsecrated at the time of the French Revolution and abandoned by the monks. Someone at Flaran obviously displeased my father.'

'Or something? He writes "Didn't like *it*", not him or her or them - *it*.'

'Maybe. Anyway, it's another piece to fit into the puzzle.'

'And what about "this place is haunted"? What place?'

'I take that to mean Le Belvédère where he was living. The house or its surroundings. He didn't believe in ghosts. Maybe he was just recounting a local superstition.'

I turned to another postcard. 'He sent this quite recently. "Something nasty in the woodshed. Sinister, you could say. Literally." He liked to use Latin expressions so I think he meant sinister as in left-handed. What could be left-handed and nasty?'

'There aren't many left-handed objects, are there?'

'A number actually. There are shops that specialise in left-handed things. For gauche people. That also means left-handed.'

'What about "in the woodshed"? Are we to take that literally?'

'I'd say not literally but near enough. Some place that could be used like a woodshed. The sale particulars say that the house has a *grenier*.'

'What's that?'

'A grain store. A barn.'

'Hiding something nasty?'

'A joke, I think.'

'Your father had a scary sense of humour.'

'He did, as matter of fact. But this is a clue, Nell. We have to take a look.'

'Sooner you than me!'

When we first met after a choir practice Nell had been impressed by my breadth of knowledge. The discovery of shared interests and ease in each other's company led to a friendship that overrode the age gap and different backgrounds - Nell, the talented but wayward daughter of a banker, and me, a high-flying civil servant whose father, a celebrated writer, I rarely saw because of his frequent long periods away from home. Despite his absences, he had been my sheet-anchor since I was a young girl.

I took an envelope from my hand bag. 'I've had a letter from Edouard. Louise told him about my work and he thinks I might help him with some research. Have you heard of an Italian sculptor called Benedetto Antelami?'

'No.'

'Neither had I. Edouard thinks the British Library might have references he hasn't found in France.'

'And have you found anything?'

'Surprisingly little for a notable sculptor. I've also been to Cambridge. Not much there either.'

'What's so interesting about this man then?'

'He's very early. Around the twelfth century and highly regarded by scholars. Edouard says he is supposed to have made a reredos for an abbey in Italy somewhere but he hasn't been able to trace it. Neither have I. My father wrote a monograph on Antelami when he was in Parma but he doesn't mention a reredos among his work. Edouard also asks me to find out what I can about a medieval chalice, a legendary piece known as the Calix Sanctitatis, the Cup of Sanctity. It's said to have been made in Ephesus in or around the year 70AD and taken to Rome some time later. In the late 12th century it was presented by Pope Celestine to an abbey in Lombardy as a foundation gift. Quite an historical piece but Edouard says it has disappeared.'

'Disappeared?'

'I concluded it had been stolen but there's no record that it was ever kept in the abbey. From the little I've been able to discover the Calix was a very important piece, not something that could vanish without trace unless it was stolen and broken up for the precious metal and jewels, which would be worth much less than the chalice itself.'

'So you're going to play detective?'

'It's interesting, as I said. And tempting. Edouard has offered me a very generous fee.'

We stepped out of the aircraft at Toulouse into blissful heat. Alastair was waiting for us. He was exactly as Nell had described him. Tall, lean, patrician and well turned out even in the most casual of clothes. Greeting us with a warm handshake, he said: 'Nell's told me about you, Julia. And about your father. A brilliant writer.' I felt myself colouring as I replied: 'And Nell's told me about *your* father, Alastair. You're very like him, she said.'

Nell filled the awkward silence by asking him about his visit to Bordeaux and saying how pleased Edouard would be that he had agreed to join us at the château. 'So am I,' she said, adding to his embarrassment with a kiss.

Alastair consulted the map briefly and quickly found the B-road signposted to Montaigut-sur-Save. The landscape as we turned westward was much as I had imagined - gentle limestone country where weathered farmhouses on hilltops could be of almost any age. It was surprisingly green for so late in the season owing, I had read, to the high water table. Thick black hose on portable irrigators spurted fountains on to flourishing crops as we drove past undulating fields of maize and nodding tournesols, through shuttered villages and across rivers that flowed northwards from the foothills of the Pyrenees. Signs on the bridges announced their names: the Save, the Gimone, the Arrats, and at last the Gers itself as we entered the small market town of Fleurance.

I marked a road which must lead to Le Belvédère. I felt a sudden shock of anticipation. This was the land where my father had spent his last days. Louise was expecting us so we wouldn't have time to go to his house till later. Alastair knew the way to the chäteau from previous visits and turned confidently through the open gates. Warned perhaps by a message from the gatehouse, Louise was below the steps at the front entrance to greet us. It was so good to see us all! She apologised for Edouard who was away until the following evening. So the four of us would be alone at dinner and we'd have all day tomorrow to talk and discover the country. There was only just time for a cool drink in our rooms and to unpack. Within the hour we were leaving for the Choir's first rehearsal at Flaran.

The golden limestone of the abbey glowed in the sun but as soon as I walked into the huge nave I was at once seized by its stark emptiness. Stripped by the revolutionaries of all ecclesiastical furniture, it was a lofty cavern with massive columns supporting a vaulted roof. The total absence of altars, chapels, screens, lecterns, statues, seating, religious images and Christian symbols promoted a feeling of cruel deprivation. It was no ruin, like Fountains Abbey or Ampleforth, but a vacant shell. I knew exactly what my father had meant by "didn't much like it".

Nell and I left Alastair to explore the abbey while we took our seats on a wooden platform at the east end below where the high altar would have stood. The director of music, Fergus Maine, welcomed and marshalled the choir.

'Before we start, I need to try seating arrangements to cope with the amazing resonance in here.'

He sang a short phrase and held his hand up for silence as the notes took long seconds to die. 'See what I mean? We need to consider tempi too or faster passages could coalesce into a jumble. If I'd known what this would be like I would have chosen a different programme. Some Gabrieli, for example. Too late now so let's try the Messiaen.'

We worked on O sacrum convivium until it was time for a

break. I left Nell and wandered further and further away from the nave, staring at all that remained of a great abbey after the monks had abandoned it to the vandals. Once or twice I looked back, feeling that someone was following me. Turning a corner towards the cloisters, I came across Jane Reeves, a buxom choir member in an inappropriate floral dress, staring at one of the pillars in the arcade with a guidebook in her hand.

'Apparently hundreds of barrels of Armagnac were stored here after the Revolution. The fumes blackened the stonework. There is something I don't like about this place. Have you been in the chapter house? To me it feels . . . well, inhabited.'

'Really Jane, you do tend to imagine things!'

'I'm sure something nasty happened here once.'

'You could say that of a lot of old churches. Like Canterbury and Thomas Becket.'

'Not the same at all. His murder has been exorcised through centuries of worship. This place was abandoned by the priests. It's a different kind of habitation now.'

'That's creepy!'

The next day the abbey was hosting a large party of Spanish pilgrims so the rehearsal was set for the late afternoon. Louise suggested we should visit the market in Fleurance. On the way she recounted a dream she'd had before going to Paris and her first meeting with Edouard.

'I was in the covered market with my friend Aude. Tame rabbits brought for sale were running about everywhere. Watched by the Gascon peasants, who sat around impassively, we were trying to catch the rabbits and tie their legs together with a huge ball of twine. The more we caught the more they multiplied and the ball of twine kept growing larger and larger. It was ridiculous.'

Nell likened the dream to the story of the sorcerer's apprentice. 'It's a serious warning. Don't meddle in things you can't control!'

'Or it could've been precognition. It was the day before you joined me in Paris and soon after I'd seen a golden oriole in the garden at home - and then Edouard brought me here, to a house called Les Loriots - The Orioles.'

'A nice coincidence.'

'An omen. A portent.'

'You're not serious?'

'Why not? The Romans divined things from the flight of birds. The augur was quite a fellow. He could decide whether the time was auspicious for any serious business, like a battle.'

'But he was a professional, wasn't he? Not an amateur diviner who doesn't know her sinister from her dexter.' I glanced sideways at Louise. 'If we could consult an augur now I'm sure he'd warn me to beware the flight of orioles and you to steer clear of foie gras, mille-feuilles and everything cooked in cream.'

Louise giggled. 'It's such fun having you here!'

The road to the covered market became impassable with people converging from all directions. Alastair parked under the shade of a huge plane tree and we strolled through narrow streets thick with shoppers and lined on both sides with stalls selling cheeses in great profusion, cured hams from the mountains, olives of many kinds, Armagnac from local producers, fresh meat and fish, foie gras, truffles and brightly coloured fungi, bunches of fragrant herbs, beautiful vegetables (which, Louise complained, were hardly ever seen on restaurant menus), live ducks peeping from baskets, their dead cousins roasting on spits, honey, strawberries, figs, blue plums, cheap clothes, boots, haberdashery, hats, garden plants, farm implements, kitchenware, underwear, music cassettes, wine - indeed, anything that a country household might lack.

Louise watched Alastair and Nell with a knowing smile. 'I shall expect you this evening no later than seven. Edouard is elsewhere tonight so I've given the chef the evening off. You'll have to put up with my cooking. Just a simple supper, but my husband's cellar is sans pareil.'

The Choir's next rehearsal went better. Never satisfied with anything much short of perfection Fergus knew how to get the best from amateurs and tempered his criticisms with sardonic humour. He was a popular director and as a brilliant jazz pianist sometimes extemporised after a rehearsal.

As we were leaving the abbey Jane Reeves asked me, in her usual direct manner: 'Would you let me have a look at your father's house? I might make an offer.'

'Really?'

'I've often thought of having a place in France. And this is such an historic area. I thought I might write about it. Try my hand at a book about the English connection. Eleanor of Aquitaine and all that. Something to do when Peter's on his travels. If you're selling, of course, but don't mention it to Peter. I want to get him in the right frame of mind.'

'Have a look, by all means, but as there's no electricity we ought to get there soon while there's still enough light.'

The house was approached down a rough track through a chestnut plantation. I felt the presence of Jane a slight intrusion but was glad that Nell was with me. I caught my breath when it came into view standing defiantly alone and tightly shuttered against the outside world. The land was seriously neglected, but at a glance the tranquil setting and sturdy structure of Le Belvédère suggested from the outside that it could, with imagination and skill, become "a country house of charm and character", as an estate agent might put it.

The entrance was up a ragged path. Climbing roses trailed in tangled disorder across the facade. The stone-flagged terrace was unsteady. Pots, urns and other receptacles contained dried up plants. For me it was a place of sad neglect. I had keys to open the outer doors which swung back to reveal a second pair with a large knocker and a small plate bearing the name BRAY. I ran my fingers over it before opening the door to the darkness inside.

'Stay there please while I open the shutters.'

There was no entrance hall. The door led directly into a heavily beamed, square room, its stone floor bare of rugs. I groped my way to a window, found the catch, opened it inwards and unlocked the shutters. There was enough light now to open the rest of the shutters on the ground floor. On a side wall of the living room a massive stone fireplace framed a blackened hearth. The only furniture was a sofa, an armchair and a small table with a lamp. There were no pictures on the walls, no decorative objects. I blinked away a tear. How could he live like this? But I knew he would want no distractions. This was not a home, just temporary lodging.

Together we began to explore the rest of the house. A door to one side of the fireplace led to another room of similar proportions also with a fireplace. In the centre was a table that could seat ten comfortably. The empty shelves of a huge pine dresser were thick with dust. Opening one of its doors, I saw a meagre collection of crockery. In a corner of the room stood a small electric cooker, a refrigerator and a china sink.

Jane was taking photographs, using flash. We went upstairs. There were just two large rooms. Only one was furnished, and that frugally with a large country-style bed, a simple chest of drawers and an ancient armoire. Hanging in the armoire was my father's faded silk dressing gown and dark green shooting jacket.

The second bedroom had been crudely partitioned at one end to form a small bathroom and a study. A writing desk beneath the window was flanked on either side by well-stocked bookshelves. Beneath one of the shelves, close to the desk, were four simple pictures hung side by side. I examined them closely. The first was just a postcard showing the interior of the church at Marcignac, the second an engraving of the Abbaye de Flaran; the third was obviously from a Spanish guidebook to Santiago de Compostela and the shrine; the last appeared to be a recent photocopy of a page of Latin manuscript.

On the desk stood the photo my father had snapped in Cambridge and above it, pinned to the wall, was a scrap of paper with four hand-written lines. I removed the drawing-pin, looked at the lines, frowned and handed the paper to Nell who read it aloud:

"One may not doubt that, somehow good shall come of water and of mud; and, sure, the reverent eye must see a purpose in liquidity." 'What does it mean?'

'A quotation, obviously, but I don't know it.'

It was getting dark. Jane was outside, quickly and confidently photographing the house from all angles. When she'd finished, we drove back to Foix and dropped her off at her hotel (her husband had refused to be billeted on people he didn't know) before taking the road back to Marcignac.

None of us took any notice of an empty car waiting near the entrance to the track.

With Alastair joining the party it was obvious Louise must be told about the mystery of "the jewel". She listened wide-eyed as I quietly related all I knew, from my near-death experience, the poignant vision of my father and the plaintive monk, the Castres connection, the message to "take care of the jewel", the discovery of Le Journal d'un Pèlerin and other documents in my father's package. I ended with an account of our visit to Le Belvédère earlier that evening and the four pictures and the scrap of paper that had been pinned up by my father's desk.

'What do they mean?' asked Louise.

'The three pictures are linked in some way to the pilgrimage - the abbey at Flaran, the church at Marcignac and St James's shrine. The photocopy could be from the manuscript of the Journal. It should be easy to check.'

'And the quotation?'

'Typical of my father. It could be a reminder to him of something special - something he didn't want others to understand. Maybe Alastair will recognise it. I'm hoping he'll agree to help us.'

For Louise's "simple supper" the curtain raiser was to be foie gras cooked very lightly in butter with sliced apples and accompanied by a well-chilled Sauternes. She would then finish off a pipérade at the stove while we sat at table, adding the eggs and topping the dish with grilled slices of jambon cru. The wine was to be a particularly good Pomerol. Alastair opened two bottles. In the kitchen Nell teased Louise as she helped unpack the purchases made in the market.

'You know, Lou, living down here in a land flowing with wine and packed with goose liver I was expecting to find you'd put on a stone at least. How do you manage to stay so trim?'

'Incentive, darling. Edouard gives me an absurdly generous

dress allowance and expects me to spend most of it in a boutique in Toulouse owned by an aristocratic cousin of his. I couldn't bear the looks I'd get from Madame if I moved up a size. So it's careful eating most of the time and an occasional splash, like tonight.'

'Don't you find his generosity a bit overwhelming? And if he really loves you, why does he leave you alone so much?'

'He has his interests, I have mine.'

'And when you're together you hold hands under the stars and listen to The Three Tenors! How romantic!'

'Nell, I'm not going to be provoked. And he's been married before, in case you didn't know.'

'No, I didn't know.'

'His wife died in a hunting accident. Broke her neck. The children were five and three.'

'How awful! I'm sorry. I really am sorry, Lou. I hope everything works out for you.'

There was a moment of embarrassed silence. Louise went on with her preparations. Nell had brought white roses from the garden and was snipping off leaves and longer stems and arranging them in an but exquisite Chinese celadon vase Louise had found for her. She went through the motions silently while Louise put on an apron, opened the jar of foie gras, looked for the copper pan she needed, asked Nell to slice the apples and put them in cold water and busied herself, much as she used to in her Sussex kitchen when friends were coming to dinner.

Nell asked: 'And when is your lord and master coming home?'

'Late this evening,' said Louise, bringing the pan to the table.

'And he's going to tell us what all this is about?'

'You'll get a folder of information after supper. I have no idea what's in it.'

She gave the same defensive answer to us at the supper table. It was not until she'd served coffee and Alastair was pouring Armagnac that she handed round buff-coloured folders tied with pink ribbon and sealed with red wax. 'Honestly, I know nothing about this. Any questions you'll have to save for Edouard tomorrow.'

The A4-size colour prints - six in all - were not the first sheets in the folder but captured attention before all else. Clearly they were of pages from an illuminated manuscript of the Middle Ages. The intricate decoration, gold leaf, brilliant colours and floridly ornamented Latin script were typical. The illustrations were certainly not. Their eroticism was beyond belief for a work of Holy Scripture. An explanation was provided in a long letter from Edouard. He wrote:

"You are welcome guests and I have asked you to stay as long as you can for a reason which I hope will intrigue you as much as it has me. Some while ago I was offered a very fine illuminated manuscript which could be from as early as the 11th century. It was brought to me by a man called André Malvin who knows of my interest in rare and beautiful things. He told me he was acting for a rich and reclusive collector who wished to sell the book privately. I hesitated because he is a man I dislike and, sadly, have learned to distrust. However he has a flair for finding quite outstanding pieces in private hands and negotiating their purchase. The manuscript is certainly outstanding and I admit to coveting it. Louise, I must say, was against me having anything to do with Malvin but, though I had reservations I decided to go ahead, provided I could satisfy myself as to its authenticity and the unnamed owner's title to it.

"I was worried by Malvin's claim that the owner wished to negotiate a private sale. Why would he wish to do so? Also, "to negotiate" is not an option. The price was set firm and it was made clear to me that there was no room for a reduction. It seemed to me that the owner would have to be eccentric and rich to the point of carelessness to offer so rare and wonderful a book privately when it could be easily sold at auction as from an unnamed vendor. Did he have something serious to hide? The manuscript seemed right to me but I felt there must be something wrong in the offer. Malvin told me the manuscript had been authenticated by

two well-known booksellers in Italy, one in Milan and one in Genoa and both of good standing. He made no objection to me borrowing the manuscript to get my own valuation, provided I insured it for its estimated value. I decided to visit Milan and Genoa and see what the booksellers remembered of Malvin's visit. They showed great enthusiasm for the book and valued it very highly.

"But there's something else. The Milanese bookseller observed that both end-papers were missing. He was sure they had been there when Malvin brought him the book because he had remarked on an inscription on one of them, dated 1217. This was in Latin and in a difficult hand. From the short time he had been allowed to examine the book, he judged the inscription to be an inventory of treasures owned by an abbey and sent away for safety at the time of a plague - a precursor of the Black Death perhaps. One must assume that the monks took this serious step in case none of them survived. I asked if he had made a copy of the inscription. He had not. He made a rather pedantic excuse for not being willing to tell me what he remembered, pointing out that the book without the end-papers was what had been offered to me. If the owner wished to retain the end-papers not shown to me he was legally entitled to do.

"That is perfectly true, but by good fortune I have now obtained a photocopy of the 13th century inscription. It was brought to me by a bookbinder who works in Marseille. His story was that he had been asked to remove the end-papers from an old book and then rebind it so that it appeared in its original condition. He seemed to know - or he guessed well - that the book was likely to be offered to me. He obviously assumed that if the end-papers were not to be sold with the book this could only be because the inscription itself must be of value. He made a photocopy before rebinding the book.

"I could tell he had no idea how to price it. Neither had I. As the bookseller in Milan told me, it's an inventory in Latin of various treasures owned, it said, by the Abbazia di

San Benedetto. The whereabouts of the Abbey was not stated. There must be a number in Italy dedicated to St Benedict. I was frank with the bookbinder. I said the inscription meant nothing to me but I would pay him something reasonable for his trouble, on account as it were, and more if the information proved useful. He was reluctant to part with the photocopy on these terms but eventually he realised he had no alternative but to trust me to be fair.

"The inventory from the Abbazia is fascinating. Each item is listed with the name of the monastery, abbey or other religious foundation - all Benedictine - to which it was sent in the year 1217. It took me quite a long time to find out where they are today. Some are still in the places where they were sent. Others are in private collections round the world. I have been able to trace all but one, a reredos supposed to have been made by Benedetto Antelami, an important 11th century sculptor. The inventory recorded it as having been sent to the Abbaye de Cluny in Burgundy. Cluny knows nothing about it. This is not surprising because the abbey was laid waste at the time of the Revolution and many of its records were lost. Before you came here I asked Julia to help me search every possible source for this supposed Antelami work. Neither of us could find any record that it ever existed.

"That, my friends, is the challenge - the mystery I would like to put to you. Will you help me solve it?"

There was one other picture in the folder - a black-and-white photograph captioned *"Deposition from the Cross. A relief in Parma Cathedral attributed to Benedetto Antelami"*.

'Perhaps,' suggested Alastair when other voices had died down, 'the reredos was diverted on the journey to Cluny for the benefit of a church or chapel in need of one. It could have been in place ever since but unrecognised as the work of Antelami.'

'That's possible,' I agreed. 'A reredos is of no use except in a chapel or church. But if your theory is right, how would you go about finding an unidentified piece of sculpture installed in the 13th century in an unknown church or abbey? It could be anywhere between Lombardy and Burgundy.'

The challenge was intriguing, as Edouard had said. We sat debating it and theorising. The candles burned lower, the stars grew brighter and Alastair's cigar-smoke curled upwards to where bats flitted silently and an occasional owl swept the velvet sky. At last I got up, saying it was all very nice but we were getting nowhere and I for one was going to bed.

The lost reredos filled my thoughts as I went upstairs. My research in England had yielded nothing. The University Library had little to offer. Equally disappointing were the notes my father had made in Parma when he was writing his monograph on Antelami. The mystery was intriguing. I was wondering where next to turn when at last the comfort of cool linen sheets and the silence of the Gascon night lulled me to sleep.

When I went down to breakfast I found my host alone on the terrace, still in his riding clothes, drinking coffee and reading the morning newspaper. After a few formal exchanges and compliments on the comfort and magnificence of the château, I asked him if he had known my father.

'Only by reputation, I'm afraid. The one time I spoke with him was after the Mass for the dead pilgrim found in the forest. I knew of him before that, of course. So did everyone in the commune. He was the only English resident. That he decided to buy a house here suggested he intended to stay. As a writer he was naturally respected and welcome. That, I think, is not the same in your country. The English do not have the same regard for literature, do they?'

It was a rhetorical question. I smiled and asked: 'Have you read any of his books?'

'The one about the Albigensians. He dedicated it to you, did he not?'

I will never forget opening covers of the copy he sent me from Italy and reading the few words he'd written.

'A fine piece of work,' said Edouard. 'That was why I wanted to meet him. I went up to him after the Mass and asked him about his discovery of the grave. I told him that as a boy I had almost got lost in the woods, and that it was a place local people shunned. We were interrupted by an English journalist who wanted to take a photograph and write a story. Your father was quite angry.'

'He hated that kind of thing.'

'And he made it quite clear. The journalist asked if he intended to write about the pilgrim. He dismissed the suggestion, saying that anything he wrote would be fiction.'

I nodded. 'Was Louise with you?'

'Not at that moment. She was talking with the Mayor, but afterwards she told me she knew you as a friend of someone she was at school with.'

'Nell Sheridan.'

'And it was from her I learned of your reputation as a researcher and wrote to ask for your help.'

I didn't want to discuss the reredos yet.

'So you know my father's house. Would you say it was haunted?'

Edouard smiled. 'There were stories put about by a previous owner to keep people from trespassing on his property. Local people believed the woods were haunted but they are naturally superstitious.'

'My father wrote to me about a place being haunted. He didn't say where.'

'I invited him to the château but he declined. Things to do, he said. There are two kinds of writers; the reclusive ones who are the more interesting if you can open them up, and the gregarious who like to talk about themselves and have opinions about everything. Your father's death was tragic and a great loss.'

I had other questions but the conversation ended with the arrival of Alastair and Nell and the service of breakfast.

Edouard convened a meeting in the library at midday. He was casually deprecating about the puzzle he had posed.

'All I've suggested is a game that might amuse you. If you don't wish to play there are many other possible diversions. Horses in my stables for anyone who would like to ride, game fishing with a cousin of mine not far away and many interesting places to visit. If you all agree you would like to play - and you must be all of one mind - you will find I have the resources here to do almost anything in the way of research. If you need to travel I will bear all expenses.'

He hesitated. 'There is something else. A marginal note in the inscription describes the reredos as the custos - the guardian - of an historic chalice known as the Calix Sanctitatis. Julia has discovered that this was a legendary cup. It is supposed to have been made in Ephesus in the first century AD and may have been used by St Paul at some time on his travels. It was therefore specially revered, hence its name, the Cup of Sanctity. The cup was taken from Ephesus to Rome and kept there until the 12th century when it was presented by Pope Celestine to a Benedictine abbey in Lombardy as a foundation gift. This pinpoints the abbey exactly. It is the Abbazia di Benedetto della Verna in Liguria. So thanks to Julia we know where to start.'

Alastair asked: 'What do we know about Antelami?'

Edouard responded. 'I've made some notes for you.'

More folders were passed round. Edouard referred us to the second page and picked out key points. 'We don't even know his birth date. It was sometime around the year 1150, probably in Lombardy. He died in Parma some eighty years later. The details of his life are just as vague. He is said to have worked as an apprentice at Arles in France, though this is not certain. One of his earliest works which is properly authenticated is a relief in Parma Cathedral - a Deposition from the Cross. You have a picture in your other folder. The relief is in the right transept of the Cathedral, signed and dated 1178. I have seen it recently. It is quite beautiful and very moving. There are also friezes said to be by Antelami in the cathedrals of Fidenza and Cremona.'

'But not authenticated,' I added.

Edouard nodded. 'The Fidenza friezes are said by commentators to be in the Provençal Romanesque style. If you turn the page you'll find photographs of the octagonal baptistry at Parma. Antelami is said to be responsible for much of the construction and sculptural decoration and also to have cast the bronze gates. And some way from Parma the church of Sant' Andrea in the northern town of Vercelli has a Martyrdom of St Andrew attributed to Antelami.'

We studied the photographs. Nell remarked that there seemed so much doubt about the work of Antelami that this could apply equally to the reredos.

'True,' said Edouard. 'We have to accept that, but what is not in doubt is his reputation as the most notable and influential Italian sculptor of his time. Julia's father made a study of him but never mentioned a reredos. Neither Julia nor I have found a record of one.'

I nodded. 'I've searched in both the British Library and the University Library in Cambridge and read through my father's notes. Antelami was the most important sculptor of his age before Nicola Pisani but only a few works attributed to him are fully authenticated.'

Nell said: 'So you agree that the reredos in the Abbey's list of treasures could be just another questionable attribution.'

'All we know for a fact is that a reredos recorded as being the work of Benedetto Antelami was included in a hand-written list of treasures sent away from the abbey in the year 1217 without explanation. The inscription is in your folder, both a facsimile of the original and a translation. As you'll see, the list includes crucifixes, patens, chalices, reliquaries, caskets and other pieces. Some of the crucifixes and chalices sold in recent times made very high prices. The abbey's treasure was of great quality.'

'No other sculpture is listed,' Nell observed. 'Only the reredos.'

'Which suggests its great importance,' I said. 'Nothing else is missing - that's after nearly nine hundred years.'

Edouard nodded. 'I accept the Antelami attribution because the date of the inscription is less than forty years after he was known to be doing great work. He may even have been alive then, in which case the abbey would almost certainly have commissioned the reredos from him directly. From what we know of his dates he may have finished it only a few years before the monks decided to send it away.'

'It may not even have been installed,' suggested Alastair. 'Perhaps the pieces of marble were on the site in 1217, ready to be assembled. Perhaps the monks then realised the reredos was so valuable they decided to send it in pieces to Cluny. That would make more sense than having to take it apart after it had been installed.'

Louise said: 'Think about it: who would want to steal a reredos? What use could it be, except in another church or chapel, as Edouard has said?'

'No use whatsoever,' I said. 'But the monks must have thought it was vulnerable. Possibly, as Alastair says, because it was still in pieces. They wouldn't have sent something so bulky and heavy on a hazardous long journey unless they rated it highly, would they?'

Alastair said: 'Yes, but there would have been a reredos in every chapel within the abbey. Maybe ten or twelve, if it's a large building.'

'Exactly,' I agreed. 'But this was the only one they decided to send away. Think of its size and weight and marble is fragile. Even if it had been intended for a small chapel it would be much more difficult to transport than paintings and church plate. Cluny is hundreds of kilometres from any part of Italy. The roads would have been rough with steep hills even for pack animals.'

While we pictured this, Louise posed another possibility. 'The list doesn't *prove* that they sent the reredos away, only that they had thought about it. Perhaps they changed their minds. Perhaps it's still in the abbey, unrecognised, like much of Antelami's work it seems.'

'But what about the Calix?' asked Alastair. 'According to the inscription the Calix was the guardian of the reredos, suggesting they were inseparable.'

'The reredos may in fact have been sent elsewhere,' said Edouard. 'Or so I've been told.'

This remark, made almost casually, provoked a flurry of questions and an objection from Louise that her husband was keeping things up his sleeve. 'If you want us to play your game, you've got to come clean, Edouard. Or are you going to keep dishing out new clues as we go along?'

Edouard waited for questions to subside. 'Let me explain. When I received Julia's notes on the Calix I wrote to various academic journals to ask if any readers could throw light on its history. Only yesterday I received an email from a lady in France. She signs herself Claudia Andrieu. She says she is a writer and had come across the story of the Calix Sanctitatus some while ago. Like me, she was fascinated by the legend and thought it might be the basis of a book. She went to Rome to do some research. The legend, according to her, is a piece of fiction though the chalice itself is real and secure. She says it is not a very early Christian piece but was made in Rome in 1197 to the order of Pope Clementine who sent it as a gift to the new abbey in Lombardy. She suggests the abbey was probably told the legend to enhance the prestige of the Pope's gift.'

'How does she support this claim?' asked Alastair.

'With what sounds like incontrovertible evidence. She found the 12th century Roman silversmith's account in the Vatican's records which also noted that the cup was sent back to Rome in 1217, for safety. There's a photograph in the archives, she says.'

'So the abbey was deceived,' remarked Louise. 'What an extraordinary story!'

Alastair said: 'We only have her word for it. Who is this woman anyway?'

'I've no idea,' said Edouard, 'except that she is a reader of one of the leading journals on Christian antiquities.'

Louise said: 'The chalice is irrelevant. It's the reredos we're looking for.'

'I wouldn't dismiss the chalice from our thinking,' said Alastair. 'Madame Andrieu's claims ought to be checked.'

I agreed. 'I'm worried about her email, Edouard. Did she say anything about the Calix's possible connection with a reredos?'

Edouard shook his head. 'How could she? I said nothing in my letter to the journals about the reredos or the inscription. Just that

I'd come across the legend and was looking for more information. I've thanked Madame Andrieu and left it at that.'

'What kind of stuff does she write?' asked Nell pithily. 'Fiction?'

13 - MALVIN

A letter from my nephew Carlo. It began straight to the point.

"My dear Uncle:

I can confirm that the medieval document you described has been found here in Montpellier in the University Library. A young graduate traced it for me. She is an historian and also a Latinist. I asked her to translate a few passages but she declined, despite my offer of a generous fee. We reached an impasse until I told her of the French translation, which she then found in the archives. This is a typescript of 116 pages bound in hard covers with the title blocked in gold - one of only ten numbered copies. I have photocopied it for you and will be sending it when I hear from you again.

As you will see, this is an account of a pilgrimage to Santiago de Compostela in the year 1212. Among the pilgrims was the writer, a monk named François de Castres. His journal is a rambling, incoherent record of the long journey from his abbey in Lombardy to the great cathedral in Galicia. It is mostly tedious, but suddenly, buried within a great deal of repetitious stuff we come to what I'm sure is the reason for your interest in the manuscript. De Castres was secretly carrying a legendary and much revered ring to be delivered to the keepers of the shrine of St Jacques in Santiago. According to the translator (a former professor at the University here) the ring is supposed to have belonged to St Jacques himself. I suspect you already know this. De

Castres fell ill on the journey even before reaching the Pyrenees and failed to complete his pilgrimage. But he did not hand over the ring. He writes with a sense of guilt, and frequently calls upon God to forgive him for unnamed sins. He was taken ill not far from Foix-en-Gascogne where you are staying. Maybe he died nearby. Perhaps you can find a record.

My student friend had never heard of this legendary ring. She dismissed the story as a medieval fiction. She may be right, but after studying the document I find it carries a certain conviction. De Castres refers many times to "le joyau". He seemed to feel that the jewel was invested with magical powers, which could explain why he didn't want to part with it. It was a ring, I am sure. The abbot who entrusted it to de Castres believed in it as a holy relic. A traditional belief, I suppose, but the abbey wasn't founded until the late 12th century. So where was this legendary ring before then? This I find difficult. One can argue that if the story is true, the ring would have been carefully guarded and handed on from one Christian foundation to another. Whether the ring carried by de Castres is what he supposed it to be can only be guessed at. But if it could now be found this document would invest it with some kind of provenance and the "joyau" would surely be of immense value. Beyond price, I would say.

Could it be found? What happened to it after de Castres' death can only be the subject of conjecture. There is nothing in the text to suggest he gave it to anyone else. If he had done so, surely this would have become known and the ring would now be a holy relic of the front rank. A careful reading of the journal leads to the clear conclusion that de Castres still had the ring in his possession when his pilgrimage ended. But where did he hide it? He wrote no more after his illness and may have survived for some while. I strongly recommend that you search local records. There is, for example, an Abbey at Flaran near where you are staying. Or you might prefer me to do this for you.

There is the slight possibility that after the completion of his journal or when he was near death he may have given the ring to someone else in holy orders to take to the shrine and complete his failed mission. I say "slight", because, in that case "someone else" has kept the secret of the ring from then until now. But his companions were devout men. Would they not have wished to complete de Castres's mission? I have made discreet enquiries of the authorities at Santiago. All my questions concerning the legend met with polite disbelief. I am confident you will reward me suitably for what I have achieved so far, and the more so if this leads to what would be a truly sensational discovery. Meanwhile I enclose a note of my expenses to date and will send you the French translation of the Latin document when I hear from you. I will of course keep all my findings totally confidential.

Your affectionate nephew, Carlo."

He enclosed a copy of his airline ticket, a hotel bill for two nights at the unnecessarily luxurious Sofitel Antigone (with the excuse that nowhere else was available at short notice), another for four nights at the Hotel du Parc, seven restaurant bills including three dinners for two people at the Michelin-starred L'Olivier, and various sundries.

This young man is getting too big for himself. He would have to be taught a lesson, but not yet. There was more work to be done. I wrote a cheque for six hundred euros and sent it with a curt note of thanks and a request that the translation of the document should be mailed by return. I underscored the words 'by return'. For the present that was as far as I would go to show my displeasure. I could not afford to offend Carlo. I had in mind that he might be able to discover the history of the so-called Calix Sanctitatis. The libraries I consulted had never heard of it. Calix is Latin for a cup. I knew that much. In the context of the other treasures sent away from the abbey it must be a cup of some value. I would ask Carlo to find out all he could - for an agreed fee to include all expenses.

There is another piece of research to be done, one I hesitate to offer to my nephew. An addition to the end-paper's inscription described the Calix as "tutela sororum Magdalae". With the aid of a dictionary I translated this as "in the care of the Sisters of Magdala". Who are they? My own resources offer nothing. I would put this to Carlo obliquely as a new task, not telling tell him the Sisters are connected with the Calix. Carlo is too clever. And sly. He couldn't be trusted with information he could use to his own advantage.

I distrust everyone, even members of my own family. Au fond they are Corsicans, natural brigands. In the early days I had asked my cousin César to bid on my behalf for a painting in a provincial auction sale. I was sure the painting had been misattributed and was greatly undervalued in the catalogue. I made the mistake of letting César know my estimate of its value. The top bidder proved to be a friend of my cousin. The nasty accident that later befell him was only a small compensation for my loss but a just reward.

I also distrust Bernard Labadie. I guessed Bernard would keep a copy of the end-papers removed from the Canticum and offer it for sale, but I would make sure the buyer wouldn't know about the Sisters of Magdala. On my next visit to Marseille I stood over Bernard and watched him carry out my instruction to obscure the crucial four words. Bernard had objected and had the impertinence to ask: 'What is the purpose of this further piece of vandalism to an historic book?'

'None of your business,' I replied. 'I pay you to do what you are told, not to ask questions.'

I wrote again to Carlo, giving him his new assignment. 'I only know of the so-called Sisters of Magdala from a brief record in Italy in the Middle Ages. It should not be too difficult for you to discover who they were. To my mind this is a simple piece of desk research which should not take you too long. If you are too occupied with other things, please let me know by return and I will find someone else.' That, I felt, was enough to keep Carlo in line.

14 - JULIA

Jane seems serious about buying le Belvédère. She telephoned this morning to ask if she could make a further inspection. 'I've found a mason who'll tell me what might need doing structurally and give me a rough price.'

I did my best to be polite and reasonable. 'Sorry, I can't manage today, Jane. I have to be somewhere else. There'll be plenty of time later.'

To Nell I said: 'I'm not going to be pressurised like this!'

"Somewhere else" was the church at Marcignac where Louise had promised to show us the pilgrim's sarcophagus.

'The sacristain is Monsieur Ferran. He is enormously proud of the pilgrim's tomb. We don't tip him, by the way. That would be an insult.'

Ferran, a small, elderly man with neatly brushed grey hair and the air of a schoolmaster, was in his garden tenderly feeding a caged family of rabbits. Yes, he would be pleased to show us the crypt. Not many visitors asked about the human remains that had been deposited there. It was a unique event, he said. Something altogether extraordinary. There had been much talk about the discovery by the foreigner of the bones of a pilgrim who, one must believe, was a man of importance - a bishop, perhaps, that his grave should be so marked.

'How was it marked?' I asked.

'With a cross naturally, Madame. And an inscription roughly carved in the stone. I will show you.'

As we made our way to the church, Ferran began explaining what we already knew about the grave in the forest. He had obviously repeated this many times. To interrupt would have seemed discourteous and even, perhaps, to have caused him to go back to the beginning of his carefully rehearsed commentary. The grave, he said, also contained a scallop shell which, without doubt, signified that the man (for the skeleton was certainly that of a man) was on a pilgrimage to the tomb of Saint Jacques. The mesdames would surely know of the famous emblem of the pilgrims of Saint Jacques? Moreover, scientific tests had determined that the bones were of a great age - perhaps seven hundred years or more.

In French he continued: 'On croit que le pèlerin a été assassiné. L'assassin est inconnu. Le pèlerin aussi, mais sans doute un homme très important. Donc, nous avons ici à Marcignac un grand mystère. Un événement qui s'est passé il y a plusieurs siècles. Prenez garde, mesdames! La crypte est sombre.'

Cautioning again that we should take care, he unlocked a door behind a curtain near the west end of the church and, lighting the way with a flashlight, went slowly ahead down a narrow stone stairway. The crypt was much smaller than the church above, faint light coming from narrow vents at ground level. The beam of his flashlight wavered as the sacristain guided our last steps and then illuminated the crypt. Four carved columns held up the stone vaults of the roof which was scarcely above head height. Several ancient tombs filled most of the floor. Tablets around the walls commemorated other graves.

'Voila!' said the Ferran dramatically, pointing towards a simple sarcophagus of apparently recent construction. 'Voila! Ici repose le pèlerin mystérieux de la fôret!'

A single slab of white limestone covered the sarcophagus. Into this had been set a small, partly broken tablet of marble bearing the much weathered but still decipherable legend:

BENEDICTUS
QUI VENIT IN N.D.

'Regardez!' said the sacristain, directing the beam to a legend carved in the slab. It read:

UN PELERIN INCONNU DU MOYEN AGE
Découvert 17 septembre 2005

Inhumé ici 21.janvier.2006

He stepped forward, struck a match and lit four candles in holders which stood at the corners of the tomb, as though placed there for some regular ceremony. Following his example, we stood in silence. Ferran crossed himself and in a sepulchral voice said: 'Kyrie eleison.' I whispered: 'Christe eleison.' Crossing himself again, Ferran said: 'Qu'il repose en paix!' To which I responded 'Amen.'

It seemed like two or three minutes before the sacristain led us back up the stone stairway. I had to ask him about "the foreigner" who had found the grave. He was a gentleman from England, said Ferran. Un écrivain. One who had not stayed long in that place but was nevertheless well respected, very well respected. Alas, soon after the discovery of the grave, the monsieur was found dead outside his house. It was thought by some that his death was somehow connected with the fate of the pilgrim.

'You believe that, Monsieur?' I asked.

'It is possible. The Englishman had been permitted to keep the pilgrim's emblem, the scallop shell, as a souvenir in recognition of his discovery. That may indeed have been the cause of his sudden demise. Also, it was understood that the Englishman was writing a book about the pilgrim of the forest. He had died before he finished it. It might be that he had discovered something sinister about the burial and that he had been prevented from revealing it.'

The sacristain crossed himself again.

We emerged from the crypt into dazzling daylight. I thanked Ferran for showing us the tomb and asked if he had met the Englishman.

'Bien sûr, madame. Il m'avait visité de temps à temps. Le monsieur était un vrai gentilhomme.'

My eyes moistened as I turned away.

A few hours later I was sitting alone in the garden thinking of my father judged to be a "real gentleman" by the village sacristain. It was a touching and perceptive remark. That was how I had always known him. Ferran said they had met "from time to time". Why?

They could not have had much in common, the simple servant of the church and the agnostic Englishman of considerable scholarship and renown.

When Alastair found me on the seat under the mulberry tree he gently steered the way towards my near-death experience, the legend of St James's ring and in particular my feeling for the Gascon house which was suddenly mine.

'Why do you think he bought it when he could have rented somewhere?'

'I think he found Le Journal d'un Pèlerin on a bookstall somewhere and was caught by the author's name. Castres is a family name. The legend of the ring and the account of the failed pilgrimage must have intrigued him. I'm sure that's why he came to the place where François died and then he learned there was once a pilgrim's hostel nearby and that the house was for sale. It didn't cost much, Alastair. Forty-two thousand euros and I think that something happened to make him want to own it.'

'What kind of thing?' Louise interposed, who had just joined us.

'Something supernatural perhaps.'

'Really?' asked Alastair, his head on one side, rather like, I thought, a supervisor of studies challenging an undergraduate's questionable assertion.

'You don't believe in the supernatural?'

'You do?'

'I can't explain my near-death experience by any other means.'

'All right. Anyway, you think your father felt there was something about the house he had to investigate.'

'And he bought it because he thought he might need to knock walls down, or excavate.'

'Are there any signs of digging?'

'Not inside. I haven't looked in the grounds yet.'

Alastair gave me a searching look. 'The legend of St James's ring is pretty incredible, don't you think?'

'Most legends are. The translator of the journal thought so too. He wrote a note saying that the legend is no more to be believed than that the saint's bones were miraculously transported from

Jerusalem to Galicia in an unmanned ship and found centuries later in the so-called Field of the Star.'

'Well, that's pretty incredible.'

'Millions of Christians have believed something like that for twelve hundred years. Thousands still make the pilgrimage every year.'

'Perhaps the translator had found the answer and wanted to put others off the scent.'

'I don't think so. He's an academic, a professor. He'd want the kudos for an important discovery, wouldn't he?'

'My belief is that as the professor got into the story he found it too incredible for publication. It was a small task he had to complete. He made only a few numbered copies of his translation. My father bought one, found this house on the pilgrim route, hunted around, found other clues and he died before he could tell the whole story, but not, I believe, before he'd actually found the so-called jewel.'

'Found it?'

'It's quite obvious to me. First, my near-death experience. I saw my father and the figure of a Cistercian monk who meant nothing to me. My father spoke to me. He said "Take care of the jewel!" Now the monk has turned up. So has the jewel - in the monk's journal. My father didn't say "Look for the jewel!" He said take care of it. Meaning he's left it for me somewhere.'

'Your father never mentioned buying a house in France to you or your mother?'

'He said little or nothing about what he was doing when he was away from home. He would send me scrappy postcards with teasing messages. Nell and I went through some of them the other day.'

'What kind of messages?'

The last one referred to the Castres connection and mentioned a medieval murder. We know what he meant now, and he wrote of "a theft that confounded the thief". That's puzzling. And he said this place - he didn't say which place - is haunted. And he wrote about going to Montpellier and coming back with a scrap of paper.'

'The photocopied page?'

'Most likely, but not certainly. Maybe something else? And there was a message about the abbey at Flaran - that it was deserted, but "not quite".'

'He meant it was haunted?'

'Could be. My father said he didn't like it at all. He didn't say what he meant by "it". Is this a lead of some kind or just another tease? And on another postcard he wrote of "something nasty in the woodshed". Something sinister, he said. But sinister, as I'm sure you remember, is Latin for left-handed.'

Alastair couldn't help smiling. 'A left-handed wood chopper?'

Louise said: 'The house doesn't have a woodshed.'

'Your father certainly was a bit of a joker.'

'But he always explained his jokes - later.' I must have sounded bitter when I added: 'This time it's too late.'

Alastair continued to play devil's advocate. 'If he'd found the jewel, as you think, why didn't he just send you a simple note, in code if need be, in case anything happened to him?'

'A simple note? It isn't a simple case. He didn't think like that anyway. He did what he could. He hid the jewel somewhere very safe - if it wasn't already hidden - and mailed the journal to England. I'm sure he's left clues for me in the house. We have one for a start - a piece of paper with a few lines of poetry. He knew I'd come here. That's why he left the house to me, not to my mother.'

'Aren't you making an awful lot of assumptions?'

'There are times when you have to. You have to make a general hypothesis and then see if the facts fit. For me all the facts fit.'

'When did he make his will?'

'The week before his accident. Leaving the house to me.'

'And what happened after he died?'

'Lots of bureaucracy, as you'd expect in France. The police interviewed the man Malvin who found him. There was no post mortem. He died of a broken neck. My mother was sent the few personal effects he had on him when he arrived at the hospital. A watch, money, a fountain pen, a signet ring. Precious little for a lifetime's work. The coffin was sent home by air. The funeral was in our parish church.'

'Nell told me about the pictures pinned above your father's writing table. What did you make of them?'

'They're all to do with François's pilgrimage. One is of the shrine at Santiago de Compostela. One is of the abbey at Flaran. That's an obvious connection with François. The third is of the church at Marcignac where the murdered pilgrim was re-interred. The fourth is a photocopied page from a Latin document. Possibly an original page from Le Journal. How's your Latin, Alastair?'

'I know names of plants and their diseases. You said there were also a few lines of poetry.'

'Something about water and mud and "the reverent eye must see a purpose in liquidity". Does that mean anything to you?'

'Nothing.'

'We need a book of quotations.'

'Edouard will have several in his library. I'll ask him tomorrow.'

Suddenly Alastair said: 'If you're not doing anything special I'd really like to see the house. Maybe we could also take a look at the site of the grave. Presumably it's marked.'

'I'm not sure. It's on private land with keep-out notices. Edouard says the woods behind Le Belvédère have always had a bad reputation. They're supposed to be haunted.'

Walking slowly, eyes to the ground, Alastair quartered the land around the house from one side to another and back again in measured strips. Louise's dog Balou - a big hairy animal with pointed ears - joined in the game, leaping joyfully around him, making wide circles, following sudden scents and racing madly to the distant boundaries before returning to the hunt.

At last Alastair reported: 'Nothing, except a small patch dug over quite recently behind the barn. Perhaps he grew vegetables.'

'Never! He was no gardener, nor a cook.'

I unlocked and opened the two pairs of outer doors. 'Stay there while I open up.' Sunlight flooded in. Alastair stared blankly at the almost empty room, but the austerity didn't seem to surprise him. He knew my father was a reclusive and self-contained man with a single-minded purpose. He would need no more than a roof, a bed and somewhere quiet to work.

We went into the kitchen. Its state confirmed my father's lifestyle. It might just pass as a place to make coffee and slice a baguette.

'What did your mother think when she heard he'd bought this place?'

'She was bewildered and very unhappy. It seemed like a deceit that he had said nothing to her. I tried to persuade her it was just for his work - for a reason I would be able to discover when I came down here. I said I was sure he would have had no further use for the house when he finished his research; that he would never have considered the need to explain it. There was no deceit. She accepted it eventually.'

'And the legend of the ring? What does she think of that?'

'It scares her. She thinks I'm tampering with something dangerous. That the pilgrim's remains might have had something to do with my father's death. There are village people who feel the same. The sacristain is one.'

'Trying to put you off, for some reason?'

'For what reason?'

'I can't imagine.'

'The sacristain who showed us the pilgrim's tomb in the church called him "le pèlerin mystérieux de la fôret". He relished the mystery. He dramatised it. He placed candles on the sarcophagus and stood there solemnly intoning the words "qu'il repose en paix!" as though he were a priest.'

'Suggesting the pilgrim was not at peace?'

'It occurred to me.' I opened one of the drawers in the dresser and started emptying it. 'Let's not talk about ghosts. There's work to do.'

'You really believe in the legend of the ring, don't you?'

'Of course. I believe what my father told me and what François recorded in his Journal, that he was carrying the "Sacred Thing" to the saint's shrine, that he became ill but failed to hand it over when the pilgrims went on without him.'

'Why do you think he kept it?'

'Perhaps he felt it would protect him.'

'It didn't protect St James, did it?' said Alastair with a wry smile.

'François was crying out for a different kind of protection. For God's mercy. I think he saw the apostle's ring as a way of communicating with the saint who would intercede for him.'

'A heavenly radio transmitter?'

'You can laugh. To a medieval monk the apostle's ring would be an object of great potential power.'

'A talisman.'

'That's a pagan concept. The ring is a Christian artefact. François would have held it in great awe.'

'Okay, but to keep it safe would hardly be a sin. Yet he felt bad about something. He was in anguish, you say. "Peccavi, miserei mei". Over and over again. If that wasn't because he'd kept the ring what was it?'

'An act of confession. He was desperately afraid.'

'Of what?'

'Eternal damnation. There was no one to absolve him.'

I let the chilling thought sink in for a moment before returning to the dresser. Its drawers contained next to nothing - a few knives and forks, corkscrews, sticky tape, candles, matches, a measuring tape, screwdrivers, a hammer, nails, a compass, sealing wax, a half-empty jar of coffee beans, string. On the dusty shelves were cups, saucers, plates, a coffee pot, a frying pan, a small saucepan, a pictorial calendar with a photograph of the cathedral at Auch, business cards from local shops, cafés and restaurants and a transistor radio.

I showed Alastair the blackened saucepan. 'My mother first had the idea he'd bought this place as a secret love-nest. Laughable, isn't it? You can see there hasn't been a woman here for years.'

He nodded. 'Is this the room where he worked?'

'No, upstairs.'

'Let's finish here first.'

'What are we looking for?'

'Something deliberately put out of place for you to spot. Meaningful disorder.'

'The whole place is in disorder. He lived like that.'

Alastair opened a cupboard. On the floor were a broom, a hand-saw, a fire extinguisher, a large portable flashlight and a wine-rack with about a dozen bottles. Hanging on a hook were two jackets, one of cream-coloured linen and reasonably presentable, the other a bright blue cagoule with a large tear in the back. As he searched the pockets of each jacket he observed: 'Have you thought, the ring could have been sewn into François's robes?'

'That's worried me. Monks were often buried in their robes.'

'In that case, if, as you believe, your father had found the ring, he would have had to open the grave.'

'That's inconceivable.'

'So François hid it somewhere else. He wouldn't have wanted the ring to be lost for all time, so he might have left a clue in the Journal.'

'Something my father deciphered? It would have been in Latin. Some kind of cryptogram which would be lost in translation.'

'Your father said he went to Montpellier. And we know he photocopied part of the original manuscript. So he had the opportunity to read it all. Would he have taken so much trouble?'

'Oh, yes. He was terribly thorough.'

Fumbling in the inner pocket of the linen jacket, Alastair suddenly exclaimed. 'Look at this, Julia! A postcard addressed to you. Stamped but never posted.'

The handwriting was hurried and shaky. So was my hand as I read it, first to myself, then aloud: 'A little saint best fits a little shrine. All my love, Dad.' I handed it back. 'Did you notice the date? The day of his accident. This is almost certainly the last thing he ever wrote.'

He touched my hand briefly, solicitously, as he read the curt message, frowning. 'Does it mean anything to you?'

'No. I clenched my fists and almost screamed: 'Why, oh why couldn't he make things easier for me? These stupid puzzles!'

Alastair tried to soothe me by saying that this particular puzzle wouldn't be too hard to solve, 'when we get the rest of the quotation.'

He turned the postcard over. The photograph was a typical tourist image of the region showing a countrywoman force-feeding a goose gripped between her knees. The picture's heading in colourful lettering was Le Gavage à la Ferme.

I pondered my father's riddle: 'A little saint? Who could that be? Not James, obviously. And Santiago de Compostela is far from being a little shrine.'

'Louise said Edouard would have a book of quotations in his library. For the present, let's go over this place from top to bottom, or vice versa. Is there a cellar?'

'No. There's a large barn.'

'We'll leave that for later.'

He finished searching the cupboard and began dismantling an ancient coffee grinder. 'The news of François's failure to complete his mission would have got back to his abbot. A search would have been instigated.'

'Yes, except if the ring had been found, it would have been taken to the shrine. In that case it would be there today but it isn't, nor anywhere else in Christendom, as far as I can find out. No one has heard of it.'

I shut the last drawer with an emphatic gesture.

Alastair remarked: 'You said François died in the abbey at Flaran.'

'That's a guess to be honest. He says he joined the brotherhood there, but there's no record at the abbey today and no knowledge of a grave. That's not really surprising after eight hundred years.'

'And what about your father's notebook? He sent nothing home apart from the journal, you say.'

'That's been troubling me. He'd have made copious notes and probably drafted several chapters.'

The search of the ground floor yielded nothing more after the discovery of the postcard. An hour had gone by. I led the way upstairs and into my father's workplace. After a quick glance round the barely furnished room, Alastair went straight to the writing table.

'Any clues here?'

'I went through his papers yesterday.'

'Find anything?'

'Only bills, receipts, my letters, a couple of invitations.'

'Who came here after his accident?'

'Only Malvin and the ambulance crew. Then the police, and they locked the place. There are no signs of any interference.'

'What did the police do with the keys?'

'They kept them until I sent proof of my title to the house. They said the house was left exactly as it was when my father was taken to hospital. I've no reason to doubt that. He wouldn't have had any valuables - nothing worth stealing except the ring.'

'And his notes.'

'Why would anyone want to steal them?'

'Where are his clothes?'

'In the chest of drawers over there. Shirts, trousers, socks, underwear. All quite neatly arranged. I don't know who did his washing and ironing. We could ask in the village. And there's a shooting jacket and a dressing gown in the armoire. His shoes and boots are downstairs. You don't need a lot of clothes in this climate. He didn't socialise.'

'Do you mind if I have a look through his things?'

'I was hoping you'd offer.'

Opening the shutters of the window by the writing-desk, I pointed across to the far boundary. 'Over there: those are the woods where he found the grave. He must have sat here often, looking out, thinking about François, wondering what happened to him.'

'He obviously made a powerful connection between François and the pilgrim in the grave. You have to ask, was that François?'

'I thought of it, obviously, yet François calls himself a puny man. The skeleton was of a giant, two metres tall. That's huge by medieval standards. His name was Magnus.'

Alastair raised an eyebrow. 'How do you know?'

'The Journal tells us. François had a close companion. A man chosen by the abbot to look after him on his pilgrimage. François named him Magnus - The Big Man. Someone killed Magnus and his companions buried him in the woods before continuing on their pilgrimage.'

'So he was a kind of security guard.'

'For François, not for the ring. Only François knew of the ring. He would have been at risk otherwise. It was dangerous country for travellers. Magnus was chosen for his stature. François calls him a simple man - a clumsy peasant, unable to read or write, though a monk. He befriended him, taught him and shared food and shelter with him. François loved Magnus.'

'Brotherly love.'

'Physical love. The love of Eros not of Agapemone.'

Alastair frowned. 'A mortal sin in the eyes of his church.'

'Yes, if it was consummated. And unconfessed, except to his Journal.'

'And therefore unpardoned.'

'That could explain his terror.'

'More than that. There were silly disputes - lovers' quarrels aggravated by the trials of the journey. Little things that got magnified. Arguments. Jealousies. Distrust. François was a complex man. Educated, thoughtful, sensitive, deeply religious, but wracked by forbidden feelings. Magnus was a simple peasant - demonstrative, virile, loyal. Things started to go wrong, and then suddenly Magnus disappears from the Journal. Nothing more is said about him. It's as though he never existed.'

Alastair frowned again, more darkly. 'You think François killed him?'

'Could he have done it? Physically, I mean? A so-called puny man overcoming a giant?'

'The skull is easily fractured. If there was a serious quarrel that flared up into a moment of violence, anger would have reinforced his strength.'

I visualised the moment. A dark night. Magnus and François lying apart from the main body of pilgrims. Magnus asleep. François awake, seething with jealousy or some other dark emotion, determined to exact punishment for some supposed wrong or betrayal, finding a weapon to hand - something sharp and heavy, like a spade - maddened by rage, losing control, standing grimly over his victim, striking the blow so hard the big man scarcely uttered a cry. Was the crime blamed on robbers? A silent attack in the night? Magnus loyally defending François and taking the blow in his place?

'It's all circumstantial,' Alastair said. 'And it hardly helps in the search.'

'I don't agree. Understanding François is important.'

Alastair turned to one of the four pictures by Dad's writing table. 'If this is from the original manuscript of the journal, why did your father choose this page?'

'Because it points to the hiding place. Why else? Perhaps it's a cryptogram, like you suggested.'

Alastair removed the framed picture from its hook and examined it closely. 'May I take it back to the château?'

'But you don't read Latin.'

'I'd just like to look at it more closely. And the journal too, if you don't mind?'

It was cool in the kitchen. He poured red wine into a goblet.

'You've earned this.'

'So have you. I couldn't have got half as far without you.'

'Half as far? We've found nothing except the postcard.'

'There's the barn still. Will you do me a favour?'

'What's that?'

'Search the barn for me. On your own.'

'Why?' Almost at once he anticipated the answer. 'Ah! The earlier postcard. "Something nasty in the woodshed". I thought it was a joke.'

'He didn't make jokes like that. Nor waste words. I had a quick look inside yesterday. It gave me the creeps. I just got the feeling that something might have happened there. So, if you don't mind. It's silly, I know, and I should have mentioned it before.'

'It doesn't matter. I don't believe in ghosts.'

I shivered, took a mouthful of wine and savoured the complexity of it before swallowing. 'That's delicious, Alastair.'

'So it ought to be. A cru classé. La Lagune. I'm taking a case home.'

'Wine's a mystery to me,' I said as I spread a cloth on the table.

'It's becoming less of a mystery, more of a science. Don't worry about the mystery, just enjoy the wine. And we'll worry about the barn later.'

I started unwrapping the ridiculously plentiful lunch Louise had packed for us. A crisp flute, butter in an earthenware pot, a coarse terrine and a smooth pâté, two cheeses, shiny black olives, golden tomatoes, radishes, salad leaves, peaches and muscat grapes. We sat opposite each other. There were plates, knives, napkins, mineral water in a flask, hot coffee in another, proper coffee cups. Alastair remarked on Louise's competence as a hostess and quizzed me about her marriage to Edouard de Marcignac.

'All I know is that she was working with Nell for a client in Paris when Edouard captured her and brought her down here. She seems to have adapted pretty well.'

'I've known Edouard for years. He's been pretty solitary for years since his wife died. No interest in other women.'

'Wife?'

'Isabella. A princess no less. I never knew her. Died in a tragic accident. One thing struck me about Louise. She is uncannily like a painting I've seen of Isabella.'

'Ah!' I nodded, as though this explained everything. I sliced the flute laterally and passed one half to Alastair. He examined the cheeses and cut into a creamy chèvre.

'Would you enjoy her situation?'

'I would never be in her situation.'

'No, of course not. You're far too sensible to take such a risk.' Seeing my sharp reaction, he hastily added: 'That's a compliment, Julia. I admire you for what you're doing.' There was a long silence. He drank some wine and topped up both glasses.

'Your father meant a great deal to you, didn't he?'

'Of course. Doesn't yours to you?'

'Naturally.'

I tasted the wine again and made a murmur of appreciation.

'Nell told me about her evening with him in Paris. La Tour d'Argent. A table overlooking Notre Dame. Red roses, champagne, the same food and wine he had there with your mother on their honeymoon. He took a chance, didn't he? Inviting a complete stranger to celebrate his golden wedding alone with him? It could have been a disaster.'

'I don't think so. My father is a shrewd judge of character. He'd spent time with Nell and saw her as a caring person.'

I realised this was as strong an admission as he was likely to make. I said: 'Nell thought your father was wonderful. I'd like to meet him one day.'

15 - ALASTAIR

The padlock was heavy but opened with a sharp click. The massive bolts were well greased and slid back easily. One of the huge doors swung outwards of its own accord. I peered into a black cavernous space. The only light was from the opening. I stepped inside and stood still until my eyes switched to the darkness after the bright sunlight. There were no windows, but a dim light filtered through gaps in the Roman tiles high above. The roof was a massive oak structure. The place smelled of old oak, rotting apples and decay.

On the floor in the immediate foreground I made out the shapes of elderly machines - a small tractor, mowers, a bicycle. There were rusty implements - a chainsaw, a brush cutter, hand tools - and several old ladders, so placed, it seemed, as to be an obstacle course to trip up unwary visitors. The tools must have been acquired with the house. I had seen no evidence that Bray had worked with any of them.

I was becoming used to the dimness now and could make out rickety tables and chairs piled high on empty packing cases. Part way along the right-hand side of the barn were wooden racks holding rows of empty wine bottles. Eight or nine dozen, at least, I estimated. How long had Julia's father been staying here? A hundred would be a bottle a day for more than three months.

The silence was palpable. It was a disturbing, neglected and sad place, though I couldn't explain Julia's reaction to it. I moved around cautiously, prospecting for I didn't know what. Hiding places? There were scores of possibilities. I looked more closely at the wine bottles. There were no labels. They had probably contained local wine bought en vrac for a few francs a bottle, but then near the end I found a single bottle with a label. A second label had been stuck to the back, not by the producer. I examined the hand-written legend thoughtfully, put the bottle to one side and began to search slowly through all the others, but found no more that were labelled.

At the far end of the barn an ancient chest of drawers stood against the wall. It was a simple country piece and had evidently once been painted blue but was now faded and scarred. The bottom drawer had lost both handles. It was wide open and completely empty. I opened each of the others in turn. The left-hand of the two small drawers at the top was full of unidentifiable bits of machinery. It also contained a sack tied with a piece of cord. I could feel something metal and sharp inside. I untied the cord, opened the sack cautiously and withdrew a rusty, sickle-shaped billhook with a worm-eaten wooden handle. The blade was sharp and had a large, jagged chip out of the edge. I put the billhook back in the sack and tied the cord.

The right-hand drawer contained a pile of old newspapers, some of them English, neatly folded over a cardboard shoe-box. I lifted the lid of the box and stared at the intact skeleton of a hand laid carefully on cotton wool with the place where the palm had been uppermost. The hand had been cut off above the wrist and the carpus was badly splintered.

Seated at the kitchen table with the sack and the cardboard box on the floor beside me I first showed Julia the bottle, turning it around in my hand. 'I counted them. Nearly two hundred. All unlabelled except this one. The label caught my eye. One of the best wines from these parts.'

'And the others?'

'Unlabelled and ordinary. I guess your father bought wine in bulk and bottled it himself, but why keep just one bottle with a label?'

'You tell me.'

'Because it bears a message. There's another label stuck on the back.' I handed it to her. 'Your father's handwriting?'

'Yes.' She turned the bottle round and read aloud. "Cellar note July 12th 2005. Château de Peyros. Vintage 2003. Purchased from Jean Cousseau. Price 40 euros. Quantity: 2 bottles. Occasion: A day to remember." 'July 12th was his birthday, by the way.' She paused with her mouth open.

'Go on.'

'Occasion: A day to remember. Guest: François de Castres! Is this some kind of a joke?'

'I don't think so. Look. Under "Comments" he's written "Sensational. Great depth. Warn JB. Cellar carefully. Third bin".'

'What does that mean?'

'JB is you of course. He's telling you to look in the cellar.'

'I've told you, there isn't one. And what did he mean by putting François's name as his guest? That gives me the shivers.'

'This might be a way of telling you he was hot on the track of François at the time. Or maybe that he had a supernatural experience when he dined here alone on his birthday. Would he have done an extraordinary thing like that?'

'Very probably, but the cellar note says two bottles. What about the other one?'

'There was only one. I searched everywhere. Maybe François got smashed at the party and. ......'

She cut me short. 'That's not funny.'

'Sorry!'

I picked up the sack, untied the cord and took out the sickle-shaped billhook. 'Careful! It's still sharp.'

Julia held the handle and examined the blade gingerly. I said: 'I'm pretty sure it's medieval.'

'Where did you find it?'

'In an old chest of drawers. Your father must have put it there. I don't think he found it in the barn.'

'Why not?'

'Because of this. From another drawer.'

I picked up the cardboard box. Before lifting the lid, I said: 'Julia, this is nasty.'

Her eyes opened wide as she stared at the cruel amputation. She caught her breath and put a hand over her mouth. 'My God!'

'François's, do you think?' I touched a joint so that one of the spindly fingers moved slightly. 'We'll have to get this carbon-dated. The bill-hook too.'

'Is that really necessary? Dating won't tell us anything we don't know.'

'It's easy to jump to conclusions. This could have come from another time. From an accident on the farm.'

'Do you really think so?'

I hesitated. 'No, it wouldn't have been kept like this after an accident. Too macabre. I think it happened near here, soon after Magnus died, and that your father found this by chance.'

'Near the house, after all those years? Surely someone else..'

'..wouldn't have been searching the way he was.'

She fingered the splintered bone. 'How awful! Would he have bled to death?'

'It was common practice to cut off a thief's hand. They used a tourniquet. Besides, if he did bleed to death, where are his remains? They'd have been found. No, I guess this was a punishment.'

'For theft? Or for killing Magnus?'

'We'll never know. Look, Julia, We've done enough here for today. Can we have a look at the place where your father found the grave in the woods?'

'I've a rehearsal at five.'

'That gives us a good hour before going back.'

She hesitated.

'Would you rather I went alone?'

'You wouldn't find it.'

I looked at her challengingly.

'All right. I'll take you there.'

I carefully put the skeleton back in its box. She stared at it - still shaken by the implications. 'You're not taking that back to the house, are you?'

'I'll put it in the drawer where I found it. And lock up the barn.'

The trees were close-packed. There were no paths except narrow tracks made by animals. Wild boar? The sky was invisible under the canopy of trees. It would have been easy to lose any sense of direction but Julia never hesitated. When I remarked on her confidence she showed me how the trail had been marked wherever there was a change of direction.

'The police did it. One of their men got seriously lost in here.'

We came across the grave without warning. Undergrowth had been cut back to make a small clearing. In the centre was a simple tablet of pure white marble inscribed only with a cross. A jam-jar containing a simple bunch of white daisies had been placed on the plaque.

I glanced at Julia questioningly. She nodded. 'No one else comes here. The villagers still think the place is haunted.'

We stood in silence for a minute or two staring at the burial place of the murdered man. Then Julia turned away. There was no reason to stay however I was reluctant to leave. Julia intrigued me. Her reticence continued to challenge me. We had spent most of the day alone together but she'd volunteered nothing about herself and had fended off my tentative approaches. Nell had said she was secretive about her work too. And was there a man in her life? She didn't wear a ring. I wished, as I had told her, that I'd known her father. She must have many of his qualities. A sharp intellect, steadfastness, courage, too. Very few women would dare to walk the woods alone. She was almost reckless in her determination to uncover the secret of the joyau.

'I told you there's nothing to see,' she said.

'I've been wondering about the Latin inscription on the grave. Who put it there, do you suppose?'

'Someone from the abbey, probably. After the pilgrims had moved on. Flaran was the only place of any consequence near here.'

'Magnus was a monk, wasn't he? Could he be the "little saint" and this his little shrine?'

'Little?'

'In saintly terms, yes. Your father was grasping at remembered quotations. He wrote that postcard in a hurry.'

'I think Magnus's shrine is where he lies. The sarcophagus.'

'Perhaps we should take another look.'

She glanced at her watch. 'We ought to be going.'

As we turned back the way we'd come, following the marked trail, I asked: 'What time does your rehearsal finish?'

'About seven, I guess. Why?'

'Will you have supper with me afterwards?'

'What about the others?'

'What about them?'

'I mean, what about Nell? I thought you were both...'

'Julia, I'm just inviting you to eat with me. Nothing more. A chance to talk about other things.'

I put out a hand. She stepped back sharply. 'I just want to help you.'

Nell was back from a sketching expedition. Louise was in a light-hearted mood after lunching with Edouard at the château in Fourcès, a rare outing. The four of us sat in the shade of the terrace where Louise had brought a pot of tea and a plate of madeleines. While she poured the tea, Julia outlined her theory about Magnus; that he had been assigned by his Abbot as François's protector on the pilgrimage; how his description in the Journal fitted that of the skeleton in the grave and my belief that he had been killed by François in a fit of jealousy. Her argument met no resistance. She produced the postcard found in her father's coat pocket. Her voice was a bit shaky. 'It's dated the day he died.'

Nell read it aloud with a blank expression. 'What does it mean?'

Louise went into the kitchen and returned with a copy of The Oxford Dictionary of Quotations. 'I borrowed this from Edouard. He asked if we're doing crossword puzzles. I said we're playing a game.'

Julia began flicking through the pages. 'Robert Herrick. "Upon a Pipkin of Jelly sent to a Lady". Just three lines. "A little saint best fits a little shrine, a little prop best fits a little vine, as my small cruse best fits my little wine."'

Louise asked: 'Does it mean anything to you?'

'Only that Herrick was one of my father's favourite poets.'

Nell remarked: 'And that's why he called you Julia!'

'Yes, as it happens.'

'Fine, but what about the little shrine?' posed Louise. 'A shrine for the Sacred Thing? The hiding place?'

'Or Magnus's resting place,' I said. 'The crypt in the church at Marcignac.'

Julia said: 'Just a wild guess.'

'Too many guesses, too few certainties,' I said. 'And now we have something else.' I described my search of the barn and the discovery of the bottle with its puzzling inscription, the sickle and the skeleton hand. 'We could get a lab test, but I'm sure the sickle is medieval. As to the hand, whose was it? The skeleton in the grave was intact.'

'They cut off robbers' hands in those days, didn't they?' said Nell.

I nodded.

'And your father wrote about a theft that confounded the thief.'

'Why did he have to be so damned obscure?'

'He was teasing you, wasn't he?'

'And one day all would have been revealed, to his great pleasure and amusement. Except it's not a joke. It's a puzzle with no answer.'

'There'll be an answer, love,' said Nell. 'I'm sure there will.'

After delivering Nell and Julia to the abbey, I changed my mind about staying to hear the choir's rehearsal and drove back to Marcignac. In the church the sacristain was placing service sheets on each of the chairs. There was to be a Requiem Mass, he explained, a much respected parishioner had died. The service would be attended by many distinguished people. I waited until he had finished his task before asking if I could see the tomb of the pilgrim in the crypt. Ferran nodded. It would be an honour etcetera etcetera. He was privileged to be the custodian of so remarkable a memorial.

The solemn performance in front of the sarcophagus was exactly as Louise described it. After the final Kyrie when Ferran was about to snuff out the candles, I raised a hand, and asked if I might take a closer look. Ferran demurred. The sarcophagus had been committed to his care. It had received the benediction of the bishop himself. No one was permitted to approach it more closely than where we now stood.

Choosing my words with care, I said I had come from England with Mademoiselle Bray, the daughter of the Englishman who discovered the pilgrim's grave. We were investigating a mystery connected with the pilgrim - a mystery to which Monsieur Ferran himself might hold the key. Mademoiselle Bray had met Monsieur Ferran here - he would remember, surely - and had judged him to be a man on whose discretion we could rely. For my own part, I would greatly value any assistance in this investigation.

I took a visiting card from my wallet and handed it over. Ferran pursed his lips and shook his head. I hesitated. Perhaps I was mistaken to suppose that Bray could have touched anything in the crypt under the eyes of this watchful man, but if the oblique reference to "a little shrine" on the postcard found in Bray's jacket didn't point to the crypt, where else? To the church itself? Ferran was its guardian, a stern, conscientious man who could be trusted. If Bray was worried about people ferreting around and needed somewhere more secure than the house as a safe deposit, so to speak, no one would think of the sacristain's house. Not for the ring; I was sure of that, but maybe for the notebook he'd finished with?

I tested this theory with a direct question. 'Un peu avant son mort, Monsieur Bray avait fait une visite ici, n'est-ce-pas?'

It was a guess, but it hit the mark.

Ferran looked at me with some suspicion. Yes, the monsieur had made a visit some little time before his death. But he made frequent visits. They were good friends. Yes, but had not Monsieur Bray, just before his sad death, given Monsieur Ferran something important to look after, either for himself to take home to England or for his daughter if she should call for it? I was sure I already knew the answer.

There was only a moment's hesitation. 'Oui, Monsieur.' With that, Ferran seemed to realise he had gone far enough. Before I could continue, he extinguished the candles and, without another word, led the way up the steps into the church.

Standing at the back of the abbey's lofty nave and surveying the great void, I wondered what became of the monks who, nearly eight hundred years earlier, had raised the massive columns of the nave stone upon stone and formed the great arches that bore up the roof. The building was now a sad witness to their life and faith, yet its solidity and the feeling that it could stand like this for another thousand years was awe-inspiring.

I stood for a while staring at the far distant choir on a wooden platform at the east end. They were singing a solemn piece. Slowly moving chords resonated against each other, vibrating and merging into a wash of sound that lifted to the vaulting high above.

At last I moved away from the nave towards where I knew, from the plan I had picked up at the entrance, I would find the cloister and the chapter house. The singing faded until the words were unintelligible. All too soon the short piece ended.

The way to the cloister and the chapter house was through a door in the last bay of the north aisle. I found the cloister to consist of only a single side with a half-timbered gallery above. According to the guide-book the rest had been demolished during the Wars of Religion in 1569 when Flaran was attacked by the Protestant Sieur de Montgoméry, Gabriel de Lorges. This Norman lord had fled to England after killing Henri II in a tourney, but came back with an army which set fire to the abbey church. The flames destroyed the archives and, I concluded, any trace of François's residence in Flaran.

There was no one about, or so I thought until I caught a momentary glimpse of a white-robed figure moving across the gallery. I waited quite a while but the man (a member of the abbey's Cistercian order?) didn't reappear. Presumably there was a staircase or a passage through which he had passed to another part of the abbey.

The little chapter house was supposed to be the most beautiful part of Flaran, with nine bays, columns of different coloured marbles and a low ceiling of complex rib vaulting. Nell had remarked that the place felt "inhabited". It was cold and empty now. Not welcoming certainly, but haunted?

I could visualise the members of the chapter at their deliberations. They must have met to debate the murder of the pilgrim in the woods. Why had they not ordered his body to be brought to the abbey for burial in consecrated ground? And had they subsequently, as Julia believed, taken François into their brotherhood?

Out of the corner of my eye I suddenly caught sight, outside the chapter house, of a passing figure - the white-robed man I'd seen in the gallery above the cloister. One of the monks gliding by with long, steady strides, his head covered and cast down and his hands tucked inside his wide sleeves.

It was an opportunity not to be missed. Though the Cistercians were a strict order, there was no harm in making an approach. The monk might be able to throw fresh light on the discovery and re-internment of the murdered pilgrim.

The ambulatory was long and straight but the man was out of sight. He couldn't have turned off for there were no doorways or side turnings. I looked back in the other direction, wondering if I had been momentarily mistaken.

I gave up. It would be simpler to ask at the information desk if there were any of the brothers I could talk to. It would soon be time to return to the nave. Julia and Nell would want a lift back and there was the question of supper with Julia. Had she implied yes or no to my clumsy invitation?

The woman at the information desk knew nothing about the monk. Flaran no longer had a religious community. The man I had seen must have been a member of the public. The abbey received many visitors from other foundations.

I went back to the cloister and made a slow circuit of all the areas beyond the nave. I met a middle-aged English couple studying the guide book and asked if they'd seen a man wearing a monk's habit. No, but wasn't this an astonishing place? You could imagine how wonderful it must have been in past times. There were echoes from the past all around, weren't there?

Nell and Julia were waiting for me by the car. I told them what I'd been doing. Nell mischievously suggested the monk was a phantom - an unhappy shade conjured up by us probing into the death of the pilgrim. I laughed a little uneasily.

Julia took the suggestion seriously. She said: 'My father wrote "this place is haunted".'

'Do you think he meant the abbey?'

She shrugged. 'I've no idea.'

I deflected talk about phantoms by telling them of my visit to the church at Marcignac.

'I thought your father's reference to "the little shrine" might point to the pilgrim's tomb. I wanted to take a close look at the sarcophagus. Ferran stopped me. I questioned him. I implied that I knew your father had given him something to keep safe for you. It was a simple guess - that your father was worried about security and needed help from someone he could trust. Someone he could rely on if he made them feel important. I was right. Ferran has something for you.'

'Not the ring, surely?'

'No, that would have been too risky. If your father found the ring that is for you to take care of. That's what he said, isn't it?'

There was no question. Julia must go at once to collect whatever her father had left in safe keeping for her. We drove straight there. It was only a slight diversion on the way back to the château. Nell waited in the car while Julia and I made our way to the sacristain's cottage. Ferran was in his garden next to the footpath round the church. He was cleaning an empty rabbit hutch. Lapin must have been on the menu lately.

He greeted us politely, wiping his hand on his apron before offering it.

Yes, of course he remembered the young lady. She had visited the crypt with Madame de Marcignac. The young lady, I said, was the only daughter of Monsieur Leonard Bray, of whom we had been speaking that afternoon.

Ferran regarded her impassively.

'C'est vrai, Ma'mselle?'

'Oui, Monsieur. C'est vrai. Il était mon père. Mon père très bien aimé. Et je crois qu'il était votre ami egalement.'

Ferran looked at her more closely. There was a certain resemblance, he remarked. In the eyes, perhaps, but Monsieur Bray had entrusted him with something of great importance. He regretted he must ask if she could show a piece of identity.

Julia opened her handbag. 'I have a picture of my father.'

It was a press cutting from the Times Literary Supplement accompanying a review of one of his books. He looked, perhaps, ten years younger - a picture that Julia had always liked more than any other. It had been chosen for the National Portrait Gallery that same year.

Ferran looked at it closely, blinking. 'Votre père, Ma'mselle?'

'Un écrivain bien célébré. Et regardez!'

She handed him a much-handled colour photograph. It showed her and her father beside a canal in Venice. They were holding hands and smiling happily.

Ferran studied the photograph for quite a while before handing it back. He seemed affected but said nothing. Asking us to wait, he went into the house. When he returned he was carrying a large package sealed with red wax. It was inscribed in black ink:

PRIVATE AND CONFIDENTIAL,
FOR MISS JULIA BRAY PERSONALLY

Giving it to Julia, Ferran grasped her hand and said; 'Voila, Ma'mselle. Maintenant c'est à vous. J'éprouve de la commisération pour vous.'

She nodded and smiled.

After a moment she managed to say: 'Monsieur Ferran, je suis très content qu'il avait eu confiance en vous.'

He straightened his back as though about to salute, touched her hand again, then turned away. When we looked back he was once more cleaning the rabbits' cage.

As soon as we were in the car Julia broke the seal on the package. It contained a very thick pile of manuscript pages and an envelope with her name on it. Without a word she opened the envelope and took out a single sheet. After a quick glance all she could say was: 'From my father.'

16 - MALVIN

Carlo had sent me a bound photocopy of Le Journal d'un Pèlerin by envoi recommandé for which I had to pay a supplement to the postman. It was accompanied by a formal letter acknowledging the receipt of his expenses "to date" and enclosing more bills.

I swallowed my anger with some difficulty and turned to the journal. It was spirally bound in hard covers with the front page bearing the stamp of the university library. On first reading it was a tedious account of an uneventful journey. I grew more and more impatient with the author's whinging. There were long and tiresome passages of self-pity and little of interest beyond revealing that the writer was carrying a jewel of some kind - the so-called "res sacra" - to the saint's shrine in Santiago de Compostela, a mission he failed to complete. Only a footnote by the editor explained what was meant by le joyau.

I read the whole text twice and parts of it a third time, searching for a hint of how the "sacred thing" might have been concealed during the journey and what happened to it after that. If a ring of such repute had been found on the writer after his death it would surely have been trumpeted far and wide by the Church. It would have become famous and widely venerated. So it was not found.

Did it really exist? If so, what of its provenance? Bray believed in it. He had written confidently: "Everything I have found in researching this book convinces me that the ring of St James was the 'treasure' brought from the Holy Land to the abbey in Liguria and subsequently given to François de Castres to take with him in secret on his ill-fated journey."

What had he found to convince him? The ring itself? The

answer must be in his manuscript. A thorough search of Le Belvédère would require the co-operation of Bray's daughter. One way or another I would have to persuade her to share what she knew about her father's work. I had heard she was staying at the château and would be taking part in the local festival. There was to be a small party to welcome the English choir of which she was a member. I would arrange to be invited.

Reading the Pilgrim's Journal once more I came to the only possible conclusion: that François de Castres had kept the joyau. If Bray knew where he had hidden it he must have told his daughter. All I needed was her co-operation, a bit of gentle persuasion.

The discovery of the ring would be an international sensation. And great prestige for me, if I played my hand carefully. I would present it to the Church. The money didn't matter. I would have plenty when Marcignac bought the Canticum.

17 - ALASTAIR

I led Julia from the terrace to a shady seat in a corner of Louise's herb garden. The fragrance of box, rosemary and lavender hung on the warm air. Branches of a climbing rose with purple blooms arched over the limestone wall behind them. I remarked that Louise had brought something of England with her to Gascony. Julia murmured agreement, but romantic ideas seemed to be wasted on her so I asked if she thought our hostess was happy as the châtelaine of Marcignac.

'Content, I would say. More or less settled, but ask Nell. She knows Louise much better than I do.'

'I have asked her. She feels Louise is nervously occupied finding her feet. Still a bit overwhelmed by what she's taken on, but no regrets.'

Julia fiddled with the gold chain round her neck. 'I think we've something much more interesting to discuss than Louise's marriage. This Claudia woman who wrote to Edouard. Do you believe her story that the Calix is back in Rome?'

'I think she is telling Edouard not to spend time looking for the Calix because it is safe.'

'She made quite a thing of her visit to Rome, didn't she? It can't be easy getting permission to search the Vatican's archives. Her assertion that the Calix was made there by order of the Pope depends on this alleged record of a payment to a silversmith in the late 12th century. If the record exists, finding it would take several days, even with the co-operation of a helpful archivist. After getting permission in the first place. Like you, I think she's deflecting further inquiries, killing the legend, stopping us going any further.'

'Why?'

'To cover up the truth.'

'What truth?'

'What really happened to the Calix. It's interesting she said nothing about the Abbazia. Did she even go there? She knew the Calix was supposed to have been there from soon after the abbey was founded but claims it was returned to Rome in 1217. For safety, she says. What does that mean? Any serious scholar would have gone to Lombardy to find out. I would.'

'And then,' said Alastair, 'she produces a photograph like a rabbit out of a hat, to prove her claim that the Calix is back in Rome.'

'A photograph would clinch it.'

'Very convenient, if there *is* a photograph, but it could be a picture of any chalice. And why has it never been published? The Calix is an historic piece.'

'Maybe it has been, somewhere. I could have missed it.'

'After all your careful research?'

She shrugged. 'I could have overlooked something.'

'Do you believe that?'

'Not really.'

'What was your most recent source, Julia?'

'An article in a popular Italian magazine.'

'The abbey was named?'

'As it was in all my sources. The magazine story was a piece for general consumption. "The Lost Treasure of San Benedetto della Verna". That sort of thing.'

'Pictures.'

'Not of the Calix. Only of the abbey. And no mention of the reredos.'

'If we're to believe this Claudia person, she didn't know about the photograph till she went to the Vatican. They would have photographed the chalice for the record, wouldn't they?'

'But never published it?'

'No need. Why publish a picture of just another medieval chalice among so many? Besides, they'd want to keep the story about the Pope's deception quiet.'

'But isn't that also a matter of historic interest?'

'It's all in the past. What I find much more interesting is why Claudia went to Rome rather than the abbey where the Calix was known to have been?'

'I agree. The abbey is where any serious researcher would start.'

'Or maybe she did go there but doesn't want to say what we know she would have found. A record that the Calix was sent away from Lombardy in 1217 to the Abbaye de Cluny in France.'

'Together with Antelami's reredos. She would have learned about that too.'

'But never said anything about it. I think she's more interested in the Calix. And I must say, Julia, so am I. If the legend is true the Calix is a unique and priceless treasure.'

18 - EDOUARD

At noon I called my guests to a meeting in the library. When all were seated and expectant I opened a drawer in my desk, took out a large envelope and placed it unopened on the table with my hand on top. Looking around to gain everyone's close attention I began the full explanation they were waiting for.

'As you know, "The Song of Songs" is a part of the Bible that stands apart because of its apparently secular subject, a young bride about to go to her husband and teasing him with her beauty. It's a charming story told in poetic and sensuous verses that seem out of place in the Bible. The monks illustrated the verses with pages of beautiful, highly erotic and imaginative pictures. Imaginative, I say, because monks are not supposed to know of such things.'

'Why not?' interposed Nell. 'Monks are not saints. Have you read Rabelais?'

I waved away her interruption. 'After I'd shown interest in buying the book, Malvin brought it here. Although he had previously shown me photographs, when I opened the covers and began turning the pages I could hardly believe what I was seeing. The booksellers I've consulted agree that, though the book's quality is outstanding, the unashamedly erotic manner of the illustrations add enormously to its value. You have seen a few of them in your folders. I have copies of the rest.'

I opened the envelope, took out a large number of colour photographs and asked Alastair to pass them round. They were viewed in total silence; there was no need of comment, the richly coloured images spoke for themselves. Here was the eager bridegroom portrayed with a frankness none could have imagined in such an illuminated manuscript of the period, let alone in Holy Scripture. Despite their frankness the pictures were also strangely innocent.

I watched impassively as Nell regarded the naked bride standing beneath a tree bearing rosy apples with the eager young man secretly watching from behind another tree.

'See,' I said. 'The fruit is ripe and tempting, but the Serpent is absent. And remember, this is an image of Man's temptation made by men who have taken a vow of celibacy.'

'Quite beautiful,' said Alastair. 'I can understand why you would want to own the book.'

'So can I,' said Louise. 'He's besotted with her.'

I gave my wife a dark look. 'I'm merely demonstrating why the abbey has guarded the Canticum so carefully that no one has recorded it until now, but the book is incidental to the puzzle I am putting to you. It was through the inscription found on one of the end-papers that I learned of the missing reredos and the so-called Cup of Sanctity. My firm belief, after much thought, is that the reredos was deliberately diverted en route from the abbey to Cluny so that it could be installed somewhere else, in its proper place behind an altar. The question I ask is which altar might that be?'

'A Christian altar?' asked Alastair.

'Not necessarily. There were secret heretical rites in the Middle Ages which may have survived, even today. And don't discount demonic practices. Obscene rites in secret places. The Black Mass requires an altar. An altar normally needs a reredos as its backing. One stolen from a Christian church would be the more potent to devil worshippers.'

It was a chilling thought. I let it sink in before continuing.

'Together you have special skills and knowledge to deduce the answer to these questions. The prize would be the recovery of a hitherto unknown work by a master sculptor. That would be a sensation in the art world. You would all share in it. I propose a secret ballot. Is it worth spending your time here, maybe many days, on an investigation? Simply write Yes or No on the slip I shall give you, fold it and put it in the bowl on the table over there. Just one thing. The vote must be unanimous if we are to go ahead.'

As the ballot papers were passed round Nell said: 'I'm voting Yes. We have to give it a go. For a while, anyway.'

'I agree,' said Alastair. 'If we've got nowhere after, say, a week, we can have another vote.'

One by one the papers were placed in a beautiful Meiji bowl that stood alone on a side table. Impassively I unfolded each slip. When I had opened the last I must have smiled broadly as I announced that there were no dissenters and that I would regard it as a privilege to be counted as an active participant.

I rang a bell and coffee was brought as we turned to the practicality of a search. First, which was the most likely route to Cluny taken by the carriers of the reredos? Perhaps, suggested Julia, the baggage train was intercepted by followers of an heretical sect and the reredos taken for use in their rites? She said the Cathars and Manichaeans came to mind. Did the Cluniac region have any followers of medieval heresies at that time? She knew of none.

If the reredos was still in proper use, as I suggested it might be, it could only be in a private place that received no visitors. And what of the Calix Sanctitatis which seemed connected with the reredos? Was it really in Rome as my correspondent claimed? We could check that, but it would take days. Alastair argued against Claudia's claims. He recounted a conversation with Julia. 'Claudia's email could have come from anywhere in cyberspace. Let's say there really is someone called Claudia Andrieu who's a subscriber to this academic journal. I guess she thinks you wouldn't spend time and money checking her story. She is trying to put you off the scent of something that is of value to her. Why all this stuff about Rome and nothing about the abbey where you'd expect her to have researched the story she found so fascinating? Our guess is that she did go there and therefore she also knows about the Antelami reredos.'

Nell cut in: 'Supposing what she says is true? In that case the Calix would also have been sent to Rome with the reredos, its so-called guardian.'

'We can discount that,' said Julia. 'If the reredos had been sent to Rome rather than Cluny it would have been installed in a church in Parma or Rome itself, with great ceremony. We more or less know the date. The year 1217 or soon afterwards. It didn't happen. The reredos is totally unknown. And the Calix with it. The abbey has to be our starting point.'

Nell observed that if Claudia knew about the reredos and the Calix she would also be in the hunt. It would be a big coup for her to bring off. They ought to assume she was a competitor.

'Possibly,' said Alastair. 'But let's get our priorities right. The first is to visit the abbey.'

'Agreed,' said Julia, 'but that's a long journey. Do we have the time?'

Alastair nodded. 'Not by road, but Edouard has already offered to pay for me to use his private helicopter service. That cuts the round trip to a couple of days, allowing for refuelling.'

'I can set it up for tomorrow,' I remarked as casually as if I were arranging a tennis match. It pleased me to see the reaction this produced.

Alastair insisted he would go alone. 'But this requires teamwork' he said. 'Julia has studied ancient heresies. While I'm gone maybe she can find a hint of some that have survived till today. Nell could work out the carriers' most likely medieval route from the abbey to Cluny. I am sure this library has all the maps you'll need. Louise could compile a list of ancient and isolated churches and chapels along the route. And most importantly, what can we discover about the sender of the email? Whoever they are they read the same learned journals as you, Edouard. Is there a line you can follow?'

I was doubtful. 'Subscription lists are highly confidential. The journal is a specialist quarterly published in Milan with a circulation of only a few thousand, but I do have some useful contacts.'

19 - JULIA

The Château de Marcignac glowed in the evening sun as Edouard's guests arrived for the festival's welcoming party. They were guided by staff from the entrance hall to the terrace, passing through a silk-lined drawing room hung with paintings which, even to an untutored eye, must have confirmed the reputed stature of Edouard's art collection. A Gauguin there above a Louis XIV commode, a couple of Toulouse-Lautrec cabaret sketches, Matisse drawings in a small group and a painting by Poussin which Nell told me was beyond price. She recounted their conversation when he found her studying it in amazement.

'Louise tells me you are an artist.'

'She exaggerates. I'm an illustrator. It gives me a living.'

'Few of the artists whose work I've bought could have said that.'

'Toulouse-Lautrec, certainly, but what about Degas? He made a good living, didn't he? I was bowled over by that wonderful pastel in my bedroom.'

Nell and I were introduced to Edouard's personal guests. An elegant French couple from Bordeaux whose name Nell recalled from cru classé wine labels, an American woman with dazzling diamonds and teeth, a distinguished-looking prelate in a beautifully made soutane, Monsieur Korelian, an art dealer from Paris, Monsieur Malvin from Cassis and a statuesque Italian woman introduced by Edouard as a cousin. Nell remembered that the style 'cousin' could be applied by French nobility to almost any remote relation.

It was Malvin who stood apart in this company, as he surely

would in any company, I thought; not for his stature, for he was of moderate height and slender, but for his head which seemed to have been transplanted from a giant. His eyes were dark and deep-set beneath thick eyebrows and his sleek hair was stylishly cut. A monocle hung from a black ribbon attached to his grey silk suit.

Champagne was offered by footmen. I took a glass and looked round the room. Alastair had gravitated towards the couple from Bordeaux who obviously knew him. Nell had drifted away and was looking at the Matisse drawings in the company of the American woman. The Italian beauty was being monopolised by the Parisian art dealer. Malvin, who had been talking to the prelate, came across the room and introduced himself in a voice that was surprisingly soft and musical.

'André Malvin, amateur d'antiquités. I am told you are the daughter of the writer Leonard Bray. I was sorry about his death. He had a great reputation here in France. A writer of integrity, I would say.'

'You have read him?'

'I have also met him. Strangely, I had been reading "Nos amis sont nos adversaires" just before his accident.'

'It's called "Friendly Enemies" in England and America.'

'A scholarly book.' He waved towards the open French windows. 'There's a fine view from the terrace. May I escort you?'

I would have liked to make an excuse but this was an opportunity to discover why he had called on my father and what, if anything he knew of his accident and the book he was writing.

I shunned his arm by walking ahead. The view was indeed magnificent. Beyond the box-fringed parterre an avenue of walnut trees led the eye to a pavilion on an island in the centre of an ornamental lake. Chestnut woodlands on either side defined a gap through which the eye was led to a distant hill crowned with a group of stone farm buildings.

Malvin turned his huge head towards me and offered the proposition that it was almost an English scene. I shrugged: 'Not with that parterre, but I know what you mean.'

He made a sweeping gesture with one hand. 'But all this! Nature enhanced by artifice. That is an English skill.'

I didn't want to spend time discussing the influence of Capability Brown. I nodded perfunctorily and picked up his opening remark: 'When did you meet my father?'

'I heard he was writing a book about Le Chemin Saint-Jacques. I've travelled some of it myself. So I went to see him. We had some interesting talks. The book will be published?'

'I don't know.'

He paused. I thought he was about to ask about the manuscript, but he took my arm and steered me down a broad flight of steps towards the parterre. I wanted to resist but this would end the opportunity to learn more of what he knew. While we walked he continued.

'There are many stories about Saint Jacques. St James the Great you call him. The well-known legend is of bones found in a field in Galicia in the ninth century which the local bishop promptly claimed were those of the saint and commissioned a shrine to be built. It is so preposterous as to be beyond belief by any rational person.'

'Millions have believed in the legend. Thousands still make the pilgrimage each year.'

'Wishful thinking. The credulity of the ignorant. All religions are based on unprovable assertions. There is a fable, is there not, that Jesus travelled to England with St Joseph of Arimathea and walked upon England's mountains green? You sing it proudly, don't you?'

'It's a stirring tune and splendid words. You don't have to believe in the story to sing it proudly.'

He was clever and knowledgeable. I was not going to be side-tracked.

'What kind of antiques do you deal in, Monsieur Malvin?'

He looked slightly pained. 'I am not a dealer. I am an adviser to collectors.'

'I'm sorry.'

'I have clients for whom I act. Collectors of rare and valuable objects.'

'Any particular speciality?'

'Ecclesiastical pieces. For their beauty and rarity. I am not a religious man.'

'Chalices, for example?' I hazarded.

'Chalices, patens, crucifixes, reliquaries. There are some great works of art.'

'With an early piece isn't it difficult to tell the real thing from a much later imitation? There are some amazing fakes in the black museum at the V&A.'

'That is true. It's easy to be deceived, as the Church has been deceived by so-called holy relics.'

Relics! I couldn't help a slight start. 'You've never been deceived?'

'You have to be on your guard. Some things seem too good to be true. A piece may be so very special you want it to be right despite the absence of a provenance. Recently I came across something quite wonderful but more or less impossible to authenticate. I ask myself is it right? Its supposed history is too obscure to verify. Yet, au fond, it's all it should be, as an object. Sometimes that makes one suspicious. Still, I get a feeling in this case - a frisson, like an unexpected physical contact. Do you understand, mademoiselle?'

I returned his gaze for a moment, then looked away.

He went on: 'I am advising my client to buy. If he does, the purchase will create a great sensation.'

'Without authentication? Without a provenance?'

'What provenance is there for, say, The Dead Sea Scrolls?'

'Are you going to tell me about this wonderful thing you have come across?'

He gave me a smile that sent a shiver down the back of my neck.

'You will hear before long.'

He returned my challenging gaze without blinking. Why was he telling me this? I had the feeling that he had deliberately led up to it. He was teasing cruelly, talking about my father, tempting me to ask the wrong questions. This was too much.

Excusing myself, I made my way back to the terrace, looking for Nell or Alastair. I found Nell with Edouard who had managed to extricate himself from the prelate and was gazing at the ceiling of the yellow drawing room. I heard her say 'Magnificent! It could almost be Tiepolo.'

Edouard smiled. 'He worked here. But only in this room.'

I could see Nell was dumbstruck. Edouard went on: 'You will have seen some of my collection while staying here, but how about a brief conducted tour?'

20 - NELL

A pair of doors opened into a room with panelling of bleached wood on which were hung a dozen or so exquisite paintings by Fragonard, Watteau and Chardin. I wanted to study them, but Edouard said he would soon have to get back to his guests. We progressed quickly from room to room. Each was dedicated to either Italian, French, Flemish or English art and furnished appropriately. I was almost dumb with astonishment as he led me along a secret corridor hung with old master drawings worthy of any national museum, through a room with illuminated shelves displaying Limoges and Sèvres porcelain and at last to the library, a room of double height with a gallery around three sides. Edouard climbed a delicately carved oak staircase and after a moment's search brought down a large volume.

'One of Louise's favourites,' he said, placing it gently on a satinwood table. 'English. A five-volume set. The Birds of Britain by the ornithologist John Gould. There are very few copies. I am fortunate to have one.'

He began carefully turning the pages. 'I'm sure you know of this. Gould was the son of a foreman gardener at Windsor and a most talented painter. This is his masterpiece. There is one plate that has a special meaning for both of us. You may guess which one I mean.'

Obedient to the prompt, I said: 'It must be the golden oriole. She found one in her garden in England.'

'Oriolus oriolus. There were many here when I was a boy. You could hear them singing in the woods but they were always difficult to see. My father named the house because of their nests nearby.'

Gould's delicate painting showed off the cock-bird in all its finery with yellow plumage, black wings and black-tipped tail. Edouard pointed a finger at the legend underneath. 'I tell Louise this should say "sometimes seen in the south of England, but more at home in the warmer climes of France".'

A broad staircase led to a softly lit central gallery and a collection of French impressionists and post-impressionists. I stood for a long time transfixed by a painting I had never seen before. It was of two solemn-faced country people, an elderly man and woman, facing each other across a rough wooden table on which was placed a carafe of red wine, a cut loaf of bread and a bone-handled knife.

Edouard tested me. 'One of my first serious purchases. It was owned by a French family and had never been on the open market. What do you think of it?'

I didn't hesitate. 'It's wonderful. So calm and touching. He's captured the essence of their life. Cézanne is probably my favourite of the Impressionists.'

'Probably?'

'Definitely. When did he paint it?'

'Sometime in the 1880s, in Aix. I'm glad you like it.'

He touched my arm. 'Please excuse me I must look after my personal guests. You're welcome to another viewing, if you can get away from the festival.'

A serious invitation or just natural courtesy? As we went down the staircase I risked a probing question.

'I was reading the other day about the legend of St James's ring.'

'His ring?'

'I thought you might know the story.'

'There are many legends connected with St James, Nell. One is that by making the pilgrimage, wearing the saint's emblem and carrying your staff and scrip you earn a remission of half the time you would otherwise have to spend in purgatory for your sins. You've been to Santiago de Compostela?'

'No. I would like to.'

'It's a hard road if you do it the proper way on foot, with your staff, your scrip and your scallop-shell in your hat, but I'm sure you know that.'

When we got downstairs he excused himself and went to speak to the man called Korelian. I found Julia on her own looking thoughtful.

'I casually mentioned the legend of St James's ring. He didn't seem to know about it. Tell me, what would a pilgrim carry in his scrip?'

'Bare essentials for the journey from one hospice to the next. François wrote up his journal day by day, so he must have had writing materials. He wouldn't have risked keeping the ring in his scrip, if that's in your mind. More likely it would have been sewn into a hem of his robes.'

'But Alastair says monks were sometimes buried in their robes.'

'That's irrelevant. The ring has been found. My father told me.'

I said nothing. Did Leonard Bray's manuscript entrusted to the sacristain point the way? So far Julia had said nothing about it either to me or Alastair. We felt she was not yet ready to share her father's unpublished revelations. The book obviously didn't spell out the secret of the ring's whereabouts or she would have said so. More cryptic clues to tantalise us? I tried another line on Julia.

'When François abandoned his pilgrimage could that have been at Roncesvalles, where the French professor said the journal was found?'

'No. François says that after Flaran he was too weak to continue.'

'So another pilgrim took his journal to Roncesvalles.'

'Not necessarily one of the same pilgrims. It could have been taken there years later, even centuries later. Roncesvalles is irrelevant. There's no point in going there.'

Trying to get to the bottom of it all was like staring down into a deep well, even though you knew there was water in the depths it was out of sight.

Julia said nothing of her conversation with Malvin. What did he know?

21 - JULIA

I didn't need to approach Malvin again. He came across the terrace towards me with an ingratiating smile. 'I hear you are a classics scholar, Ma'mselle. Cambridge, wasn't it?'

I bridled. 'I was at King's. Not a scholar in the sense of having won a scholarship, but yes I did read classics.'

'And you were awarded a first-class degree,' he said with a sketchy smile that eluded his eyes.

How did he know that? Maybe by talking to Fergus Maine. Obviously he'd been asking questions about me.

'Are you a classicist?' I asked him.

'Only in the sense that I love Greek and Roman art, among other periods.'

'The Middle Ages?' she ventured.

'Of course. Italy most of all for its sculpture. The early masters in particular. Wiligelmo in Modena and Antelami in Parma were the leaders. Your father did a study of Antelami, he told me.'

'Yes.'

'Antelami's work in Parma Cathedral is his masterpiece.'

Was this a prompt? Malvin knew, of course, about the reredos because he had paid Bernard Labadie to remove the end-papers from the Canticum. Did he also know that Labadie had visited Edouard and given him a copy of the inscription? Were they, as Louise suggested, accomplices? I decided to steer clear of the lost reredos. Instead I reverted to something he had touched on.

'You seem to be contemptuous of holy relics, Monsieur.'

'Most are beyond belief, like the bones of St Jacques, as I said, or the innumerable pieces of the True Cross, or the Crown of

Thorns exhibited in the treasury of Notre Dame in Paris.'

That lip-curling smile again. More like a sneer, I thought. He went on: 'When I talked with your father about the bones in the forest grave I put it to him that they were of a man who, like millions of others, had been duped by bishops and priests into believing in the bones of Saint Jacques. The entire wealth of Santiago de Compostela rests on that fraudulent claim. Can you dispute that, Ma'mselle?'

I shrugged. 'And what did my father say?'

'He agreed. But then he told me of a little-known relic which he seemed to believe in quite passionately. An extraordinary story. He must have told you of it?'

It was phrased as a question and he looked at me searchingly.

'What would that be?'

'A ring. Connected, they say, with Saint Jacques.'

My mind was whirling. I said nothing.

'He found the story in Montpellier. A record made by a pilgrim while travelling on the Rue St Jacques. He showed me a translation of it.'

No! It was impossible to believe that my father would have shown François's journal to Malvin, a man I was sure he would instinctively distrust, but how else could Malvin know of the journal?

'When was that?'

'I can't remember exactly. We had several conversations before his tragic accident.'

Totally bewildered by what I'd heard, I grasped at this lead. 'It was you who found my father.'

He lowered his eyes. 'Truly I wish it had not been.'

'Do you know what was he doing up the ladder? It's quite unlike him to try to fix anything. He was not a practical man.'

'I really have no idea. There was a window open on the upper floor and it was not stayed. Perhaps he was fixing something. The ladder fell with him onto the terrace.'

I managed to say: 'Was he alive when you found him?'

'No. I'm sorry, Ma'mselle. He was beyond help. I called for an ambulance at once, but that was only a formality.'

He held out his hands in a gesture that might have been seen as an attempt at comfort. I took a step backwards. He lowered his hands.

'It was terrible. I cannot say how sorry I feel, Ma'mselle. I believe your father was on the verge of making an important discovery. You could complete that for him.'

'What makes you think that?'

'The pilgrim's record he showed me. By a monk called, as I remember, François de Castres. It is still a family name known in this region.'

My pulse quickened and I took a deep breath.

'Where did he show you this?'

'In his work-room. It must be there still.'

22 - LOUISE

Soon after dawn I was awakened by Edouard creeping out of our room. About two hours later I met Nell on the terrace where we saw the helicopter land in the paddock. A few minutes later it lifted off above the trees, circle and swing away towards the south-west. Nell shaded her eyes against the sun to watch it disappear. She looked fresh and relaxed in a green cotton dress. As we walked back to the château I wondered if she or Alastair had made use of the communicating door during the night. I put the question obliquely.

'Did you sleep well?'

'Wonderfully. Until cock-crow.'

'It's Edouard who usually wakes me when he goes into his dressing room. He's an early riser, but rather later than the roosters.'

'So you're still sharing a bedroom?'

'Of course. I've told you, I like being properly married.'

'I see,' Nell said, without obvious conviction.

She avoided my eyes and looked out across the park towards a distant avenue of chestnut trees. A single horse and rider could be seen moving towards them at a slow canter.

'This is such a beautiful spot, Lou. I'm so glad for you. Really.'

We were interrupted by a footman who brought orange juice, coffee, a basket of croissants, pains au chocolat, brioches, hot rolls, butter and pots of preserves. When he had laid everything in its place and left us alone, Nell said: 'It's like living in the grandest of hotels, isn't it?'

'Not at all. This is a home, not an hotel. *My* home. I'm terribly lucky.'

133

Julia joined us. As she sat down she asked: 'Did you hear the helicopter? Eight o'clock I made it.'

'He should be back early tomorrow, Edouard says, barring......'

I stopped short before using an unfortunate word.

Julia kept silent while we discussed our thoughts about the reredos which Edouard was pursuing - whether the carriers might have had an accident on one of the mountain passes, whether it might have been stolen for some irreligious purpose or destroyed by vandals. Some extraordinary event must have taken place. How else could so substantial a piece vanish without trace or record? The mystery was as baffling and intriguing as a Torquemada crossword clue.

Rather tentatively I pointed out that Malvin must also be in the hunt and he had a head-start. 'He may know things we don't know. Could he lead us to the reredos?'

Julia said: 'I was talking to him last night. He seems to know everything we know. He says my father showed him the French translation of the Journal. He said enough to make me sure he must have seen it.'

'Seen it? But how could he...?' Nell left the question hanging.

'I've been worrying about it all night. He knows about the ring. He said my father was near to making an important discovery. He says the answer is in the house. There's something there, he says.'

'But you and Alastair searched it from top to bottom,' I said.

'Something could still be hidden. Malvin says he's sure it's there.'

Nell stared at her. 'You don't believe him, do you?'

23 - ALASTAIR

The pilot took a direct route to the coast near Béziers and then turned east over the Mediterranean. The tiny Robinson R22 maintained a steady 85 knots. We had nothing in common save the journey and barely spoke. There was little to look at as we flew out of sight of land until the port of La Spezia came into view. Changing course towards the north, the pilot dropped altitude as clouds gathered and approached the hills of the Costa Castagnolasca. Soon, turning to me, he jabbed a finger in the direction of a fold in the land.

'The abbey should be somewhere around there, Monsieur.'

I looked to the left as the helicopter began a steeply banked turn. I raised a hand and said: 'I see it! A large basilica and a group of buildings at the top of a narrow track. Trees all around.'

The pilot said. 'Okay. I'm descending.'

The landscape was steep, rocky and thick with closely planted conifers. Even at a few hundred feet I could see no possible landing area. There was no sign of life, neither animal nor human.

'I'm going to follow the road until there's an open space,' the pilot said. 'We can't risk a landing here.'

We had covered about two kilometres when a farmstead came into view from behind a small bluff. Close to the house was what appeared to be a fairly level piece of fenced land. The pilot pointed. 'Let's have a closer look.'

We dropped another hundred feet or so, turning sharp left at the same time and leaving my stomach behind.

'No good. Animals.'

'Mules.'

135

'We'd stampede them. Could be costly.'

We made another turn and climbed. Beyond the bluff there now appeared a piece of barren, rock-strewn land no larger than fifty or sixty metres square.

'This will have to do. I'm going in. Hold on.'

The machine hovered and manoeuvred just above ground among rows of young cypresses. There was just enough space between large boulders. When the pilot put the skids gently on the ground I complimented him.

'Routine, Monsieur.'

He switched off the engine and the blades gradually stopped rotating. The only sound was the susurrus of the wind in the cypresses.

I opened the door. 'It could be a stiff climb to the top. I shall be gone for at least two hours, maybe three. Please be here. We'll find somewhere to stay the night near where you can refuel for the journey back tomorrow.'

It took a good half-hour to skirt the hill and reach the farm. I became aware that my approach was being watched from some way off by two men. They held farm implements in what might have been a threatening manner. Doubtless they connected me with the helicopter - and unfavourably. Their faces as I came nearer were a study in dour suspicion. Guessing that with my briefcase I was probably marked as an officer of some unwelcome agency such as the revenue, I greeted them as best I could in my sparse Italian, saying I was an English professore visiting the Abbazia di San Benedetto. This announcement, aided by much hand-shaking, slowly took the chill off my reception. Using a few key words from my limited vocabulary, coupled with gestures in the direction of an elderly pick-up standing nearby and the casual display of banknotes, I was able to get the younger of the two men to agree to drive him up the hill to the abbey. More money, I decided, would be needed to persuade the driver to wait during my meeting with the abbot and to bring me back to the farm.

It was a high-speed, heart-stopping journey up a snaking track. An avenue of trees invited disaster. The driver steered with one hand on top of the wheel and his elbow on the window ledge. He whipped the pick-up round blind bends with some skill but alarming bravado, throwing sidelong glances at me as if to gauge the effect. Holding on to the door-handle (there was no seat-belt) and determined not to respond visibly to this test of nerves, I attempted to look cool as I opened my briefcase with one hand and ruffled through the papers inside.

The driver asked a question. What was it? I made a vague gesture which could have been taken for ignorance or incomprehension and continued to look among my papers. Why had I volunteered for this mission in a land where I didn't speak the language? Surely there would be a French or English speaker in the abbey?

The hair-raising drive lasted a mere ten minutes before we came to a sliding stop at the end of the track. I got out, thanked the driver and said a silent prayer of gratitude to St Benedict for our safe arrival. Using my watch to indicate the time I expected to return and displaying more euros, with nods and grins and salutes I seemed to have secured the undertaking I needed - to be met at this same spot in an hour's time. It was already noon.

Leaving my chauffeur to reverse the pick-up down the track to a place where he could turn (which he did with spectacular élan), I set off up the rough path to the gateway of the abbey.

The doorbell was answered after some delay by an elderly monk who looked at me enquiringly, said nothing, but nodded when I asked if he understood English or French. I assumed this meant both and offered, in English, a true account of my identity and requested the favour of a brief meeting with the abbot on a matter to do with the abbey's records. There was a moment's hesitation before the monk murmured that it was the hour of the midday meal. Nevertheless, indicating that he should be followed, he led the way along empty corridors, at last opening the door into a lofty hall which proved to be the refectory.

About twenty monks in robes of the Benedictine order sat on either side of two long tables. No one spoke other than a monk who sat apart, reading aloud from a book placed upon a lectern. A few heads turned towards me before they returned to the slow rhythm of the meal.

My guide indicated that I should sit at the end of one of the tables. A bowl, a plate and a cup were placed before me and, without a word, a thick soup of beans and pasta was ladled into the bowl. The monk seated next to me offered bread from a basket and poured red wine into my cup from a large pitcher. Only the rise and fall of the reader's voice broke the silence.

The soup was good and welcome after six hours since a hurried breakfast. I glanced around the room. It was a scene that must have changed little over centuries. Nothing of the present day seemed to have penetrated this gaunt simplicity save that some of the monks were wearing modern spectacles and most wore wrist-watches.

It seemed that the abbot was not present at the meal, or if he was he neither occupied a prominent place at table nor wore distinguishing robes. This was confirmed almost before there was time to finish the bowl of soup. My guide returned, stood beside me and again silently indicated that he should be followed.

Perhaps the abbot was fasting, for there was no sign in his cell of food having been served. He was tall, thin and sallow-faced. Immediately he rose from behind a plain table and offered a bony hand. In rather halting English he apologised for the delay in receiving a guest. 'You ask about our records, signor. Another of our brothers may help. He speaks good English.'

As if a bell had been pressed, the door opened and a young monk with an earnest expression came into the cell. He introduced himself as the abbey's librarian and asked what assistance he could give. I had decided on the most direct approach. Addressing the abbot, though knowing that the librarian would be the one to answer, I said 'Father, there is a record that the abbey once possessed a reredos of the 12th century, supposedly the work of the famous sculptor Benedetto Antelami and a rare piece. All trace of the reredos has been lost.'

The librarian looked at the abbot with a puzzled expression and repeated the question in Italian. I observed a momentary reaction from the abbot at the mention of the word reredos. His reply, after a moment, was given with a sad smile. The younger man turned to me and said: 'The name Antelami is familiar to the reverend father for we had a recent visitor so-called, but he has not heard of the sculptor. Neither have I, signor. Nor of a reredos in the abbey of any importance. If there were such a rare piece we would certainly know of it.'

'I was sure of that,' I said, 'but I have good reason to believe that long ago, perhaps soon after the abbey was founded, the reredos was here and that it was then sent away for safety's sake at the time of a great plague, together with other treasures.'

The librarian relayed this to the abbot and, after an exchange, said: 'That is all most interesting, signor, but unknown to us. Perhaps you will tell us why you believe this.'

'Because I have seen a record of the treasures that were removed from this abbey at the time of the plague in the year 1217 and the reredos was listed among these.'

I paused and rehearsed in my mind the argument I intended to put to the abbot. 'I can tell you, Father, that all the other treasures on this list have been located. Many are of great value and are safe at present in other Benedictine foundations. It is possible - I emphasise "possible" - that they could be restored to you if it can be proved that they once belonged here. As I've said, of all these treasures only the Antelami reredos has not been traced. Naturally I thought it must still be here.'

There was further conversation in Italian before the librarian said, with some deference: 'The reverend father asks if you will kindly say where you have seen this record.'

I hesitated. The point was critical. 'May I first ask you another question? Does the reverend father know of an illuminated manuscript of the Canticum Canticorum?'

It was the turn of the librarian to smile. 'I can answer that. The reverend father does not know of it, but I do. I have only just catalogued it in our library. It seems to be a most unusual book.'

'You have only just catalogued it? Surely it is of very great age. Has it not always been in the library here?'

'Very probably, signor. We have no records to show otherwise, though I must say that our records are not in good order. That is why I have been given the task of making a new catalogue.'

'And the Canticum?'

'What of it, signor?'

'Did you not observe an inscription on one of the end-papers?'

'On an end-paper? Strangely, there were no end-papers. I noted that and recorded the fact in the catalogue.'

I thought carefully before responding. 'Please tell the reverend father that I know what has happened to that end-paper and why.'

Speaking in short sentences so that the librarian could translate as I gave my account, I told of how the Canticum Canticorum had been shown privately to a distinguished French collector by a dealer from Corsica and offered for sale; of the Frenchman's doubts because the agent was a man of poor repute and would not identify his client; of the manuscript's verification by a most reputable expert and its valuation at maybe two million US dollars; of the discovery that the end-papers had been removed before the manuscript was offered and the confirmation of this by a bookbinder who had been asked to remove it; and finally of the inscription that had been discovered with its account of treasures sent from the abbey in the year 1217 to other Benedictine foundations in Italy and France.

There was a long silence. At last the abbot asked, in English: 'My son, this is the truth?'

'The absolute truth.'

There was much conversation, questions and answers in low voices. The young librarian took off his glasses, wiped them and put them on again.

'The reverend father says he knows of a document which may throw some light on what you have told us. The document is in our archives and, as far as the reverend father recalls, is of about the same age as the inscription you say you have seen. Until now it has meant nothing to us. It is a letter from the Comte de Toulouse giving an account of the death of one of our brothers long ago.'

After a delayed flight because of a threatened storm I was back at the château the next day in time for a late supper. To celebrate my safe return Louise had asked the chef to prepare papillote de coeur d'oies aux cerises, a local dish which, despite its peculiar main ingredient, was much approved. Over the coffee I gave an account of my trip.

'At first I was sure I must be in the wrong abbey. It was a sad, run-down ruin of a place. You couldn't imagine it might ever have possessed a rare and valuable reredos. As I expected, the abbot said he had never heard of Benedetto Antelami. I did notice that he reacted slightly when I mentioned the word reredos.'

'In what way?' asked Julia.

'Mostly he was impassive, then there was this flicker of recognition or puzzlement but he made no comment.'

'You think he was concealing something?'

'There turned out to be a very interesting explanation.'

I savoured my Armagnac, holding my audience in suspense before continuing. 'It was also hard to believe the abbey had a library that might contain treasures such as the Canticum Canticorum. When I spoke of it, the abbot looked as blank as ever, but the librarian, who was my interpreter, said he had recently come across it while making a new catalogue. He called it "unusual" but said he'd not had time to study it. When I asked him if he had noted the inscription on one of the end-papers he said that the book had no end-papers. He had made a note of this for the catalogue.

'Before I left the abbey I was invited to see the library. It's quite a large collection. I'm not competent to say whether there are any books of special interest but the young librarian showed me the Canticum. The book is even more astonishing than the photographs suggest. I asked him about visitors. He doesn't have many visitors but he remembered Malvin because he'd asked if there were any illuminated manuscripts of the fifteenth century.'

'Fifteenth?' asked Julia, frowning.

'He remembered because this was one of the his own special interests.'

'That must have put Malvin on the spot,' said Louise.

'I doubt it,' said Nell. 'He's so slippery I'm sure he'd bluff his way out of that. But why the fifteenth century?'

'Just an opening gambit, I imagine. I guess he would come round to questions about earlier manuscripts gradually, as if by chance.'

Edouard remarked that at least we now knew the book was safe.

'And we also know,' said Julia, 'that Malvin was offering it for sale without the abbot's knowledge. How did he think he could get away with it?'

'I can only guess his plan was that when Edouard agreed to buy he would put himself forward to the abbot as an agent for a rich client. They could have no idea of the book's value and would probably have agreed to settle for much less than Malvin was expecting to receive.'

Edouard touched Louise's hand. 'I should have listened to you, chérie. You warned me about that man. I was, as you say, besotted with the book.'

Intervening I said: 'Well, the Canticum needn't concern us now. What matters is the reredos. As I've told you, the abbot betrayed a flicker of interest. He asked the librarian to show me a letter that has been in their archives since 1218 - the year after we believe the treasures left the abbey. The three of us went to a room where the abbey's records are stored. The librarian produced a splendid key and unlocked a magnificent chest covered with ornate metalwork. Spanish, I was told. There were many old documents. The letter of 1218 was in good condition, written by a scribe in Latin on parchment and signed and sealed by the Comte de Toulouse. I couldn't read the medieval script but was told by the librarian that the letter simply informed the abbot that one of his brethren, a monk named Pietro, had been set upon and killed near the town of Vaison-la-Romaine and had been given Christian burial there. Vaison was part of the Count's domains at that time. Brother Pietro was described in the letter as Custos Reredorsi - the custodian or guardian of the reredos.'

No one spoke for a moment. Edouard congratulated me. 'A positive lead,' he observed. 'Well done!'

'Our *only* lead,' I replied. 'But I learned something else. The librarian told me that Malvin turned up again several weeks after his first visit. I guess this may have been when he secretly returned the Canticum he'd taken to Genoa and Milan before showing it to you. He spent the best part of the day looking through documents in the archives, with the help of the librarian and he was accompanied by an elderly priest. They had come from Genoa, the priest told the librarian.'

'A priest? Not Malvin's style, surely,' remarked Nell.

'Think about it,' I said. 'Malvin would know that the abbey's earliest records would be in Latin, so he took someone who could read them.'

'Wasn't the librarian suspicious?'

'Why should he be? It's a librarian's job to provide access to enquirers. Malvin had already gone some way to establishing his bona fides by his previous meeting with the abbot and pretending an interest in old manuscripts. He told the librarian his specialist period was the early thirteenth century. He wondered what the archives might hold covering the first two decades from the year 1200.'

'When the letter from the Comte de Toulouse was received.'

'Exactly. I asked if it was shown to him. It was. He examined it but said it was of no interest; he was looking for records of a plague during those years. The librarian knew nothing of a plague.'

Julia asked: 'The abbey has no record?'

'None as far as I could discover. I am sure they aren't hiding anything. Why would they? Nor would they have been surprised that Malvin showed no interest in the Comte's letter. Until my own visit, it had meant nothing to anyone in the abbey.'

One thought must have been in everyone's mind. Nell voiced it. Malvin now knew that the reredos had got as far as Vaison. 'And what about the priest? Another competitor in the field,' she remarked. 'Isn't this a mistake on Malvin's part? Or do you think he's deliberately involving the church for some reason or other?'

I shook my head. 'It took Edouard and Julia a lot of research to learn that the reredos never reached its destination. Malvin could have gone over the same ground and come to the same conclusion.

Otherwise he wouldn't have had the end-papers removed from the book. In any case, an elderly cleric would be quite easy to hoodwink. According to the librarian the old man was pretty simple, but what interest could Malvin have in the reredos? I think that finding the Calix is his motive. It would be easily portable and, if the legend's true, enormously valuable.'

Edouard interposed: 'You have competition nevertheless. Malvin knows as much as you do. What will he do now, Alastair?'

'He'll go to Vaison. He's probably there already.'

'He can't be,' said Julia. 'I've agreed to meet him at Le Belvédère tomorrow.'

24 - JULIA

We had been stunned by Malvin's claims. Alastair suggested he was bluffing. I was sure he was not. He knew too much, but how much?

He was waiting for me outside Le Belvédère. When I had unlocked and opened the doors he blinked his way into the darkness of the entrance hall and stood there while I unbarred the shutters. I confronted him at once.

'This document you said my father showed you, when exactly was that?'

'I can't be exact. We met now and then. Not long ago. I could look in my diary.'

'Can you describe it?'

'There were a hundred or more photocopied sheets stapled together in sections. The text was in French, typewritten with double spacing. Very neatly done with no corrections. It was an account of a medieval pilgrimage to Santiago de Compostela. The author was named on the first sheet as François de Castres. There was an introduction and a commentary by the translator, a professor at Montpellier University.'

He was looking at me closely.

'My father let you read it?' I must have sounded incredulous.

'Not right through. There was no time, and naturally he wouldn't part with it. He told me he was mainly interested in the legend of Saint Jacques' ring. I got the impression that he believed it. Indeed, he said as much and he seemed to think that the ring must be hidden somewhere hereabouts. He implied he was on the verge of a major discovery; whether the ring or something else I couldn't say. Surely he told you this, M'amselle, his favoured daughter?'

I coloured. He knew that too. I said nothing.

'He told me that the pilgrim's tale will be a part of his new book.'

'He said that?'

'I recall a draft he showed me saying that everything he had found convinced him that the ring was the treasure, as he put it, brought from the Holy Land and secretly taken by François de Castres on his ill-fated journey. That was the word he used. Ill-fated.'

My thoughts were racing almost out of control. I remembered a passage much like this in my father's manuscript, but he would never have shown it to this man? Or had I completely misjudged Malvin? Surely not?

'He showed you his manuscript? The book he was working on?'

'Briefly, M'amselle. A few pages only, for my comments. I offered some thoughts on the provenance of the ring, based on my professional experience.'

I shook my head. He could take this as disbelief or just unwillingness to comment. He asked if he might look at my father's workroom again. Maybe there was something I had overlooked. I asked what he expected to find. He shrugged. Was there any harm in looking? My father had so nearly reached the conclusion of his quest for the truth - his personal pilgrimage as it were. Now this task was handed on to me. He could help with what he knew. Together we could complete my father's work.

Work with Malvin? Never! Oppose him? Only with great care. He was devious in every way. Louise had known this from the first and had warned her stubborn husband to have no dealings with him. Edouard had been dazzled by the beauty of the Canticum. He was still blinded, I felt, to the extent that, with Malvin alone able to negotiate its purchase, Edouard would have no option but to keep in touch.

Was the Canticum worth it? To my eyes no, but the market had spoken and money has a loud voice.

25 - ALASTAIR

Bray's neighbour, Eugène Pontet, received me cautiously but politely. He was a large man with thick curly hair and a face weathered and worn by work. His thick forearms were as burned as the Gascon earth, his eyes were as dark as his hair and there were deep furrows beside his eyes. I introduced myself as a friend of the baron and of the daughter of Monsieur Bray who had died so suddenly and so sadly. It was on account of Mademoiselle Bray that I would be most grateful for a word with Monsieur Pontet.

My careful approach softened Pontet's manner and I was invited to take a glass indoors. There seemed to be no one else in the farmhouse. The remains of breakfast were scattered untidily on the kitchen table - half a pain de campagne, butter in its wrapping, a coffee pot, a knife and a white bowl with traces of coffee grounds.

Small glasses were brought and filled to the brim with a colourless eau-de-vie from a bottle with a hand-written label. After exchanging mutual wishes of good health and two sips of the fiery liquid I went to the point. 'May I ask, how well did you know your neighbour Monsieur Bray?'

'He was a writer, well-known in England, they say. I like to read crime stories and he got me books by English authors translated into French. We often talked over a glass in the evening and sometimes I made a daube or a cassoulet. I am alone here, Monsieur. My wife died four years ago. And Monsieur Leonard was away from his wife. He was interested in my work and I was interested in his. For an Englishman he spoke good French, as you do, Monsieur.'

'I come to France often. I come to the Gers to visit the vignerons who grow the tannat grape and make the Madiran.'

'Ah, then you feel at home here.'

'Yes, I like the Gers, but I am more at home in the Médoc. I advise Monsieur de Marcignac on some of his purchases from Bordeaux.'

Pontet waved a hand dismissively. 'That is another country, Monsieur.'

I duly smiled and returned to my careful questioning. 'Do you happen to know what Monsieur Bray was writing at the time of his death?'

'He told me it was a book about this part of France and the pilgrims who come this way. I asked him if it was un roman. He said it was a true story but so extraordinary it would seem like un roman. He promised to send me a copy when it was published. It would be printed in French as well as in English, so he must have been a good writer to get published in France.'

'Did he tell you what was extraordinary about the book?'

'No. He preferred that I should wait to read it.'

'When the pilgrim's grave was discovered near here did you not think this might be part of the story?'

'How could it have been? He finished the book before the grave was discovered.'

'You're sure of that?'

'Quite sure. We celebrated its completion with a good wine, Château de Peyros '88, and my best Armagnac.'

'The wine was his?'

'No. He didn't buy good wine. It was from my cellar. I keep it for rare occasions. I don't have many visitors.'

'Did Monsieur Bray have visitors?'

'Only the postman.'

'What about the man called Malvin who found him after his fall? He used to call sometimes, did he not?'

'Maybe once or twice. One evening, soon after Monsieur Leonard finished the book, I took him some foie gras and the man Malvin had just called, but I didn't meet him.'

'He didn't tell you why Malvin had called?'

'No. I remember only that Monsieur Leonard was happy to have finished the book and to be going home soon to see his daughter. He was very proud of her. She works for your prime minister, is that not so?'

'For another minister, in fact.'

I drained my glass as Pontet had done, blinked and asked: 'This man Malvin, has anyone in the village spoken of him?'

Pontet refilled both glasses.

'They say he is from Corsica and deals in rare old antiquities for collectors like Monsieur de Marcignac. I don't know why he called on Monsieur Leonard who collects nothing but ideas for his stories. Perhaps because they are both educated men. It was not for me to ask, but I could tell that Malvin was not welcome.'

When we had again emptied our glasses the visit was over. As I went to the door, I remarked casually: 'They say the woods behind Le Belvédère are haunted and the house too.'

Pontet looked at me sharply. 'The woods maybe.'

'Not the house?'

'I don't know. I've seen nothing. The grenier perhaps. People have said so.'

'Monsieur Bray said so?'

Pontet smiled. 'He liked to tell ghost stories and he was good at telling them. He told me there was a troubled spirit haunting the grenier. Sometimes it's difficult to tell fact from fiction, isn't it?'

26 - JULIA

Pontet's story was credible; Malvin's was not. Nevertheless he must have seen a copy of the Journal or at least a part of my father's manuscript. I met Alastair and Nell in the small dining room where I removed the thick pile of manuscript from the envelope Ferran had given me and placed it on the table.

'Sorry to have kept this from you so long. In part my father's book is his view of St James, his martyrdom and all that followed: the bones found in the Field of the Star, the 'extravagant' cathedral built as a sanctuary for them and the centuries of pilgrimage. It's also a picture of our kinsman François de Castres, as much as can be gleaned from his writing. Essentially though it's a personal account of my father's lifelong pilgrimage. It's a valediction, as if he somehow foresaw an early death.'

'How sad,' said Louise. 'And how terrible for you to read it now.'

'That was the word he used to describe the outcome of his search.'

'And the ring?' posed Nell. 'What of that?'

'He writes about finding the Journal and then the legend of St James's ring, but there's nothing beyond what we already know.'

Alastair said: 'That's not surprising. According to Pontet your father finished his book some time before stumbling on the pilgrim's grave. The two of them celebrated its completion with a bottle of Château de Peyros. That was the empty bottle I found in the barn. It was from Pontet's own cellar. So it looks like the message on the label was just another of your father's teases.'

'No,' I said firmly. 'He wouldn't lead me up the garden path.

150

The message means something.'

'He wrote "Cellar carefully. Third bin." There's no cellar under the house.'

Nell said: 'Perhaps he meant Pontet's cellar. Do you think he told Pontet about the jewel?'

'No,' said Alastair. 'They sometimes had supper together and he liked Julia's father to tell him ghost stories. I asked if Le Belvédère was haunted. He thought not, but people say the woods are and the grenier might be.'

'There's something else,' I said. 'My father's letter. There was a postscript. His postscripts were always meaningful. This one suggests I should take a good look at the photocopied page he brought back from Montpellier. I have done. I found one word decorated with florid curlicues. Not obvious at first. He must have used a calligrapher's pen with ink to match the photocopier's printer.'

Alastair asked: 'What does the text say?'

'François is being penitential, as usual. Crying out to the Lord. "My soul thirsts for God like a man looking for water in a desert. The wells are dried up and I am sorely troubled. Why have you abandoned me in my distress? Hasten to deliver me lest I be consumed and eaten up".'

'It sounds like one of the psalms.'

'François would probably have known the psalms by heart.'

'What about the word that's been decorated?'

'Quemadmodum. It means "in the manner of". I've seen it printed somewhere recently. I wish I could remember where.'

'A family motto? Or part of one?'

'In a book, I think. Something to do with music.'

'An instruction to the performer? Quemadmodum scherzo.To be played like a scherzo.'

'You'd write quasi scherzo, wouldn't you?'

'If you say so,' said Alastair dryly. 'You're the scholar.'

I pulled a face at him. 'You once asked me why my father used such an arcane way of alerting me to the joyau when he could have sent me a simple note in a code I'd recognise. This could be it. The crucial codeword.'

'But you don't recognise it.'

'It'll come to me. It's musical, I'm sure. Fergus ought to know.'

Jane had used every argument to persuade her husband that a small house in France would be a valuable asset. (Accountancy-speak had always been the best way of putting arguments to him.) She told me how Peter had set up all sorts of obstacles.

'I shall commission a full professional survey - top to bottom,' he'd said when he finally acceded the point in principle. 'As soon as I've got a list of all the defects I will make a provisional offer.'

Jane told him I will want a firm offer. 'That's reasonable. She's a friend, not an estate agent.'

Peter said nothing could be definite until he knew exactly what needed to be done to put the place right and roughly what it would cost. Jane said this would take too long.

'There's a great deal to do. Julia knows that as well as we do. The kitchen is dreadful, for a start and we'll need at least one other bathroom.'

Peter said he was not talking about improvements. He was talking about the condition of the roof and the timbers, the stability of the stone walls, the drains, the electrical wiring, the pipework, the possibility of underground springs and anything else that could cost him a mint of money. And legal implications. 'Believe me, Jane, once the lawyers get involved anything can happen.'

After getting as far as this with Peter, Jane was not going to risk pushing him too far. And I had still not committed myself to selling. Why was I hesitating? I didn't want a holiday home, and it was unlikely I could afford to put the house into a state that would make it lettable. The sale would give me a useful sum of money to invest, but Le Belvédère was linked so strongly to my father that I would find it hard to sever the connection.

I was the last to arrive for the afternoon rehearsal in the abbey. Jane Reeves had some "good news" for me, but there was no time before Fergus called for silence and asked for a pile of sheet music parts to be handed round.

'Change of programme. As you've heard, the intimacy and subtleties of the Elgar part songs get lost in all this space. So I've decided to give our French audience what I believe will be a ravishing new experience for them - the Byrd Great Service. Few will have heard it before, and probably not at a live performance. Let's run right through the Kyrie. Follow my hands. Watch the phrasing. Remember your breathing. A real pianissimo, please.'

He discarded his baton, raised his hands, looked around and when all eyes were on him, indicated the tempo. Our voices stole into the huge arena as if from nowhere. We had sung the Service during Lent in Ripon Cathedral. I was soon swept up in the reverential music. It went smoothly and magically until the last gradual diminuendo. In the ensuing silence we could hear the final chord vanishing into the distance.

Fergus waited a long moment, smiled broadly and said; 'Thank you. Two minutes.'

'We'll pay cash, of course,' said Jane to me as we took our seats again. 'Forty thousand pounds,' she added, committing her husband beyond the possibility of his reneging. She enthused about the house. It was just what she'd always wanted. She didn't mind the seclusion. It would be a peaceful retreat from London when Peter went away on long trips abroad. Somewhere she could write and paint and get to know the French. The house needed a lot doing to it but it had great opportunities. And of course I would always be welcome to come and stay.

I was taken aback. I knew that ultimately I would have to sell and the offer was a good one. Not having to use an agent was a real advantage. I could persuade Jane to delay completion until I was ready to hand over the property. That meant, of course, the completion of our search for the joyau. A successful completion. Finding the ring. Nothing less.

The programme at Auch was to be mostly the same as at Flaran except that Fergus had reinstated the Elgar part-songs which he said would sound fine in the less resonant acoustic of the cathedral.

There had been much debate about whether the concert should begin in the early evening or after dinner. Fergus was fiercely resistant to a late start. How could we give of our best with their stomachs full of rich, half-digested food and our heads fuzzy with alcohol? But expatriate English members of the Festival Committee gave expert counsel and the concert was scheduled for 9.15pm.

Alastair had booked a table at the Relais de Gascogne for seven o'clock and was already there when Louise, Nell and I arrived. Edouard, who had quarrelled with Louise on some trivial domestic matter, had gone to Tarbes - to see a business friend he said.

I was still worrying over Malvin's professed relationship with my father. They met after the Requiem Mass for the pilgrim when Edouard introduced Malvin. 'That,' I said to Alistair 'would give him a seal of approval. If, as he claims, Malvin has a copy of François's Journal he could have guessed what my father was doing and made all the same connections - that the joyau must have been hidden by François near here and that my father may have found it. Perhaps he hinted at this and offered help as one of Edouard's trusted advisors.'

'A lot of 'ifs' there, Julia,' said Alastair 'Don't you think your father would have summed up Malvin pretty quickly and shown him the door, like Pontet said? I'm sure he didn't trust anyone with the secret of the joyau. He didn't even tell you while he was alive.'

It was an obvious truth. I suppressed a sharp response and switched the conversation to the alteration to the photocopy.

'Does it mean anything to you, Alastair?'

'I wouldn't expect it to. Your father's package left with Ferran was for your eyes only. Even then he didn't tell you where to look for the joyau. Quemadmodum is meant for you to understand and you alone.'

'Well, I don't! Why the hell didn't he trust me? It's been the same all along!'

Alastair was soothing. 'It wasn't a matter of trust. Your father had to be sure that anyone else who read his letter wouldn't understand it.'

Nell also tried to lift my spirits. 'Honestly love, he was doing everything he could for you. He had to be secretive. Maybe because of pressure from Malvin.'

Theories about the deceitful Corsican dominated our conversation. Louise, who admitted to the row she'd had with Edouard, was mostly silent. Everyone was glad when it was time to leave. We walked up the narrow street from the restaurant and turned into the small square where the Cathedral of Sainte-Marie stood in gothic splendour among little shops and cafés. I paused to take in the magnificence of the west front with its twin towers, but there was no time for study. Following the others, I threaded my way through the traffic across the street and entered the cathedral's dim interior.

How different from the Abbaye de Flaran! It was smaller, though the height of the arcades made it seem large enough and unlike Flaran, this was a basilica that spoke of continued worship through the centuries. Its chief treasures, my guidebook told me, were from the early sixteenth century - eighteen luminous windows by Arnold de Moles and choir stalls sculpted with a hundred and thirteen figures in wood, an array that was said to be the finest in France.

The choir was to sit at the east end of the nave. I followed Nell, took my seat, arranged the music on the stand and looked around. The cathedral was filling up. Alastair was standing alone, glancing towards Louise who was near the west door talking to a tall young man in jeans and trainers. It was already past the advertised starting time. Fergus was nowhere to be seen. Puzzled by his absence I consulted Nell who reminded me that he would be in the organ loft.

'Had you forgotten? This is his big moment!'

The opening item was announced in the programme as "Allegro maestoso de la Sonate No. 1 en sol majeur pour l'orgue de Sir Edward Elgar, interpreté par Monsieur Fergus Maine, Maitre Musicien de Londres". There was also a note on the Grande Orgue built, it was said, between 1688 and 1694 by Jean de Joyeuse. Fergus had been unable to resist the opportunity to get his hands on this historic instrument. Admitting it was a piece of self-indulgence, he said the Elgar would be a way of introducing the French to some thrilling English music they wouldn't know.

As soon as the first great chords burst from the massive pipework spread across the west end I shivered. Fergus was right: the music *was* thrilling. A joyful noise suited to this brilliant instrument built by the well-named Monsieur de Joyeuse.

27 - LOUISE

I was not listening. My mind was wholly on the chance meeting with Jake Lowell who was sitting in the row ahead, a little to the left so I could see his tanned profile without turning her head.

Handsome young Jake, an American friend of my son James. I remembered how Jake had taken me to the Wallace Collection and how I flirted with him and in his gaucheness he had not known how to respond to this middle-aged Englishwoman. I now learned he had spent a year in France after coming down from Cambridge. When he approached me just now he'd grinned and taken my hand and asked what I was doing in France, was I with my husband, and didn't I look just great? He said he'd often thought of our afternoon together, and why didn't we make a date, do a gallery, have lunch? I hardly got a word in.

He'd often thought of me? That was absurd, but I'd certainly often thought of him, which was just as ridiculous. The chemistry of that brief encounter in London had been instantly reactivated by the touch of his hand, the look in his eyes, the warmth of his voice. I had answered his question about Geoffrey and said I was now living in France, not far from Auch. He didn't enquire about James or Hugh. He repeated that I looked great. And then it was time to take my seat. Alastair gave me a quizzical look. A college friend of my son's, I explained. Such a nice boy.

The movement from the Elgar sonata ended to appreciative applause and Fergus descended from the organ loft to take the baton for the next item, which was the Elgar part songs. Alastair was sitting on my left so it was impossible to glance at Jake without him noticing. Why should I want to anyway? The answer troubled me.

Now I was wondering how I might avoid Jake during the interval. Alastair would be sure to notice my confusion in his presence.

Before the applause died away at the interval I was out of my seat and making my way towards the choir to congratulate them.

Nell asked: 'Who was your young friend?'

'A Cambridge chum of James's. Quite a coincidence.'

I remarked on Fergus's performance on the organ. 'Wasn't he good? I've never heard him play before.'

Nell said the organ had made her think of Alastair's father. 'He would have enjoyed that. I must send him a postcard.'

I said. 'I need fresh air. We've time for a stroll outside, haven't we?'

Alastair joined us. I was glad he didn't ask about Jake.

We left by a side door that led to a corner of the *place* on the south side. There was a vantage point at the top of the monumental staircase with a panoramic view of the lower town and the River Gers. We leant on the balustrade enjoying it. Jake had followed us out of the cathedral. I saw him standing quite close, looking out over the view. Quickly I turned away and pointed out to Nell a statue on a landing near the top of the staircase.

'D'Artagnan. Edouard says he was a real man called de Batz. D'Artagnan was his mother's name. The stories are mostly fiction, but he's a local hero still. The James Bond of the Gers.'

Jake was looking towards us. I turned away and said: 'We could walk down and look at the statue. Not all the way. There are two hundred and thirty-two steps to the bottom. When Edouard was a boy he and his chums used to race up and down.'

Why did I keep talking about Edouard? I wanted to put him out of my mind. No one seemed inclined to go down the steps. I took Nell's arm and led her back towards the cathedral, staying close to her and chatting inconsequentially about how much I liked Auch, until it was time to take our seats again. Jake was already in his place. As I sat down he turned his head and smiled at me. I gave him a nod of acknowledgement and picked up the programme to divert my mind. An anthem by Purcell, Debussy's Trois Chansons de Charles D'Orléans, the piece by Olivier Messiaen that had given the choir such problems at Flaran and some English folk songs arranged by John Rutter. The Purcell sounded very well in the loftiness of the cathedral. The Debussy was unfamiliar and languid.

I couldn't help my attention drifting to Jake Lowell. It was flattering and disturbing that he should suggest an outing. He was doing some historical research, he said and he'd found a picture in Foix that he was thinking of buying. Would I like to see it?

The Rutter arrangements brought the loudest applause of all. Fergus took three calls before departing towards the sacristie. Julia seemed in a hurry to follow him.

28 - JULIA

Members of the choir were gathered outside the west door where the coach that would take them back to Foix was already waiting. Louise and Nell were saying goodnight to friends when I came out of the cathedral. I must have been smiling broadly and looking radiant because Nell asked: 'What's happened?'

'He *knew*! I said he would. We've got it!'

'Who knew what?' asked Alastair.

'Fergus knew quemadmodum. It's in the Book of Common Prayer. The leading word in Latin of one of the psalms. Each of the psalms has a Latin heading, in case you've never noticed. Fergus knew this one because we sang the Howells setting a couple of years ago. I should have remembered. Number forty-two. "Like as the hart desireth the water-brooks". It's what we've been looking for.'

'How so?' asked Alastair.

'There's a verse that always made us giggle in chapel. My father shared the joke. It goes: "One deep calleth another, because of the noise of the water-pipes." The plumbing in school was like that.'

'Plumbing!' exclaimed Nell.

'Exactement, mon enfant!'

'The cistern!' cried Alastair. We never thought of the cistern!'

I was all for going to the house directly, regardless of the hour. It wouldn't take long to get into the attic and uncover the cistern.

'You'll need lights, a ladder and tools,' said Alastair. 'And a handyman. Why not leave it till the morning when we can see what we're doing?'

My impatience was calmed by his logic. The house was securely locked. No one had been inside since my father's death except the police. No one except the sacristain could know of the existence of my father's letter unless Ferran had broken his trust, and even if someone such as Malvin had sniffed it out and contrived to see it, the oblique reference to Psalm 42 was so private as to be unfathomable.

'Everything has been totally wrapped up beyond anyone else's understanding except yours,' said Alastair. 'Your father was obsessed with secrecy.'

'It was his nature. As I've said, he never talked about his work till it was done.'

'But he told you quite a bit, didn't he? Those teasing postcards.'

'That was a game we played. He liked to test me.'

'I just wonder how much more he would have told you had he lived. Would he have said nothing till he came home with the manuscript and, as you believe, the ring? Or would he have taken the game to its conclusion - inviting you down here so he could enjoy watching you unravel the clues? He couldn't mail his last postcard, but he'd taken the precaution of leaving his last clue with Ferran in case the others eluded you. It was a final way of pointing you in the right direction.'

'Yes, but still cryptic. Do you remember the book about the golden hare that was buried somewhere for the first person to find if they could solve the author's puzzle? My father was fascinated by the whole idea. I seem to remember that the author had to do something to stop people digging up the country.'

'This is a different kind of treasure hunt. The clues are for you alone. Why don't you sleep on it, Julia? The prize will still be there in the morning. And it's a lot more precious than the golden hare.'

Alastair arrived at Le Belvédère in a pick-up with a ladder tied on the back. There was room for only two passengers on the front seat. Nell volunteered to go in the back with the tools. Louise had said she didn't mind not going on the expedition. She needed to go to Auch. 'In any case, I don't think I could stand the suspense. What if there's nothing there?'

'There's got to be!' I said with outward confidence. 'The noise of the water-pipes has kept me awake half the night.'

The attic was reached through the ceiling of the second bedroom. Alastair climbed the ladder and lifted the trap-door. Standing on a rung near the top, he shone his flashlight into the loft. The water tank was in the far corner. He called for me and Nell to follow him and warned us that the floor wasn't boarded. 'Watch where you put your feet or you'll go through the ceiling below.'

While we waited he went back down the ladder and picked up the box of tools he'd borrowed. The loft smelled musty. Small gaps in the Roman tiles let in cracks of light. After the glare of the morning sun my eyes needed to adjust to the darkness. Guided by the beam of Alastair's flashlight, we moved gingerly, steadying ourselves against the roughly hewn oak trusses and braces which supported the weight of the beams and tiles.

The water tank was boxed in - perhaps to prevent mice or bats from falling into the water. The lid was nailed on. It was a simple matter to prise off the boards. We stared inside. There was no glint of water. The tank had been drained. The beam of light revealed only spiders' webs, small bits of debris and a decomposed lizard.

Deflated and dispirited, we made a fruitless search of the roof space. There were no other hiding places. Disappointment hung over us like a black cloud. Back in the living room, we sat gloomily side by side on the sofa. Nell broke the silence.

'Well, what do you think? Wrong clue, or has someone been here already?'

'The tank hasn't been touched,' said Alastair. 'You can't lever off the top of a box like that without making some marks.'

'Wrong clue, then?' suggested Nell.

'I don't think so,' I said. 'We shared the joke about the water-pipes. My father knew how much it appealed to me.'

'The pipework, then?'

'He wouldn't have known how to get it apart, let alone how to put it together again. No more would I.'

'So where do we go from here?'

'We use our intelligence. The cistern seemed obvious, and

maybe he did intend to use it as a hiding place but couldn't get the lid off. After he'd pointed me to quemadmodum he had to find somewhere else connected with water pipes.'

'Or just water,' said Nell.

'Water and mud,' posed Alastair, reminding us of the obscure quotation.

'Mud rules out the cistern.'

'It's all too damn clever,' complained Nell, not for the first time.

29 - LOUISE

I often enjoyed the narrow medieval streets of Foix-en-Gascogne and lingering in the market square with its shady arcades. Founded by Henry II of England in the 13th century, Foix is one of many fine bastides in the Gers bypassed by most tourists hurrying south to the Pyrenees or west to Biarritz, St-Jean-de Luz and Spain. There is not a building less than three hundred years old, including those which at street level now serve as shops, butchers, bakeries, hairdressers, cafés and restaurants.

The church of Sainte-Marie-de-la-Fontaine dates from the eleventh century. Students of Romanesque architecture come from far away to see its beautifully proportioned apse and the low-relief marble panels depicting the miracles of Jesus. Opposite the east end is a popular café that spills onto the pavement. Just to sit there contemplating the church is enough to lift the spirits.

I had forgotten it was market day. I threaded my way though the stalls, pausing to exchange a few words with vendors I knew. As I reached the Place de la Résistance the church clock struck twelve. Already many of the stall-holders were beginning to pack up. Shoppers drifted away to their midday repas. I crossed to the café and looked for a table in the shade. Jake stood up from where he was sitting and raised a hand to attract my attention.

As he moved over to let me take a seat, he said: 'You look wonderful! And so chic. France suits you.'

Yes, I thought, that's young Jake! Full of bullshit. He asked what I would drink. Just mineral water, I said. Badoit. He ordered, to my surprise, a pastis for himself, asked for the carte and enquired about the house specialities. I remarked on his fluency and good accent. He said his mother was French, from Toulouse, and had always insisted that he and his brothers keep in touch with their Gallic heritage.

He asked: 'How's James? Still at Cambridge? I haven't heard from him.'

'He's doing a PhD. I haven't seen him for a while. Geoffrey and I parted,' I explained. It was easier to say than that I had walked out on him. I asked about his research.

'The French Middle Ages. Wherever I look round here it's like a page of history, but I guess you see it differently.'

Throughout lunch he hardly took his eyes off me. He asked about my life, whether I had French friends, what the baron was like and the château. He asked which local places he ought to visit for his studies. I said I was sure he knew far better than I did. I teased him a bit and was quite indiscreet, telling him about Edouard's art collection and his distinguished guests. 'Your ambassador stayed at the château a few months ago and Gérard Départieu came down with some friends for a weekend. Edouard loves the cinema.'

'Things are quite lively down here then?'

'We have our moments of excitement.'

I told him about the grave in the woods and the pilgrim's re-interment in the crypt at Marcignac. He put down his fork. 'None of the guidebooks say anything about that.'

'The locals don't talk about it to strangers. They're worried about encouraging a flood of tourists. It's a very private place.'

'That's so unlike the French. What an opportunity! You'd expect them to be telling the story in a Son et Lumière spectacular at seventy euros a seat.'

'You couldn't do that at Marcignac. It's tiny and enclosed. There are only about a dozen houses. The church is proud of the sarcophagus but they treat it reverently.'

There was no harm in telling him about the discovery of the skeleton hand at Le Belvédère and the laboratory report that dated it as medieval.

He listened raptly. I couldn't resist embroidering the story. 'The place where the grave was found and the house of the man who found it are supposed to be haunted. He was a writer, the father of a close friend of mine. Soon afterwards he fell off a ladder and died without speaking.'

The idea of a 'malignant spook' captivated Jake. When was I free to go to the church? In the morning? We could take a picnic. He would put it together and drive me there. I backed off as gently as I could, pleading the needs of our house-guests.

'There's a concert at Flaran tomorrow and a reception by the Mayor afterwards.'

He brightened. 'I'll see you at the abbey, then. We can talk about the sarcophagus later.'

I said nothing. I was doubting the wisdom of meeting Jake. His impetuosity and energy were difficult to resist. I was not sure I wanted to resist. Already I was being caught up anew by his charm and enthusiasm.

As we said goodbye and I eventually withdrew my hand from his tenacious but gentle clasp, he repeated his suggestion that we should go to the crypt together.

When I left him and crossed the road to make my way back to my car, I caught sight of a man standing on the opposite pavement looking in her direction. Malvin! The last person I would want to meet at that moment. Had he seen us together? What if he had?

Driving home, I didn't think of Malvin, I could think only of Jake and how he had made it clear, not in words but in every other way, that he wanted me.

The concert at Flaran was scheduled for the late afternoon. There was to be a final rehearsal after a picnic lunch in the grounds of the abbey. I declined Nell's invitation to join the choir for the picnic, pleading that Edouard was due back from his visit to Tarbes. It was a small deceit. He had telephoned before breakfast to say he would be late and would miss the concert. Again! Just like at Auch. He could have been there but chose not to be. I gently reminded him that he was the patron of the festival. He said no one would miss him and he had important things to do. I asked if he'd had a successful trip. Yes, quite successful. He asked how I was. I was fine. Much of our conversation these days was like this.

Jake called shortly afterwards. I fluttered about in the bedroom, doing things to my face, my nails and my hair, changing my outfit for the second time, checking my appearance. Just for a picnic! No, not just for a picnic. For a man who wanted me in a way I had forgotten.

I parked my car near the church. His was already there. He came towards me with his usual broad grin. I took his hand, he held it firmly and made a slight pressure, as if asking a question. I responded with a like pressure.

I suggested he should wait in the church while I went to look for the sacristain. When I came back with Ferran, Jake was standing with his hands in the pockets of his jeans reading the legend on the war memorial. He greeted Ferran in French even before I introduced him. He explained he was studying medieval history, was staying in Foix and had heard from Madame de Marcignac about the remains of the unknown pilgrim buried in the crypt. Would it be possible to see the tomb?

Ferran said he would be proud to conduct the young monsieur. The discovery of the pilgrim's grave was, he said with pride in his usual manner, an extraordinary event. The sarcophagus was unique in the whole of France. Continuing with his routine, he lit our way down the narrow steps and asked how it was that a young American should be staying in such a little known place. It was by chance, said Jake, and by another chance he had met Madame de Marcignac, the mother of a good friend of his at Cambridge University. I wished Jake would be less forthcoming. Our visit might be reported to Edouard.

The performance in the crypt was even more dramatic than usual. Ferran was clearly trying to impress this American student of history. To his well-rehearsed presentation he added an account of the foundation of the village and something of its past. At last he extinguished the candles in their gilt holders and said: 'Suivez-moi, s'il vous plâit, m'sieur-dame.'

As we climbed the steps I was conscious of Jake very close

behind me. His hands were on my hips as though steering me. I was happy to be steered.

On the way out of the village, Jake said he would like to see the site of the grave that Leonard Bray had discovered.

'You'd never find it. It was in the woods behind his house. People get lost in there, besides, there can't be anything to see now.'

'We'll go to the house, then.'

He would drive and I could collect my car on the way back. I persuaded him it was not a good idea. My car was well known. Left there for several hours it would invite questions. He drove behind me along the lane from the village and down the rutted track. We parked the cars side by side on the grass in front of the barn.

The house was shuttered. We walked all round it on the rough terrace. Jake asked if I had the keys.

'No.'

'I would like to have seen where he worked.'

'It's very simple inside. Nothing to see, really.'

I told him about Bray's work-table and the pictures he had pinned to the wall. There seemed no harm in telling him. He was interested in the pilgrim's journey.

We sat behind the barn. He spread a rug on the grass and laid out the picnic he had brought; bread, butter, terrine in a jar, a Pyrenean hard cheese, a ewe's milk cheese called Esbareich, a bottle of Madiran, figs and peaches. We talked about the murder of Magnus and François's sense of failure.

'He must have been very near here at some time,' Jake asserted.

'Why do you think so?'

'He must have been, if he killed Magnus. You said there was a hospice of some kind here. He came this way so he probably stayed in it.'

'But not in this house. It isn't that old.'

He opened a plump fig and pushed the pink flesh into my mouth. I bit into it and the juice ran down my chin. He leaned forward and licked it. Then he kissed me. He said: 'You're lovely.' I said: 'Thank you, young sir.' He looked at me seriously. I countered by being flippant, teasing him, holding him off. It was a game reminding me of when we met in London and, because of my disappointment with Geoffrey, I encouraged his gauche but harmless advances. This time he was more mature, more forthright and more confident. It was a dangerous game.

Suddenly, to my astonishment, he took a large key from his pocket, went across to the barn and unfastened the padlock that secured the hasp of the large door.

I stared at him. 'Where did you get that key?'

'Found it this morning,' he said with a grin. 'Under a rock. Dumb place to hide it.'

'This morning? What were you doing here?'

'Looking for François.'

'François?'

'De Castres, or whatever his name is. I guess he's some place round here. Bray must have thought so. Did you know the barn was once a pilgrim's hostel?'

'I've heard it said.'

'I can prove it. And did you know it has an undercroft?'

'You can prove that too?'

'Sure.'

He opened the door of the barn and held out a hand. 'Let's go take a look.'

'You're joking, aren't you?'

'Like hell I'm not.'

I stood immobile. 'Jake, before I set foot in there you've got to tell me what's inside.'

'Nothing but a lot of old lumber, as far as I can see, but François can't be far away.'

For a moment I was speechless. Jake was incredible. Ever since we'd met again he'd been setting a breathless pace. He would have to be stopped somehow before I got myself into deep water.

He said: 'Come', and held out a hand again.

I let him draw me behind him through the door into the dark interior. For a moment my eyes could make out nothing but vague, shadowy shapes. After the heat outside it was cool and dry. There was a not unpleasant musty scent. The darkness was eerie. Gently, he led me past the scattered implements and other obstacles spread across the floor. He was steering me towards the farthest, darkest corner of the barn.

There was an ancient armoire up against the wall partly obscured by a pile of tea chests. He had his hands on my hips and backed me gently against the armoire. He kissed me again but this time full on the lips. He moved his hands upwards and cupped my breasts. I took them away.

'We shouldn't be doing this.'

'Why not? Don't you like it?'

'Yes, Jake, I do. That's why.'

He was pressing himself against me. He was so tall that I had to turn my face upwards to receive his kisses. On my lips, my eyes, my cheeks, my ears, my forehead, the tip of my nose. He said I was beautiful, a goddess. I was Hera and he was Zeus. He was squeezing my bottom (did Zeus do that?) and stroking the back of my neck. If he went on like this I would be lost, but I didn't try to stop him when he began unbuttoning my blouse. His hand slipped inside and round the back. I didn't have to help him undo my bra. I shrugged my blouse off my shoulders and leaned back. He buried his face between my breasts. When his tongue found one of my cherries I thought I would die.

It was madness. But I didn't want it to stop. I was unzipping him. He was hoisting my skirt. As he stepped back to unbuckle his belt I suddenly became aware that one of the barn doors was slightly open. I put a restraining hand on Jake's arm, looked towards the doors and whispered to him to stay still. A man's figure was dimly silhouetted against the daylight. The man stood for a while peering into the barn. After an age the man withdrew, leaving the door open.

I was nearly late for the concert. The choir had already taken their places on the wooden platform at the west end of the abbey and Fergus was making his entrance. There was an empty chair on the end of a row next to an English couple I knew slightly. They smiled a greeting as I took my seat and the concert began.

I closed my eyes as though rapt in the music. My mind, though, was struggling with everything that had taken place - most of all, who was the man at the door of the barn and what had he seen? I had been mad even to consider meeting Jake again. Madder still to give in to my impulses.

In the interval I wandered away from the crowds and found my way to the empty cloister where I sat on a stone parapet and wondered what to tell Nell, my closest friend.

Distant singing intruded. The concert had restarted. I recognised the piece. Delius. 'To be sung of a summer night on the water'. An idyll that was more French than English, I felt. It reminded me uncomfortably of when Edouard in Paris wanted to take me to a secret place by the river where, he said, you could see otters and kingfishers. Instead he took me to Gascony with the promise of golden orioles, but the orioles had flown.

Sitting quietly clarified my thoughts. I would tell Edouard something about Jake - my chance meeting with this Cambridge friend of my son. I would tell him about Jake's interest in French medieval history and our lunch together in Foix. That would be enough. I rang the château on my mobile. They told me Monsieur de Marcignac was in the garden. I asked for the telephone to be taken to him. I told him I was coming over. Where could I find him?

He was sitting under a small walnut tree on the edge of the park - a tree I had persuaded him to plant in memory of his wife. He'd never thought of commemorating her with something living. I told him this was what an English gentleman would do. A walnut tree would bear fruit for his children and grandchildren and give shelter to them and their children. I had encouraged his interest in smaller gardens rather than parks. We had been to Giverny together. I often talked to him about making an English garden in this corner of the park where there was shade from the summer sun. There would be thousands of bulbs in spring, then swathes of lilies, banks of irises, oleanders, fuschias and plumbago, peonies among clouds of crambe and a golden haze of the poppies I had loved at Giverny. Above all there would be masses of roses, for no other flower that I grew in England seemed so able to cope with the difficult soil of the Gers and as a concession to French tastes, I suggested rows of white wooden containers with orange or lemon trees flanking a wide path. They could be moved to shelter in the winter months.

'Oranges or lemons?' I asked.

He smiled. 'Either would be splendid.'

'The leaves of orange trees set off the colour of the fruit better, I think.'

'Oranges, then.'

'In a few years it would be beautiful, Edouard.'

He nodded. He was so indulgent and I was deceiving him. We walked down towards the lake. He asked about the concert at Auch. I told him about my meeting with Jake Lowell. 'Such a nice boy,' I said, echoing my words to Alastair, and I told him everything I'd intended. 'He knew Leonard Bray's work and had heard about his discovery of the pilgrim's grave. He asked to see where he worked. So I took him there.'

Edouard nodded as if in agreement. 'I haven't seen the house for years. When I was a boy it belonged to a strange old man called Cussac. He was very protective of his property and I'm sorry to say we liked to bait him. We openly stole plums from the trees behind the house. This was quite unnecessary because there were masses of windfalls all around - and here too, of course - but we enjoyed the terrible threats he issued when he chased us away.'

Cussac. The name on one of the documents sent home by Julia's father.

I asked: 'Did Cussac have a daughter?'

'Sabine. She inherited the house from him. A bit of a witch. No one wanted to marry her despite her property.'

'And what were her father's terrible threats?'

'That we would be locked in the haunted cellar until the police came to take us away. We didn't know the house doesn't have a cellar.'

'But Jake says the barn has an undercroft.'

'An undercroft? What makes him say that?'

'He has studied medieval architecture. He's quite sure.'

'Really? Well, perhaps we should meet this clever young friend of yours. Jake Lowell, you say?'

29 - JULIA

Clouds were sweeping in from the south, covering the stars. It was hot and humid. Louise said there was going to be a storm. Our discussion lacked energy and momentum. Old questions were rehearsed and new ones raised. About the house, the barn, the possibility of other clues in the text of the psalm, the postcards, the pictures and the strange verse by the writing desk. We were going nowhere.

Louise asked me if I had taken any photographs of the house.

'Jane did. She gave me some prints at the Mayor's party. I haven't looked at them yet.'

I found them in my handbag and passed them round with brief comments.

'I can see him at his table there looking out of the window and thinking about the pilgrim's grave and all it led to. That's the living room. Very gloomy. The kitchen's much better, with its beautiful fireplace. That's a good shot of the front of the house. Very overgrown. And that's round the other side. What a view! The terrace could be super with a lot of work. Jane says it needs masses of plants in terracotta pots.'

'Pots need endless watering,' said Nell.

Louise handed back one of the pictures. 'That looks like a water-butt under the low eaves there.'

The photograph was handed round. Against the back wall of the house and partly concealed by brambles was a shape that certainly looked like a water-butt. It would have been so easy to lift the lid without being observed and drop a waterproof package inside.

Nell insisted we should go there at once. Alastair said it would be wise to wait for daylight. It was already raining quite hard. The track down to the house could become a quagmire. He wouldn't want to tackle it in the dark. I said we were wasting time with negative thinking. We could be there and back in half an hour.

Alastair shrugged. 'Go, if you want to but be careful. It's up to you. If this is really going to be the moment of discovery you three ought to share it together. I'm an interloper.'

We couldn't persuade him. I suggested we should take Balou to keep watch for us. Nell drove with me beside her and Louise on the back seat, more or less submerged beneath the excited, hairy and smelly bulk of the dog. The road was empty. The storm was building up. The world outside the car was a Wagnerian scene. Nell turned the windscreen wipers to full speed and pressed the car forward as fast as she dared against the driving rain. Almost continuous flashes of lightning silhouetted the distant Pyrenees and floodlit the banks of cumuli. The wind was driving huge banks of cloud towards us from the south and swaying the trees on either side of the road. Balou quivered with excitement.

There were runnels of water loosening the surface of the track. Nell took it very slowly in bottom gear and at last brought the car to a standstill by the barn. She had hoped to manoeuvre it into a position where the headlights would light the back terrace, but the darkness and gathering storm made it too risky to go further, with the risk of grounding or getting stuck. Our flashlights would have to serve.

We stepped out onto sodden ground. It was crazy to have come. The first rumble of distant thunder seemed like a warning from on high. I went ahead lighting the way as we stumbled through long grass and over the uneven flags of the terrace. The beams of our torches searched along the wall until there, to cries of triumph, stood the water-butt, overhung by a network of briars and brambles. It was much weathered, with rusty hoops and a cracked lid. Ignoring the driving rain, we stood in silence, like explorers in some remote jungle face to face with a shrine that was the object of their quest.

Gingerly, Nell pulled back the briars with a piece of broken guttering she'd found lying around. The lid of the barrel was in two pieces. One came off without much difficulty. Three beams of light were directed inside. Three heads peered over the edge. The barrel was full to the brim and covered with a dark layer of slime. Nell fiddled with the tap at the base. The spigot broke off in her hand. The bung proved to be immovable without something to grip it. No one had thought of that.

A huge sheet of lightning lit the whole sky and was immediately followed by a heart-stopping crash of thunder. Startled faces were frozen as in a camera flash. It seemed that the stage was being set for some kind of dramatic revelation. Soaking wet, we joked about the storm but our laughter was forced. It was not the moment to give in to primitive fears.

If the barrel couldn't be drained, the obvious answer was to tip it over. The downpipe from the gutter had first to be uncoupled. After several futile attempts, I suggested the pipe was so corroded it would break off when the barrel was overturned. This was another problem. There wasn't space to get behind and push and the surface was so slimy and wet it was impossible to get a grip and find the strength to pull it forward. Even if we could push or pull, the weight of hundreds of litres of water would defy all our efforts. Breathless and frustrated, we stood back. The water-butt hadn't moved an inch.

In despair, Nell cried out: 'Alastair, where are you?'

I said: 'Come on, let's think properly. There may be an axe in the barn we could use to smash it.'

Nervously we agreed to go into the barn together, with Balou on a slip-lead. I found the key under the rock where Jake had left it and unfastened the padlock. Slowly we walked side by side with the beams from our torches probing the darkness like searchlights. Moving shadows cast by the objects on the floor seemed almost like ghostly figures. Balou bristled and barked once or twice at hidden enemies and was sternly but shakily silenced by Louise. It was an alarming place.

Lightning flashes pierced narrow gaps in the roof and were reflected through the open barn door. We searched as quickly as we could, eager to be done and to return to our task. No axe was found, nor any other tool that was likely to smash the barrel. But Nell, rummaging among a pile of broken tiles, called out and emerged with a length of scaffold pole. It would serve as a lever, she said. Hurriedly we stumbled back to the terrace.

It took our combined strength, disciplined heaving and the leverage of the long pole to lift the barrel, first a few inches from the stones on which it stood, and then with another heave to tilt it slightly. Another aching effort with concerted shouts of 'One! Two! Three! Now!' tilted it further, and the water began slowly to tip over the edge. The tip became a cascade and the waterfall gained its own momentum and the tilt of the barrel increased with the loss of water.

Suddenly it went over. I was on the wrong side and had to step back quickly to avoid its fall and the wash of water across the flags. Despite its rusted hoops, the barrel stayed in one piece and rolled drunkenly in all directions until it came to rest just off the paving.

Balou paddled around happily and drank from the rivulets running across the terrace onto the grass. Spontaneously and in silence we gathered round the open end of the butt. Our torches searched its dark depths. I leaned forward. My heart was thumping as I stooped, eased my head and shoulders inside the barrel and reached out as far as I could. The next moment I backed out holding a parcel covered with filth and cried out 'Water and mud!'

'It was larger than I had expected - an oblong shape wrapped in something that showed a hint of blue through the slime. I held it high in triumph. We were all laughing and crying, taking no account of our soaking state and the rain cascading down our faces.

The storm was right overhead now. We could hardly hear each other for the wind and the thunder. 'Well, are you going to open it?' Nell shouted.

I shouted back. 'Not here. This is not the place.'

Picking our way carefully, we started back towards the car. We had taken only a few steps when Balou growled, stood rigid with his ears pricked, his body quivering, pointing towards the barn. The door was open.

Louise grabbed him and slipped the leash over his head. Nell thought she'd seen something. Anxiously, we looked and listened. The howl of the wind covered all other sounds. Balou growled again. The ridge hair on his back bristled. Then he began to howl like a wolf. We froze.

Louise turned to me. 'Did you close the barn door?'

'I think so. But I didn't lock it.'

'The wind could have opened it.'

'I hope so,' said Nell with a wry laugh. Then she pointed in the direction of the car.

'What's that?'

The wavering beams of the torches hardly penetrated the driving rain but for a moment there seemed to be a faint figure beside the entrance to the barn. My elation had turned to cold fear. We had to get away as quickly as possible. Taking a step to one side, I tripped and let the slippery parcel fall from my grasp. In panic, I dropped to my knees and scrabbled around in the mud. It took a few frightening moments to find it.

Balou's howls had died to a whimper. The image had faded. Or maybe the rain had changed direction.

'It's nothing,' said Louise with a show of determination. 'Balou hates thunder. Let's go!'

He was reluctantly coaxed forward, his tail lowered. But then as quickly as he had shown fear, he relaxed and moved ahead of us, stopping now and then only to shake the water from his coat.

Led by the dog, we got back to the car. Gratefully on board, we locked all the doors. Nell started the engine, put the car in gear and steered shakily towards the track. The hill, as Alastair had predicted, was treacherous. As we reached the first gradient the wheels spun. Nell changed to a higher gear, let the car roll back and tried again with slower revs. The front wheels began to grip and pull the car forward.

The windows had steamed up. I did my best to clear the windscreen as Nell peered ahead, finding rougher surfaces beside the muddy track. We slid sideways into a deep rut and had to drop back for another attempt. Contrary advice from the passengers drew from Nell the threat that she would get out and walk if the bloody backseat drivers didn't shut up.

Calming down, and encouraged by supportive remarks, she steered an almost crablike course with the nearside wheels off the track, dangerously close to clumps of coppiced trees. The car tipped precariously as it mounted the bank to avoid a sea of mud. At last we felt tarmac beneath the wheels.

The return journey was calm and reflective. None of us doubted for a moment that we were bringing home the prize.

It was accepted that, though the contents of the package were to be revealed in the château I was to direct the proceedings. I decreed that the opening ceremony would take place on the terrace where we had enjoyed convivial meals together, but nothing would be done until we had all bathed and changed.

Alastair and Edouard were waiting anxiously. Our glowing faces told them all they needed to know. I insisted the men should join us at the table when we were changed. Louise suggested champagne to celebrate success but I declined. This was to be a solemn and magical moment. I asked for a dozen candles. These were placed in a circle around the table. While the men watched in silence, each of us women lit one candle with a taper and passed it around four times until the ring of light was complete. I then placed the packet on the table in front of me. It had been washed and was now seen to be wrapped in a bright blue waterproof material raggedly cut from an anorak or cagoule and haphazardly fastened with broad strips of tape. The parcel was untidily made, as if in a hurry, but perfectly secure and watertight.

The tape was cut with scissors and the package slowly unfastened by each of us three in turn until I cut the final strip of tape and opened the ragged parcel. It had been weighted with a terracotta tile that must have come from the terrace. A second waterproof packet inside contained a large notebook, a sealed envelope addressed to me and a small box fastened with adhesive tape.

For a while all eyes were on the box which was slowly passed around. There was no hurry. Somehow the occasion needed to be prolonged. At last I opened the envelope, took out a sheet of paper and began to read it. My eyes misted. Struggling, I blinked and handed the sheet to Nell. 'I'm sorry. I can't see very well. Please read it for me.'

After quite a pause, Nell took the letter. 'It's from Julia's father,' she said. 'This is what he has written. "My darling daughter. I know you will find this. I know that you will have followed the same trail that led me here and that at last you will have uncovered the secret that our kinsman François de Castres carried with him to his grave. Whether or not this is the true ring that once belonged to St James the Apostle of Christ others must judge but I am sure that François and his brethren believed this to be so. I had hoped to take the ring safely to England and then go with you to the shrine of St James, as François intended. If you are reading this letter it is because something has prevented me from undertaking the final task. Do this, then, for François, for me and for the unnumbered multitude of pilgrims. Your ever-loving Father."

I broke the silence, clenching my fists angrily. 'Why did you have to die on me?'

I glanced quickly through the notebook and without another word began to peel off the adhesive tape from the box. Heads leaned forward. The inside was packed with bits of newspaper in the centre of which I slowly withdrew, between finger and thumb, a complete but quite small scallop-shell, the two halves sealed by a yellowish substance.

'Yes! Of course!' I murmured as if to myself. 'Why didn't I think of it? He had it with him always. Or rather, Magnus did. No one would have given it a thought. And no one realised the shell was of any value when they let my father keep it as a souvenir. When we talked about how François might have hidden the joyau on the journey I never thought of this.'

I remembered my father's obscure message about "a theft that confounded the thief". Was he suggesting that Magnus stole the scallop-shell and its treasure from François? What an irony that it was buried with him!

Slowly I turned the shell round in my fingers close to one of the candles so all could see it. After a while I held it to my nose and sniffed. 'Beeswax. My father must have resealed it.'

Louise said: 'I'll get an oyster knife.'

With very gentle prising, the shell was separated into two halves. But still its secret was not revealed for the inside also proved to be packed with beeswax.

'Hot water,' said Louise. 'I'll put a pan on the stove in the kitchen.'

At last, a little before two o'clock in the morning, I carefully wiped away the last remnants of wax and the glint of gold shone in the candlelight.

No one could speak. The ring - for it was indeed a ring - was slowly passed round hand to hand so that each could hold it and examine it closely. The gold was seen to be delicately incised with the simple outline of a fish. I explained as Edouard nodded. 'In the early days of the Church followers of Jesus risked the death penalty under Roman law. They met and worshipped in secret. The symbol of the fish was a secret sign of their faith. The ancient Greek word for fish is Ichthus. The Greek letters I, CH, TH, U and S spell out the words Jesus, Christ, God's, Son, Saviour.'

'It looks absolutely right to me,' said Nell, turning the ring round slowly in her fingers.

'I agree,' said Edouard. 'I've seen gold pieces of the period.'

Alastair got up from the table. Silently but grinning broadly, he embraced each of us in turn, me last of all, holding me in a bear hug and lifting my feet off the ground until I broke away laughing and protesting.

There was no need for words. We continued to pass the ring round in wonder, our faces glowing in the candlelight, our voices instinctively lowered to a near whisper.

'The end of the trail,' said Louise at last.

'Not the end,' I said. 'Not yet. I shall write to the Bishop in Santiago de Compostela and tell him I propose to bring him a relic of the utmost importance and in great secrecy, and to ask that this may be suitably received. Meanwhile I trust you all to say nothing whatsoever to anyone until it is safely delivered. I thank you, each and all of you. Nell, Louise, it would please me greatly if you will accompany me and the ring on its last journey.'

They agreed with the utmost enthusiasm that this should be done, and that when a reply was obtained we should meet somewhere in Spain and carry the ring along the Pilgrim's Road to its proper home.

'How will you protect it till then?' asked Nell, practically.

'Rather it shall protect me,' I said. 'I shall wear it on a chain round my neck, night and day. But we still have work to do. It was obvious tonight that François is not at rest. My father said so. I felt the same. The place must be exorcised.'

Breakfast was very late. When we had exhausted all talk of the ring, Edouard gently reminded us of the mystery of the reredos and invited me to report on what I had learned. I brought a sheaf of notes to the table.

'So far I've found only one possible connection between Vaison-la-Romaine and an heretical movement there at some time. It's an extremely slender connection - merely a footnote in a chapter on Manichaeism. Vaison was said to be the location of an active Manichaean school in the third or fourth century. There were many such schools in France. The faith or sect flourished and faded a very long time before the treasures were dispersed from the abbey in Lombardy but I've found nothing to show that the Manichaeans were still around at the time the reredos disappeared.'

'Who were the Manichaeans?' Louise asked.

'Heretics from early Christian times. They spread far and wide. They were dualists or gnostics like the Cathars, who probably stemmed from them. Their founder was a Persian prophet called Mani. I've made some brief notes but if you want to read it up I can give you chapter and verse.'

Alastair said: 'Just your notes please, Julia.'

I put on my glasses. 'Mani was born in Mesopotamia in the year 217 and was brought up as a Christian. His doctrine was uniquely based on the combined teachings of Zarathustra, the Buddha and Jesus. His followers, the Manichaeans, believed that human souls have fallen out of the spiritual world into the material world and are trapped in a perpetual cycle of reincarnation unless roused and saved from the power of the Prince of Darkness by knowledge of the Light. This knowledge is to be gained through a Saviour sent from the Father of Greatness.

'You can see the Buddhist and Christian connections, but that's a very simplistic summary of their beliefs. This was long before the Albigensian Heresy challenged the Roman Church. We know what happened to the Albigensians, but the Manichaeans seem to have just faded away or been absorbed within other heresies.'

'Do we know where the Manichaean school was in Vaison?' asked Alastair.

'No. I've told you all I know. It's not much. Probably a red herring. I wouldn't have mentioned the Manichaeans except that I've found nothing else.'

Alastair persisted: 'But from what you know about them, could they have had a church in or near Vaison?'

'You could call their meeting place a church, I suppose.'

'Do you think they would they have wanted it furnished in the Christian style? A font for baptisms, an altar for sacrificial rites, a reredos as a focus for the altar?'

'I've no idea. It's plausible, but not based on anything I've been able to discover. I've only had a few hours in the library, but I've consulted all the most likely sources.'

There was a rather dispirited silence.

Then Edouard said: 'Thank you, Julia. This Manichaean stuff may not be relevant, but we can't afford to ignore it. When you get to Vaison you may be able to pick up some echoes of those times.'

'Where would we start looking?'

'There's one possible line to follow.'

'What's that?'

The list on the end-paper shows that a crucifix was also sent to Cluny. It must have been disposed of by the same people who took the reredos, perhaps for money or just as a gift to some church to salve their consciences. We know it's now in private hands in Texas. A piece of that quality will have been handled by leading salerooms so it must have a documented history. If we can trace it back to the time when it left the abbey, or soon after, that would give us a clue.'

It was a couple of hours before the time difference made a call to the Texan owner of the crucifix possible. While Edouard was gone Alastair suggested we might hone our minds over a few hands of bridge. We cut for partners. Alastair drew me and was the dealer of the first hand. He opened the bidding with one spade. Nell on his left bid four clubs. I bid four hearts, Louise passed and Alastair bid four no trumps, asking me to show the number of aces I held; I responded with five hearts to indicate two aces, whereupon Alastair bid seven no trumps. Nell doubled and all passed.

Nell led the king of clubs. As dummy, I laid down my hand, showing two spades to the jack, six hearts to the ace, four diamonds to the queen and the ace of clubs singleton. A few minutes later Alastair took the thirteenth trick with the king of diamonds in hand and observed: 'Grand slam doubled. Maximum points. A good start, partner.'

'A lucky start' Nell riposted. 'I had nine clubs to the king queen.'

'But nothing else. A rash double. The ace was against you. You could never have got in, could you?'

Louise said: 'Well done. You two make a good partnership.'

Lucky at cards...' said Nell, leaving the old saw unfinished. I smiled.

It was more than half an hour before Edouard returned and reported the outcome of his telephone call.

'An American called Robert P. Keppler bought the crucifix in Paris three years ago. He still has it. He paid seven hundred and forty thousand euros for it. Mr Keppler is faxing me a photocopy of the page in the sale catalogue and a colour photograph. He says the provenance goes back to the fourteenth century when the crucifix was in the possession of Guillaume de Malaucène. There is a town of that name close to Vaison-la-Romaine.'

The fax from Robert Keppler arrived within half-an-hour. Edouard brought it to the table.

'There are five pages. You're welcome to read it in full, but the essential facts of interest are these. The catalogue entry reads: "A very fine crucifix of silver and gold, ornamented with precious stones and enamel. 77 centimetres high. Italian 13th century." The provenance is remarkable. It starts with Guillaume de Malaucène. On his death in 1249 it passed to the Abbey of Cluny for which, as we know, it was originally intended. It remained there until 1789, the year of the Revolution. The Abbey was closed the following year and mostly demolished soon afterwards. The crucifix then came into the possession of a Monsieur Fréderic Rosteig and remained in his widow's family, named Duvivier, until 1913, when it was bought at auction in London by the Trustees of the Hart-Rosefield Estate. They paid a very modest price for it at a time when ecclesiastical pieces were not much regarded by collectors, and they made a huge gain when it was sold to Mr Keppler three years ago in New York.'

He handed the fax to Alastair, who glanced quickly through the pages.

'Where is Malaucène, Edouard?'

'About ten kilometres from Vaison. Not an interesting place, except for a fortified church built in the 14th century by Pope Clement the Fifth.'

Alastair checked the map. 'Obviously we must go there. It could be where the custodian of the reredos was killed. I'm puzzled why the Comte of Toulouse, a man of power, wealth and position, took the trouble to report the death of an obscure monk to his abbot? Did his letter hide something? Could he have had a personal interest in the treasures being sent to Cluny, something he couldn't risk committing to paper but the abbot would understand?'

Nell said: 'A secret conspiracy?'

'Not necessarily to kill the custodian. That could have been an accident, but there may have been an agreement to divert the treasures intended for Cluny.'

'Why would they do that?'

'Maybe the Comte wanted the reredos.'

I said: 'And we know Guillaume de Malaucène wanted the crucifix.'

185

Casually Edouard remarked that he had a cousin living near Malaucène.

'My husband has cousins in every corner of France,' said Louise. 'When we travel we stay in draughty châteaux without central heating or swimming pools, and seldom with a good chef.'

Nell intervened. 'You're not proposing that we should *all* visit Edouard's cousin in Malaucène, are you?'

'No. Just you and I. We should leave as soon as possible. It'll take at least six hours so we won't get back till the day after tomorrow at the earliest. Let's hope we pick up the trail.'

Edouard suggested a time limit. 'If you've not come across anything significant by Sunday, I think you should come back and spend the rest of your stay enjoying yourselves here.'

'We *are* enjoying ourselves,' I protested. 'At least *I* am. And while Alastair and Nell are in Provence we could try to unravel the mystery of the Calix.'

30 - ALASTAIR

Nell and I left for Vaison immediately after breakfast. Our route by-passed cities which had witnessed turbulent chapters of France's history. After a quick cross-country drive to Toulouse we joined the Autoroute des Deux Mers and followed its wide sweep across the Languedoc towards the Mediterranean; past the vast medieval fortress of Carcassonne with its fifty towers; past Narbonne and the Archbishop's palace close to the golfe du Lion; past cathedral-dominated Béziers where in the 13th century there had been a ghastly slaughter during the king's crusade against the Albigensians; past the elegant university city of Montpellier; past Nimes, "France's Rome" with its huge amphitheatre; and at last, crossing the Rhone near the ruins of the Pont d'Avignon, we came to the city that was the ancient seat of the Popes during a dispute with Rome.

'I thought we might stop for a simple lunch at Christian Étienne,' I said. 'It's right by the Palais des Papes. I've booked.' Nell gave me a knowing look.

We were shown to a table on the terrace. When I had ordered a kir royale for Nell and Badoit for me and the waiter had handed us the cartes, Nell remarked 'Did you notice the dark green Clio that went by rather slowly as you were parking? It passed us a couple of times on the autoroute going at quite a rate and it was behind us in Toulouse and again near Béziers.'

I said: 'Yes. Three men.'

We ate modestly - grilled red mullet, a sorbet and cheese and talked about everything but the challenge we'd been set. When the coffee was brought Nell lit a cigarette and teased me. 'You're enjoying this, aren't you, Alastair? This is your métier - the scent, the pursuit, the kill. You're the huntsman, we're the pack, but you'd be in the chase even if you were alone. I think Edouard has set it up entirely for your pleasure.'

'What nonsense!'

She smiled at me across the table. 'All right, then. How long would you be staying at the château were it not for the challenge of the hunt?'

'Why do you think I accepted the invitation?'

'Not on my account.'

'Certainly on your account.'

'I find that difficult to believe.'

'You're being provocative and feminine.'

'I am feminine, haven't you noticed?'

As we drove out of the car park I made a point of waiting a while before edging into the place de l'Horloge. Almost at once the small green car appeared as if from nowhere but hanging back so there were two other vehicles intervening.

'Can you see anything?' I asked.

'There's too much traffic, but he's behind you.'

I took a right out of the square and right again into the rue Racine. The Clio followed. I made several more sharp turns through the narrow streets and joined the ring road near the Pont St-Bénézet. Glancing into my offside mirror I said: 'They're some way behind and keeping their distance.'

'Can you lose them?'

'Not without attracting a lot of attention and risking a big fine.'

The car on our tail was unexpected. Why had Malvin, if indeed it was Malvin, not made straight for Vaison, as I had predicted? Maybe he thinks we have a more precise destination and if you don't know the way you follow someone who does.

'The next exit from the motorway is coming up soon,' said Nell. 'You could lose him there.'

'I don't want to. We need to know who they are.'

She said: 'You mean you don't know?' in a tone that implied my infuriating certainty was failing.

When the motorway merged with the Autoroute du Soleil the Clio was several vehicles behind. As we slowed at the approach to the péage Nell glanced back and said the green car had joined a parallel queue of vehicles waiting to pay the toll, where it was hidden by one of Norbert Dentressangle's huge camions.

'Perhaps he's staying on the motorway,' she said.

'I don't think so.'

Instead of taking the ring road around Orange, I drove slowly into the centre of the town. The Clio tailed us. It was all too obvious, but our followers had no choice if they were not to lose contact.

'Let's take a break,' I said and pulled off the road by a café in a small square where plane trees provided shade. As I parked Nell looked back and said: 'I can't see them.'

'They're still with us. Probably round the corner in the next street.'

We left the air-conditioned comfort of the car for the sudden blast of the Provençal sun, like opening an oven door, and made for the shade of tables set out under the trees.

I ordered thé au citron for us both and asked Nell: 'Have you seen the Roman theatre?'

'Do we have time?'

'Plenty. We can be in Vaison in half-an-hour. It would be amusing to treat our friends to a bit of culture.'

Nell smiled. 'I've seen the theatre. Very early one summer morning, a few years ago. I sat on the very top tier and sketched the great bowl and the stage and tried to remember the colour of the shadows and the depth of blue in the sky.'

'For a commission?'

'For pleasure, to make a spontaneous impression. Later I added some colour washes and showed the sketches to Patrice. He offered me quite a lot of money for them.'

'Did you accept?'

'No, I turned him down. I enjoyed turning him down. He thought he could buy anything he wanted.'

'But you didn't always turn him down.'

'Are we going to look at the theatre or not?'

I placed coins on the table and got up. 'Take me to where you made your sketches and don't look behind you.'

I led the way out of the shade into the dazzling brilliance of the afternoon sun. It was only a short walk through narrow streets to the entrance of the Roman theatre. I took her hand and pulled her up behind me as we climbed one of the steep stone staircases that fanned out from the level of the stage to the top of the huge amphitheatre. When we reached the uppermost row of stone benches I said: 'You can turn round now.'

There were perhaps fifty or sixty people scattered around the auditorium. Two young men were standing on the stage far below, sharing a book and declaiming lines in what Nell recognised as Latin to an audience of their fellows seated high up. Every word was audible.

The scena behind the stage was like the facade of a great palace, its doors, windows and ornaments thrown into hard relief by the sun. I tried to picture an audience of seven thousand provincial citizens packing the benches along the curving tiers. How extraordinary that a town which was once so glorious and important should now be just a tourist attraction. 'And how inappropriate,' Nell said, 'to name a beautiful town like this after a fruit! Though I suppose the stone has that colour.'

'No connection,' I said. 'Orange was named for the Prince of Orange. The fruit's name comes from the Arabian naranj. Hence naranja in Spanish. It was first known in England as a norange, not an orange. Useless information, but a nice tease, you might think.'

'Shouldn't we make a move?'

'No hurry. Let's see how long it is before they can't bear waiting outside any longer and one of them comes in to find out what we're up to. The others will stay to watch the exits in case we slip out by another door.'

After a few minutes I said: 'Look. Just inside the door where we came in. Two men. Can't see their faces from up here.'

They were of different ages. One was a dark, curly-haired young man of athletic build wearing a yellow tee-shirt, blue jeans and trainers, the other lean and stooping and wearing a check shirt and black trousers. Neither showed any interest in the great theatre but stood by the entrance, scanning the steep tiers of seating from side to side.

'Recognise either of them?'

'No.'

'The third man must be Malvin. He knew we would spot him so he's staying out of sight, with the car probably.'

'You're very sure.'

'Who else would follow us all the way here?'

'And his passengers?'

'Underlings, to keep track of us while Malvin stays in the background.'

'I got a quick look at one of them when their car passed us. Could be the smaller one there. Balding man with large ears. Middle-aged. Moustache. Face like a ferret.'

'Sounds like Edouard's description of the bookbinder. Malvin may have brought him along because he wants to keep an eye on him, or Labadie may have insisted, for the same reason. They've both seen the inscription on the manuscript and they distrust one another.'

'You're pretty good at this game, Alastair.'

'It's an excellent game. Don't tell me you're not enjoying it.'

She had to admit she was beginning to do so. The hijacking of an ancient church treasure and its unknown fate presented so many intriguing possibilities. She'd always enjoyed expeditions with unforeseeable twists and turns and hazards. Like Malvin. This posed a question. She asked it.

'What interest does Malvin have in the reredos?'

'None, in my opinion, but he knows something we don't know, so he stays on our heels, waits his moment and grabs the prize, if we're not on our guard.'

'What prize?'

'The Calix obviously.'

When we'd checked in at the Hotel Beffroi in the haute ville of Vaison-la-Romaine, I telephoned Edouard's cousin Henri. He was expecting my call. In perfect English he said he and his wife would be delighted to receive us at any time. Indeed, would we not prefer to stay the night with them rather than in an hotel? It was a drive of only twenty minutes. I declined with thanks. We had some things to do before leaving Vaison but would be pleased to call the following morning. Eleven-thirty? I noted down the directions to the château. Reporting the conversation to Nell I added suggestions for some amusement during the rest of the day.

'First, a visit to the Roman remains. As tourists we mustn't miss so important a site.'

'Tourists?'

'Perhaps we can persuade Malvin and his friends they've made a big mistake and are wasting their time; that our journey is just a cultural trip. They must have wondered why we stopped to see the theatre at Orange. When they see us doing nothing in particular in Vaison they might begin to wonder if we guessed they would follow us; that we are decoys, luring them away from whatever the others are doing back at Marcignac. Let's keep them guessing.'

'Nell said: 'You've a devious mind, Alastair Hadley.'

'We're dealing with devious people. In any case I'm sure you'll find the Roman town fascinating. The two sites are very exposed so it will be fun to see how our escorts try to stay out of view.'

'Okay, and what then?'

'This evening a short journey to the hill village of Ségurat for dinner. I doubt if Malvin and his companions will dare to dine at the same restaurant, so they'll either have to hang about for a couple of hours somewhere nearby or risk losing contact. Later we might take an evening stroll around Vaison and separate for a short while to see who follows whom and whether they're any good at it.'

'What fun!' said Nell sarcastically. 'Has it occurred to you that these are villains and we might be in some danger?'

'Nonsense, they're amateurs, but if you'd rather not play along, we can dine here in the hotel. Malvin got out of the car as we came up the hill. I saw him go into a small hotel. His two chums are sitting in their car outside so it will be a very boring evening for them unless we give them something to do. Besides I thought you'd enjoy the truffe soufflé en coque d'oeuf at Ségurat and the pigeon with figs.'

'We had a good lunch,' said Nell.

'An omelette in a bistro, if you prefer. Then we could come back and have an early night.'

Nell hesitated. 'What do you know about the truffe soufflé?'

'A speciality of the chef and the cellar has some rather good Rhone wines.'

'Give me time for a cool shower and to change into something more suitable for exploring ruins.'

In my room I made a call to Edouard. After a brief report of our journey I asked: 'The little bookbinder from Marseille - what does he look like?'

As I expected, the description tallied with that of the ferret-faced man seen by Nell. So why was Labadie in the party? I took a shot in the dark.

'Could you ask Julia to have a very close look at the photocopy Labadie brought you? I have a feeling it might have been tampered with.'

'How do you mean?'

'That some connection with the reredos might have been removed from the original. Just a hunch.'

'I didn't notice anything myself.'

'Please call me on my mobile if Julia finds anything.'

31 - JULIA

Edouard gave me Alastair's message.

'He could be on to something. Suppose the photocopy you were given by the bookbinder had been doctored to hide something much more interesting to Malvin than the reredos - something small sent from the abbey to Cluny at the same time as the reredos and the crucifix?'

'And which, unlike the crucifix, has never been catalogued.'

'And unlike the reredos, could be sold on the open market.'

Edouard had interesting news concerning his correspondent Claudia Andrieu. The journal in which she'd seen his letter was circulated only to subscribers. A call to the subscription manager confirmed that the lady was known. By encouragement and flattery of the kind that Edouard practised with aristocratic ease, the manager was persuaded to reveal that Madame Andrieu had lived in Provence for many years. Her address, of course, was confidential.

'I had no difficulty in finding her in local directories. She has a house just outside Carpentras.'

'A few kilometres from Vaison. A coincidence?'

'I wonder. Let's see what Alastair and Nell can find out.'

'So long as they're discreet. If this woman is anxious to discourage your interest in the Calix, we ought not to let her know we're in the field.'

'But what's her motive?'

'To put us off the scent.'

Meanwhile we turned to Alastair's request to examine the photocopy of the inscription provided by Bernard Labadie. Sitting side by side at the long table in the library and taking turns to scrutinise the difficult script through a powerful glass, we studied the text line by line.

After a long while Edouard said: 'I can't see anything.'

'I can.' I pointed with my pencil. 'Here, half way down. The note about the reredos being the guardian of the cup. This line contains only two words with ascenders - *color* and *forma*. Throughout the document all the letters 'l' and 'f' are elongated so that they almost touch the line above; but the ascenders on this line have been very slightly cut off at the top of the stroke. You could easily miss that.'

Edouard took the glass from me and examined the letters I indicated.

'You're right. Sharper eyes than mine! No one would notice unless they suspected something.'

'Someone has made a photocopy of the original, sliced out a piece at the end of the description of the reredos, put the two bits together and photocopied them once more.'

'But if you do that you get a faint line where the join is made.'

'You remove the line with erasing fluid, photocopy the document a third time and you get a clean copy. If you're careful no one can see what you've done. What gives this away is that the tips of the "l" and the "f" have been very slightly clipped in the process.'

Louise came into the library to suggest that we should go riding before dinner. 'You're wasting a beautiful afternoon.'

'Far from wasting it, my dear,' said Edouard. 'I've just received a lesson in observation and deduction. Julia has shown me how the inscription has been tampered with. Malvin knows something about the Calix we don't know.'

32 - ALASTAIR

We led our faithful shadows on foot through the busy streets of Vaison-la-Romaine and eventually to the Quartier du Puymin, the larger of the two excavated sites. Aware that Labadie and the third man (who was he?) were within the gates but out of sight, we made our way to the Roman theatre. Just as we got to the top tier, Edouard's promised call came through. After a few minutes quiet conversation on the mobile I switched off and told Nell what Edouard had learned about Claudia Andrieu and of Julia's discovery that the photocopy had been falsified.

'So you were right. What do we do now?'

'I suggest we leave Claudia for later. As to Malvin, we must obviously confront him and get at the truth.'

'Confront him? With what?'

'The prospect of a hefty spell in jail. We've got enough on him to scare him. We know he stole the Canticum.'

'Borrowed it.'

'With intent to deceive. He removed the end-papers and kept them. Criminal damage and theft. He misrepresented himself as the agent of the owner for personal gain. Fraud. There are plenty of reputable witnesses. Baron Edouard de Marcignac, the Abbot of San Benedetto della Verne, the booksellers in Genoa, Milan and Paris.'

'I don't think Malvin's easily frightened and even if you scare him, there's no way of getting him to tell you what he erased from the inscription. It could be a dangerous move.'

'We've no choice. I'll have to risk it. How else can we find out what he's hiding? At the moment we're just playing into his hands.

Somehow he'll steal the prize from under our noses. And my guess is that, considering the time, expense and cunning he's put into this, the prize will be very special.'

'It might not exist.'

'We have to assume it does.'

Two hours later, the friendliness of our welcome at La Table du Comtat in Séguret prompted Nell to ask: 'How do you know this place?'

'I usually eat here when I go to Gigondas.'

'To see a lady friend?'

'To taste the wines.'

Apart from our table and one other, the restaurant was full. Then, just as we were sitting down, Nell looked up and she pointed to a smartly dressed couple who had just arrived. The man immediately came towards her with outstretched hand and a quizzical look. Glancing at me he said: 'Nell, my dear, I thought you were staying at Marcignac.'

'We are,' said Nell, 'but our host has sent us on a treasure hunt. We've got rather stuck here. I don't think you know Alastair Hadley, by the way. Patrice Roussillon.'

He regarded me coolly and said: 'You seem to be covering a lot of ground.'

I said: 'There are no limits to the scale of Edouard's invention. Perhaps you can help us. Nell tells me you have a place near here. Do you know anything about the Manichaeans - an ancient sect? They were supposed to have been active around here centuries ago.'

Patrice shrugged and looked at his wife who was clearly uninterested.

'Manichaeans you say? I've never heard of them.'

Fortunately our tables were widely separated and no further exchange took place. I studied Sophie Roussillon. She looked cool, classically beautiful, perfectly turned out from her immaculate coiffure and finely arched eyebrows to her gold-tipped shoes. It was difficult to imagine anyone touching her.

The meal was as delicious as I had led Nell to expect. I was attentive to Nell throughout dinner but I could tell she was distracted by the presence of Patrice, who was in her line of sight.

It was nearly eleven o'clock by the time we left the restaurant. As we went outside I pointed out the green Clio parked a short distance away but without any attempt at concealment. I'd seen it arrive soon after us.

'Why didn't you tell me?' Nell objected.

'Because Malvin is an unpleasant intruder. Knowledge of him hovering nearby could spoil your dinner, if it hasn't already been spoiled by the presence of that man Roussillon.'

Speechless, she followed me to our car. I opened the passenger door for her and said: 'Stay here please. I won't be long.'

'What are you going to do?'

'Confront him. This silly charade has gone on long enough.'

'Be careful!' she said anxiously.

'Don't worry.'

The car was in a patch of darkness. I approached it quietly from behind. There was no one in the passenger seat. I guessed that Labadie and the other man had been left in Vaison to share watches on the hotel. I relished the thought of Malvin's wasted, hungry evening outside the restaurant. How alert would he be after so long with nothing to do?

But it wasn't Malvin. The top of Labadie's bald head glistened in the faint glow of a reading light. So the little bookbinder had drawn the short straw to follow us while the others dined in Vaison.

I quickly opened the passenger door, said: 'Bon soir, mon ami!', reached across, took the key from the ignition and climbed inside. Labadie stared at me in terror, his eyes bulging, his mouth quivering. I casually took my cellphone from my pocket and switched it on. I pointed to my wristwatch.

'You have just one minute to explain yourself, my friend. If I don't like what I hear, I shall call the police.'

Labadie managed to say: 'I have nothing to explain. I have done nothing wrong.'

'Nothing wrong? Criminal damage? Fraud? You're in the shit up to your armpits, my friend, and you'll get what your friend

Malvin is going to get unless you tell me here and now what I want to know. You've already wasted twenty seconds.'

The little bookbinder was pale and shaking visibly. At first he seemed incapable of speech, then he managed to say: 'What can I tell you? I know very little.'

I gripped Labadie's right arm above the elbow and pressed my finger-tips hard into the muscle, such as it was. 'That's fine, Bernard, because I'm wanting very little. Just a few words. I want you to tell me the words - the exact words which you removed from the photocopy of the inscription you sent to Edouard de Marcignac.'

'I don't remember. It was Malvin made me do it. I don't know why he wanted me to tamper with the book. The inscription was in Latin anyway. I don't understand Latin.'

'What a pity, because you have only twenty seconds before I make this call. The police won't be interested in what you don't remember. They will be interested, however, in other things. Your deliberate damage of a highly valuable book and the theft of the end-papers. Your conspiracy with Malvin to defraud the baron. We'll think of other things and in case Malvin hasn't told you, there are plenty of reputable witnesses. Experts who saw the book before it was damaged, the librarian of the abbey from which it was stolen. Your time is up, Bernard.'

'I've told you, I don't remember. It was all foreign to me.'

'Nonsense! Malvin's friend from Genoa translated it for you. We know much more than you suppose, Bernard. You removed a line from the description of the Antelami reredos. What did it say? In French, as you don't remember the Latin.'

He stammered: 'Malvin will kill me.'

I started pressing buttons on my mobile. 'He's planning to do that anyway, isn't he? Do you think he brought you along to share in the proceeds? Bernard, you're an idiot. Malvin doesn't need you, except as a watchdog. You've done all he needed from you. He brought you here because he couldn't risk leaving you behind to get up to the kind of things I'm sure you're good at - deceit, treachery, informing. You've been inside, haven't you? He picked you for this dirty work because you've got a record, so he can lean on you.'

I held the phone to my ear and increased the pressure on the little bookbinder's arm.

'He'll certainly kill you if you stay till he's got what he wants. This is too big for him to share. You know that. He'd never trust you not to say anything.'

Labadie was looking in the driving mirror and from side to side as if in hope that some kind of rescue would appear.

I spoke into the telephone. 'Police? Hold on, please.'

'All right, I'll tell you.'

I switched off the mobile but held it under Labadie's nose.

'The truth, Bernard. I know enough already to tell if you're lying or holding anything back. What were the words you removed from the inscription?'

There was a long silence while Labadie kept swallowing and rubbing his face. He looked as though he might be sick. His voice sank to a whisper.

'The words, as I remember them translated into French were "in the care of the Sisters of Magdala", whatever one may understand by that.'

'Nothing more? Just that? In the care of the Sisters of Magdala?'

'Just that.'

'Say it again, Bernard.'

'In the care of the Sisters of Magdala.'

I dug my fingers harder still into Labadie's arm. 'The truth, Bernard. You know what will happen to you if you're lying?'

Labadie whimpered. 'It is the truth.'

'Who are the Sisters of Magdala?'

'I don't know. Nor does Malvin.'

'They are here in Vaison? Is that why you came to Vaison?'

'I tell you I don't know. We simply followed you.'

I tightened my grip. Labadie squealed.

'What else, Bernard?'

'There was a letter Malvin saw in an abbey. A letter mentioning Vaison. I haven't seen this letter. I've told you everything I know. It's the truth. You're hurting me!'

'If you've lied, Bernard, I will do more than hurt you.'

'You're not going to call the police?'

I got out of the car. 'Listen. Malvin's on to something much too big to share with anyone. There's nothing in it for you, nothing. Believe me, he wants you out of the way, permanently. Cut your losses, Bernard. The baron promised you some reward if the information you gave him pays off. So far it has. He'll be very angry to have been deceived by you, but he's an honourable man and will keep his word. It's your choice. A few hundred euros from Marcignac or a nasty end from Malvin'

I hesitated as I opened the passenger door. 'My advice Bernard, is drive away. Don't go back to Vaison. Forget everything you've heard and get home as fast as you can. Your best hope is that Malvin is behind bars before he can catch up with you.'

Labadie swallowed. 'This isn't my car,' he said pathetically.

'Compared with your other problems, why should that worry you?'

I was about to hand over the keys, then had a thought. 'Before you go, Bernard, who is your young friend?'

'My young friend?'

'Yes, your young friend who has been having a good dinner back in Vaison with Malvin while you've been stranded here. Who is he?'

Labadie almost spat out the words. 'He is Carlo. Malvin's nephew. An arrogant little shit. He's the one you should be getting at, not me. He's the one.'

I threw the keys on to the passenger seat, slammed the door and stood watching as Labadie switched on the lights, started the engine, somehow managed to reverse without hitting anything, put the car into forward gear and with a squeal of tires swept off down the hill, narrowly avoiding the parapet.

'Will he go back to Malvin? Nell asked as soon as I had given her a brief account of my confrontation with Labadie.

'I doubt if he'll have the courage not to.'

'And do you believe what he told you? "The Sisters of Magdala", whatever that means.'

'It's not something you could make up on the spur of the moment, is it? I doubt if Labadie has that kind of imagination. It rings true.'

'But what does it mean?'

'A geographical feature perhaps? We need to check maps and guide books.' I started punching keys on my mobile.

'Who are you calling?'

'Edouard.'

'It's nearly midnight.'

'This is a crucial lead, Nell. We can't afford to waste time speculating. Malvin may already know the answer.'

33 - JULIA

Despite the late hour I was still in the library poring over reference books when Louise came in with Edouard. He brought news of another email from Claudia Andrieu.

'She's sending me a photograph of the Calix.'

'The Calix? A photo could be of any old chalice. The only way to verify it is the one she claims was made for the abbey would be to search the archives in Rome. She's trying to deter you from going there.'

Edouard frowned. 'Why would she do that?'

I swallowed my irritation. Surely Edouard realised Claudia was an unreliable witness? Setting aside one directory and opening another I asked if he knew the present Comte de Toulouse. 'One of your numerous cousins, perhaps?' I asked with a teasing smile.

Edouard shook his head. 'The last Comte died in 1737. He was the son of Louis the Fourteenth, and the Marquise de Montespan, one of the king's mistresses. Louis-Alexander was the last of seven children the king fathered on the Marquise. Eventually he got tired of her. She swapped the court for a convent where she became the Mother Superior. It was a colourful period in our history.'

'Colourful indeed!'

That ended our exchange.

The call from Alastair came through on Edouard's mobile. He listened intently, nodding once or twice and repeating the word "Magdala". When he switched off he said Alastair had discovered a new line to follow and more work for me.

'His guess was brilliant. The photocopy has been tampered with. Labadie admitted Malvin told him to delete a few words. They were in Latin, appended to the reference to the Calix. Labadie said they mean "belonging to the Sisters of Magdala" but couldn't explain it.'

'Sounds like a religious order, doesn't it?' I said. 'Sisters in the religious sense.'

'Alastair suggests it might be the name of a local feature, like caves or hills.'

'Does he believe Labadie?'

'Could he have made that up on the spot? Alastair thinks not.'

Louise agreed. Labadie was sly but not that clever. I said it shouldn't take long to carry out a search. I wasn't persuaded to leave it for the morning. 'This is too good a lead to go to sleep on.'

34 - NELL

It was a clear, star-lit evening as we drove back from Séguret to Vaison. We crossed the Ouvèze below the Haute Ville. At the bottom of the street leading up to the hotel. I asked Alastair to stop so I could look at the historic Roman bridge. 'I'll walk back, don't wait. I could do with some fresh air.' Alastair objected, but mildly, knowing he couldn't prevent me from doing what I wanted.

I watched the car until the rear lights vanished round the bend. The best view of the bridge would be from high above. I walked a short way before stopping to lean over the parapet. The river flowed calmly far below the graceful arch. In 1992 it had raged in a wild torrent that flooded the riverside houses and much of the industrial part of the town. The Roman structure stood firm as it had done for nearly two thousand years, surviving the flood that destroyed the modern bridge. Beyond the trees on the river bank and the lights of the town centre was a dark patch which must be the Quartier de Puymin where we had led our followers a dance that afternoon. The only sign of life was down by the river itself where a few couples sat or strolled in the shadows.

At last I turned away and began the walk up the hill. The road to the hotel was empty. All I could hear was the hum of traffic below and my heels clicking on the pavement. Suddenly there were other footsteps. I glanced over my shoulder to see the shadowy figure of a man maybe fifty paces behind. He must have come out of a door or passage-way as I went by. What was he doing there at this time of night? Going home like me, of course. Or was he?

Taking a deep breath, I increased my pace. The hill was steep. He was closing on me. I quickened my steps and crossed the road.

He also crossed. I was almost running when he took hold of my arm, gripping it with steely fingers. Angrily I turned to face him. Malvin! I caught my breath and only just managed to cry out: 'Let me go!'

The street was empty and the houses dark and shuttered. How stupid I'd been! Even if I screamed he could drag me somewhere out of sight, down some alley-way, before anyone took any notice.

He read my mind. 'It would be very unpleasant if I had to silence you.'

I took a deep breath. 'What do you want?'

'To talk. Not here. In my hotel.'

I must stay calm, keep him here in the street. Alastair would come back and look for me if I didn't show up soon.

'Let me go. I promise not to make a noise.'

He still kept hold of my arm.

'This way, if you please.' He turned me back across the road, the way we had come.

'My friend will be here any moment,' I said.

Malvin took a mobile from his pocket: 'Monsieur Hadley? I think not. He has gone up to his room.'

How could he know? Who could have called him? Labadie? Alastair seemed sure he would have been too scared to desert Malvin. Was Malvin bluffing? I thought not, he was too assured, too confident that I was helpless. Hoping to stall him till Alastair came back to look for me I turned to face him. 'What do you want to talk about?'

'Things I am sure you want to know. Something you are looking for.'

'All I am looking for is a quiet time alone with my friend.'

He laughed unpleasantly and propelled me forward again. He quickened his steps, forcing me to keep up with him. Once or twice I caught my heels on the uneven pavement. The strength of his grip kept me from overbalancing. His fingers dug into the flesh of my upper arm. I winced with the pain.

His hotel was no more than a guest-house quite near the Beffroi. He had a latch key that opened the front door. The minuscule reception area was empty. Simple places like this didn't have night porters, nor a bar where guests might still be up. If I shouted for help what would he do? My throat was dry.

'This way, if you please.'

If you please! His politeness was ironic.

He took a room key from one of the hooks behind the desk and pushed me into the tiny lift. There was barely space for one person with baggage. When he closed the folding door I was pressed hard against him face to face. I couldn't move except to turn my head. I felt stifled. He'd been eating something garlicky and evidently didn't use deodorants. I tried to hold my breath as the lift slowly ascended. Think clearly. There would be guests sleeping nearby. When we got out of the lift I only had to start shouting and making a lot of noise. I could cry 'Au feu!' People would come running, wouldn't they?

'It would be wise not to make a disturbance,' he said, reading my thoughts. 'We don't want the police to get in the way, do we?'

He was right. We were both on the same quest. Police involvement was the last thing Alastair would want. Delays, interviews, my word against Malvin's, everything would come to a stop. Malvin knew that. He was clever, also unpredictable and dangerous. If I provoked him, I was sure he could turn violent. The thing was to stay calm, bluff my way through, play along with him.

The lift crawled its way upwards. Third floor. Fourth floor.

'I don't wish to hurt you, Madame. Just to talk. To exchange information, then you can go back to your lover.'

I flushed angrily. What could he want to talk to me about? He couldn't have planned this. It was a meeting by chance.

The lift shuddered to a halt. He pushed open the door and gripped my arm again before I could think of pressing the ground floor button. Resistance would have been useless anyway.

Room 43, fourth floor, third bedroom. He pushed me inside and locked the door behind us. It was a single room with a bed against one wall, a dressing table, a wardrobe and a small chest of drawers. Not Malvin's style but perhaps the only place he could get a room close to the Beffroi. There was only one chair. He gestured towards it.

'Please sit.'

Stay calm, don't provoke him. I sat. He stood by the window using a toothpick to extricate part of his dinner from a hidden molar with a hand over his mouth.

I decided on a direct attack. 'You've been following us ever since we left Marcignac.'

He paused in his dental exploration and asked in a casual tone: 'What were you looking for in Orange, Madame?'

'We went to see the Roman theatre, what else is there to go there for?'

'And Vaison?'

'The same, to visit the Roman town.'

His eyes narrowed. 'I am not stupid. You are wasting time. I know what you are looking for.'

I shrugged. 'As I've said, all we're looking for is a brief holiday. Peace and quiet, and to be left alone.'

'As lovers? You don't share a room.'

How did he know that?

'It is more discreet not to.'

'You are smart, Madame, but I don't believe you. You are here in search of something very remarkable.'

I managed a smile. 'So are you.'

'Indeed. And what for?'

'I don't need to tell you.'

'Please do.'

'Okay. The Antelami reredos, if it exists.'

'Just that?' He laughed.

'Of course. Look, we're just playing a game devised by the baron. A kind of treasure hunt. Everyone is given clues and you have to find something hidden at the end of the trail. That is the truth. Have you never been on a treasure hunt?'

He regarded me superciliously.

'And the treasure is this reredos?'

'Exactly.'

'Nothing else?'

'I've told you.'

He half turned his back to look out of the window, watching perhaps for Alastair's car. Casually he asked: 'What do you know of Guillaume de Malaucène?'

I frowned. 'Who is he?'

'Please don't pretend. Why else have you come all this way?'

'I told you.'

'You're playing a game, a treasure hunt you say. We can play too and when you find your treasure, we shall be there. You can be sure of that. So why don't we reach a friendly agreement? It would be so much more civilised to share what we find. More sensible, don't you think, than getting into a dangerous contest? Who knows how that could end?'

The threat was chilling. I thought hard. Though I was locked into this cheap bedroom with this horrible man, I didn't feel any great sense of danger. Malvin was far too smart to attempt anything beyond making these quiet threats, enjoying the power he had gained over me for the moment.

'Well then, what would you do with half a reredos?'

'You know that is not what I'm talking about.'

I flushed. 'I am not pretending. I have no idea what you're talking about. We have nothing to discuss, so please unlock the door and let me go.'

'Not until you have agreed that we share the treasure.'

'What treasure.'

'The Calix Sanctitatis.'

I managed to remain silent.

'It's no use pretending. Equal shares, yes? It will fetch a very big price.'

'No.'

I stared defiantly at him. He glared back, put the toothpick in an ashtray and moved away from the window.

'I don't think you understand my offer, Madame. To the present owners the Calix is just a nice piece of church silver. They cannot know its history otherwise it would have been sold long ago. We can buy it for very little and sell it for a fortune, maybe a million dollars. Maybe more. One half to you and your friend, one half to me. Otherwise...'

I laughed outright. 'You're mad.'

For a moment I thought he was going to strike me. Instead he took the key out of his pocket and jabbed it at me menacingly. 'Just tell Monsieur Hadley, equal shares or nothing. That's a promise. It's also a warning. Take it seriously.'

He unlocked the door and held it open.

Thoroughly shaken, I was on the point of saying something rash - to repeat Alastair's charge of criminal damage, theft and fraud - but checked myself in time. Instead I got to my feet, walked through the door without looking at him and made straight for the staircase.

Alastair was waiting for me in the foyer. When I came through the door, he could see at once I was controlling myself with difficulty.

'What happened? Are you all right? It's been half an hour.'

I told him everything. 'He knows about the Calix. He says it's worth a million dollars.'

'He can't know what it's worth.'

'Okay, but how does he know about Guillaume de Malaucène?'

'The same way as we do, from the provenance of the crucifix. Easy, considering how much else he's found out, but I doubt if he knows any more about the Calix than we do. That's why he wants to make a deal.'

'I was really scared. That man is capable of anything.'

He was soothing. He reasoned that Malvin wouldn't do anything that caught the attention of the police. Like us, he thought he was on the trail. He'd got as far as Vaison by the same kind of deduction as we had and needed only a few more clues or lucky breaks to locate the reredos.

'He's such a horrible man, Alastair. Can't we pin something on him and tell the police?'

'I'd rather keep the police out of it.'

He took my hand. I said: 'It was my fault. I was mad to go off on my own.'

'We'll stay together from now on, I promise.'

'Malvin believes we're lovers but he knows we're not sharing a room.'

'Do you want to? Tonight?'

'I'm all right.'

'You're sure?'

I nodded.

It had been a long day. When we reached my room he gave me a gentle kiss and said: 'I think you need a good night's sleep. Malaucène tomorrow.'

35 - EDOUARD

It was nine o'clock when Julia brought the notes she'd written in the early hours. 'Magdala,' she said, 'was a village in Galilee in the first century. As you know, Mary of Magdala is more usually known as Mary Magdalene. She was the first of Jesus's disciples to see the resurrected Jesus after his tomb was found to be empty. So I thought the suggestion that the Sisters of Magdala might be a religious order looked good, but the prime source, the Dictionary of Religious Orders, doesn't record it. If it were a proper order it would be listed there.'

'What about it being the name of a local geographical feature?' asked Louise.

'I wondered about the Dentelles du Montmirail, a chain of hills near Vaison. The guidebooks describe them as a ridge of jagged limestone pinnacles in an empty and picturesque landscape. Dentelle means lace, as you know. The ridge is eroded so that the peaks are delicately pierced like lace so I hoped to find that some of the peaks have been given feminine names. They haven't, but I have found something else, something intriguing, though you may not want to go down this route.'

'Intriguing?' I asked.

I think so. There's a reference to a so-called Tour Magdala built by a priest in the village of Rennes-le-Château in the Languedoc more than a hundred years ago. The story of strange happenings in the village has been the subject of best-selling books. You know the story. A nineteenth century priest named Béranger Saunière became hugely and inexplicably rich after discovering four ancient parchments in the church. They were in ciphers and codes and pointed to mysteries far beyond the ones we are trying to solve. Could the Tour Magdala at Rennes-le-Château somehow be connected with the so-called Sisters of Magdala and the Calix Sanctitatis? I've found nothing else.'

There was a long silence. I knew what each of us was thinking about. None of us voiced it. I thanked Julia and said I would call Alastair and pass on her report.

'Maybe he'll pick up something else from my cousin in Malaucène.'

36 - NELL

The moment we left the Beffroi I observed that the green Clio had taken up station about a hundred metres behind us. There was no attempt to keep out of sight. Malvin was driving, Labadie was sitting next to him. So he had not gone home after all! Carlo must have been left behind for some reason.

'Can you shake them off?' I asked Alastair.

'I doubt it. It's only ten kilometres to Malaucène and the road's too busy to take chances.'

'You could make a detour and find a faster road.'

'I don't think I'll bother. They seem to know where we're going anyway but they won't get into the château. I'll make sure of that.'

Edouard's cousin Henri lived a little way outside the town. The sturdy west front of the château was out of sight until we were some way up the long drive. The Clio pulled over on to the verge soon after we went through the gates.

'There must be another way out,' Alastair said. 'We could lose them when we leave.'

Henri de Sault-Benoit-Roaix must have observed our approach. He came down the grand stone staircase above the parterre with a pair of dalmatians at his side. They would have made an imposing cover photograph for a society magazine. Tall and lean and casually dressed in an English-style tweed jacket and light-coloured trousers, he appeared at least ten years younger than his cousin Edouard de Marcignac. He welcomed us warmly and led us through several rooms to a terrace on the other side of the house.

When coffee had been brought and pleasantries exchanged, our host said: 'I hear from Edouard that you're researching ancient heresies, the Albigensians and all that. I'm afraid I know very little, nothing you couldn't find in libraries.'

'What about the Manichaeans?' Alastair asked. 'I was hoping they might have left traces in this area.'

'That was even longer ago. My mother might know something. She'll be joining us soon.'

I wondered if Henri was married. Edouard hadn't said. The château was in fine order. Someone was looking after it well and everything spoke of money.

When the comtesse arrived and introductions had been made, her son excused himself to make a telephone call.

Eleanor de Sault-Benoit-Roaix was tall like her son with handsome features, beautifully coiffed silver hair and a cool aristocratic bearing that signalled "approach with caution!" She conversed in perfect English that was only slightly accented. She liked England, she said, and asked me where I came from. London? She didn't much care for London but she'd stayed in some famous country houses where she had many friends from her childhood. 'There is a mistaken view, you know, that the French and English do not like each other. That depends on who you are. People of our class are as comfortable with our friends in Norfolk as we are with those in Normandy.'

Lunch was served in a charming, oval-shaped room with blue toile de Jouy fabric on the walls. The service was by a young woman in a black dress and white apron. The meal was simple and delicious - a delicately flavoured tarte à l'oignon (which the comtesse declined), veal with wild mushrooms, cheeses and wild strawberries. Towards the end of lunch Alastair steered the conversation away from the wines of Gigondas and Vacqueyras to local customs and legends. He made the easy transition to sects and heresies of the past, such as Manichaeism. One of the clues Edouard had set us might be linked to Manichaeans during the Middle Ages.

Henri nodded: 'Edouard said he'd set you a bit of a competition, with a time limit.'

'And time is running out,' I said.

'There is a prize for the winners?' asked the comtesse.

'A piece of silver.'

'I'm sure it will be splendid. Edouard has some very fine pieces.'

'You can imagine how keen we are to win.'

'And this is what brings you half way across France?'

'We've picked up a strange story from the thirteenth century about a certain Guillaume de Malaucène.'

'A forebear of mine,' said Henri. 'Not a lot is known about him except as a warrior. It was a time of many wars.'

Alastair spun his story carefully. 'By some means Guillaume acquired a very fine crucifix. It belonged to a Benedictine abbey in Lombardy and was sent from there, along with other treasures, to the Abbey of Cluny in France at a time when the monks were threatened by a plague. Somehow the treasures were diverted on the way to Cluny and disappeared. We are trying to find out what happened to them.'

The comtesse wiped her lips on her napkin and placed it on the table. 'And what has the lost crucifix to do with old heresies?'

'The crucifix is not lost,' said Alastair. 'On Guillaume's death it was finally sent to Cluny and remained there until the Revolution. It passed through various hands over the years and is now in a private collection in America, but other Christian artefacts from the abbey were also diverted and have not been found. Our theory is that they were taken by Christian heretics separated from Rome who wanted them for their churches or meeting places. Manichaeans, for example.'

'Manichaeans weren't Christians,' said the comtesse rather sharply. 'They brought together other beliefs.'

Alastair was disconcerted to find himself unexpectedly challenged by someone who knew about Manachaeism. He wished he'd listened more carefully to Julia's briefing. Stalling, he said: 'That is true, but a crucifix is a potent symbol, even to non-Christians and if the Manichaeans were not involved, maybe the Albigensians were. The Cathar church included disaffected Roman priests and even bishops.'

The comtesse was dismissive. 'Catharism hardly touched this

region of France. I'm afraid your theory is a bit far-fetched, Monsieur.'

Alastair shrugged: 'We have to explore every possibility.' Hesitating for a moment, he added: 'I've been told of a lady in Carpentras who might help us. Claudia Andrieu. Would you know her by chance?'

The comtesse laughed. 'Claudia? Ask her about Sèvres and Limoges porcelain and she'll talk all day. Catharism? I don't think so!'

'I would also like to ask her about a legendary chalice known as the Cup of Sanctity. Does that mean anything to you?'

The comtesse pushed back her chair and got to her feet: 'Why don't we go into the garden?'

Henri offered me his arm and led me out of the French doors. Alastair escorted the comtesse. As we walked, she began talking about her family and the history of the château but suddenly, without a break, asked who had recommended that he should meet Claudia Andrieu.

'It was Edouard.'

'Because of her interest in French porcelain, perhaps?'

'Very likely, he didn't say.'

He spoke of Edouard and his art collection. 'He has the most exquisite things I've ever seen in private hands.'

'And a new English wife. She is an exquisite thing too, yes? I have not met her yet.'

Alastair laughed. 'She is charming.'

As we walked the comtesse pointed out the distant line of the Dentelles de Montmirail. 'It is a beautiful, unvisited area. Quite small, with rugged tracks. You can see it only on foot and need good boots. I wouldn't risk it alone today. A man was attacked by a sanglier only the other day.

From that distance the Dentelles were like pointed teeth. Alastair asked if any of the pinnacles had names. The comtesse said she was not aware of any, but the rock climbers who went there on summer evenings might know. Why did he ask? I judged her to be a complex, highly intelligent woman and that she was holding something back. Her brusque dismissal of Alastair's theory about heretical groups in the region, whether past or present, had raised a barrier. It would be rash to persist and lose her co-operation. Meanwhile, as I had said, time was passing too quickly. Tomorrow was Saturday, we had almost reached the limit set by Edouard.

We leant on a balustrade watching a spectacular fountain in the centre of a large pool. Henri began to explain the hydraulics which propelled the jet high into the air. The comtesse interrupted. 'Henri, women are not interested in such things.' She took my arm and led me away.

It was some while later that I found Alastair alone, still by the pool, leaning over the balustrade and looking intently at the water beneath as if, I suggested, searching the depths for an answer to the mysteries that baffled us.

'If there's anything here,' he replied with a wry smile, 'I think our hostess is keeping it from us.'

'So do I,' I replied, and gave him an account of my conversation with the haughty Eleanor de Sault-Benoit-Roaix. 'She quizzed me. She asked if I'm a Catholic. Apropos of nothing.'

'Strange, she asked me too. I said you were a Protestant.'

'I told her I'm nothing in particular. Church of England by upbringing. By her reaction it seemed important to her that I'm not a Catholic. I countered by asking about her own faith. She says she left the Catholic Church some years ago. When we got off the subject of religion she asked me some more very personal questions. I was interrogated, Alastair. There's no other word for it. She wanted to know about where I'd been in France, how well I know you, how well I know Edouard, what he and Julia are doing while we're away, what I meant by "time is running out" and so on. I don't know what Edouard told Henri about you and me but something seems to have got to his mother. It was a probing but gentle inquisition. She seems to be quite a warm person despite the aristocratic manner. I can't fathom why she's interested in me. As you said, I think she knows something about Guillaume, the crucifix and local heretics but won't talk about them.'

'She was testing us, or you at any rate.'

'When she asked what brought us here I said it was just the competition and the little we'd learned about Guillaume de Malaucène. I'm sure she didn't believe me.'

Alastair said: 'So what now? Henri professes to know nothing about Guillaume, and his mother knows something but is not telling.'

'There's Claudia Andrieu. I asked if Eleanor could give us an introduction. There was no harm in that, was there? She said she thought she might be away. In a matter of fact way I also asked if she knew of a church around here dedicated to St Mary Magdalene.'

'And does she?'

'The question disturbed her. She said nothing for a moment, then she just shrugged and suggested I ask the tourist office.'

'Well, let's do it. Henri has invited us to stay another night. It's Saturday tomorrow so unless we come up with something by the end of the day we shall have to go back empty-handed. We could spend the morning in Vaison and visit the tourist office and then go on to see Madame Andrieu in Carpentras.'

He got down from his perch, took my hand and led me towards an arbour with a seat.

'I've just had some interesting news from Julia. The photograph from Claudia has arrived. A picture of the chalice she says she found in the Vatican. Edouard says the cup is certainly Italian and of the right period, but he recognised it as one sold in Paris in 1987. He still has the catalogue. The buyer was a London dealer. Wherever it may be today, it's unlikely to be in the Vatican and is positively not the chalice presented by Pope Celestine to the newly founded abbey in Lombardy. So Claudia lied. Our meeting could be interesting.'

Having said goodbye until the evening, we drove out of the gates of the château. There was no sign of the Clio. This was worrying. If Malvin no longer needed to follow us he might have discovered something we didn't know about the Sisters of Magdala and was already on the trail.

None of the information offices in Vaison had heard of the Sisters. A young woman in the tourist office suggested we ask in a church. 'Perhaps it's a charity of some kind. A church may know.'

'You've never been asked before? In the last few days, perhaps?'

The young woman dismissed the suggestion. She would have remembered, but yes, she did know of at least one church dedicated to St Mary Magdalene. 'My parents were married there, near my grandmother's home. It's a long way from here, in the Lubéron hills. Very old and small. The parish no longer has a *curé.*'

She unfolded a map, pointed out the area and marked the best route by road. 'There may be others, of course. We only cover the town and notable sights around here,' she added with a smile as she handed over the map.

As we left the tourist office I asked: 'What do you think? It was just an idea.'

We went to a café where Alastair began picking apart the argument for going to the Lubéron. The journey would take several hours there and back. The connection between the Sisters of Magdala and a church dedicated to St Mary Magdalene was no more than a hunch. If there was a connection it would be more likely with a church, chapel or other so-named foundation in Lombardy where the inscription was written rather than in France where the reredos was ambushed.

'We don't know where the inscription was written,' I objected. 'It was long after the book was made, and in any case there's no proof that it was made in the abbey where Malvin found it. You were told it was never catalogued, so only the date of the inscription is known.'

We agreed to put the question to Julia. Was there a religious foundation dedicated to St Mary Magdalene in the Lombardy region? If so, would it be worth the journey?

There was no mobile signal so Alastair telephoned Claudia Andrieu from the café. There was no reply for at least a minute and he was on the verge of giving up when a woman's voice answered, asking who was calling. In English he introduced himself as a friend of Henri de Sault-Benoit-Roaix visiting Provence and wondered if he might call on her briefly that day before leaving the area. She asked why he wished to call. Alastair said he was also a friend of Edouard de Marcignac with whom she'd been in correspondence.

This registered. After a moment's silence, she said: 'Yes, I remember, the chalice. Frankly, it's not very convenient at the moment, but if you can be here this afternoon at four I will receive you.'

'Very formal and cold as ice,' Alastair said as he put down the telephone. 'Four o'clock this afternoon. We've time to spare. Let's go to one of the churches.'

But no one there had heard of the Sisters of Magdala. Helpful suggestions were made, the Archdeacon might know. He knew most things, but he was away until Sunday. Or one of the nuns perhaps, though there didn't seem to be any of them around at the moment. Could we come back at the time of the evening mass when there would be several clergy there? No, regretfully we were unlikely to be able to come back. Smiles, apologies, but a complete blank.

Would it be worth going back? Alastair thought not. He was getting testy. The pursuit, which had seemed full of promise and interest when he made the flying visit to the abbey, was losing momentum. It was too much to expect that a cryptic few lines found in an early medieval manuscript could point the way to the discovery of something that had been lost for eight hundred years, if indeed it ever existed. I reminded him that, by deduction, scholarship and dogged persistence, Julia and her father had uncovered an unimaginable treasure from centuries back. Alastair was being defeatist, but if he wanted to call off the hunt and go back to Marcignac for the rest of our holiday, that was all right by me. I must have had a note of contempt in my voice, and a different note when I added that though I had been seriously threatened by our opponent, I was game to carry on.

Alastair was chastened. 'Okay. We've three hours before we need to leave for Carpentras. There's a starred restaurant called Le

Moulin à l'Huile near the Roman bridge. Let's see if we can get a table.'

As we crossed the road, I touched Alastair's arm and said: 'Don't turn round. That creep Malvin and his sidekick are parked across the road. They've changed their car or hired another one. Take a quick look when you can. It's a black Peugeot. I caught a glimpse of Labadie as he was getting into it. Maybe he followed us into the building. There's no sign of the third man at the moment.'

'So they're still watching,' said Alastair. 'Looks like they're going to have to wait while we eat. Too bad!'

37 - JULIA

'More about the Calix,' said Edouard coming into the library where I was looking for a book. 'A fax signed by E.L.Respighi of the University of Bologna. He says he saw my letter in the journal and assures me the Calix is safe in the Vatican. Just as Claudia Andrieu claimed '

The text, in English, was short, hand-written and to the point.

Dear Monsieur de Marcignac,

I read your letter in the Society's Journal. The Calix Sanctitatis has a most interesting history. It is said to have been made by a silversmith in Ephesus and presented to Saint Paul, but I am sure you know that. It was taken to Rome at some time, There is a record of it there in 1197 when it was presented by Pope Celestine to the Abbazia di San Benedetto della Verna in Lombardy. Not long after its presentation the abbey was threatened by a plague and the monks prepared to disperse the finest of their treasures to other foundations as a precaution. Hearing of this, the Pope demanded the return of the chalice to Rome and sent a delegate from Santa Maria Magdalena to receive it. I found an account of this at the University here and was enabled by a friend in the Vatican to see the Calix there. I can tell you that it is a beautiful piece, 28cm high and with a base 15cm in diameter and in good condition despite its travels. I hope this is of interest.

Cordially yours, E.L.Respighi, Universita degli Studi di Bologna

I handed the fax back to Edouard. 'You know the writer?'

'Never heard of him.'

'Him? Looks like a feminine hand to me. And what about Santa Maria Magdalena. Some connection with the Sisters of Magdala? One thing for certain is that both your correspondents want to save you the trouble of looking for the Calix.'

'Is there a Santa Maria Magdalena in Bologna?'

'Easy to check. If not I'll have to scour the whole of Italy. Maybe that was intended. The writer also makes it clear the Calix is not for anyone to see.'

'The University of Bologna is the oldest in the Europe. It is also very large. Where would we begin and how long would it take?'

'Exactly.'

'Meaning?'

'We are being intentionally misled.'

'And the reredos?'

'If we accept what Respighi says, the reredos can no longer be the guardian of the Calix. They've been separated.'

'In that case the reredos was stolen for itself.'

I shook my head. 'Not necessarily. Whoever attacked the carriers may not have known the Calix had been sent elsewhere, if indeed it had. Because of its supposed connection with St Paul the chalice must have been prized beyond all else in the abbey. It would have been a kind of talisman, protecting the abbey and everyone in it. Perhaps they hid it inside a section of the reredos before it was assembled. That would explain why the reredos was the only piece of sculpture sent away. No one would have known what it concealed.'

'Clever,' said Edouard. 'But it seems someone did know. The secret must have been betrayed. The carriers were attacked near Vaison and the custos was killed. The thieves knew what they wanted. If they destroyed the reredos to get at the Calix that's why it hasn't been seen since. They left the marble fragments where they lay to be covered up by the forest growth, like so many other ruins.'

'I'm afraid you could be right. All the other valuables sent away from the abbey have been traced. We've considered the possibility that the Calix was stolen not for its value but for a secret religious purpose.'

'What kind of purpose?'

'Heretical rites? For use in the Black Mass? Satanists need a chalice for the blood of a sacrificial victim. A Christian chalice would be prized as a deliberate act of blasphemy. Often the victim would be a goat, a child of the Devil, or a human being. A female, inevitably. It's been said that in the 14th century the Knights Templar practised secret satanic rites here in France and there are reports of such things still going on today.'

'You really think the Calix might have been taken for such a purpose?'

'We have to consider everything.'

38 - NELL

Edouard's call to Alastair reporting the content of the fax came through just as we were being shown to a table at Le Moulin à l'Huile. There was no time to discuss it before we were approached by a young man I instantly recognised as one of the two who followed us into the theatre at Orange. Looking nervous, he introduced himself as Carlo Seta, a nephew of Monsieur Malvin.

'I need to talk to you about the Calix.'

A waiter approached and asked Alastair if he wanted another place set at the table.

Alastair turned to Carlo: 'You will join us for lunch, Monsieur Seta?'

The young man glanced over his shoulder. 'I have no time.'

'What a pity. Anyway, what is this Calix you want to talk about?'

'There is no need to pretend, Monsieur. I know as much as you do and what you know has put your lives in danger.'

Alastair managed a slight laugh. 'In danger, Monsieur?'

'Seriously. I overheard my uncle talking about you with Labadie. You know Labadie?'

'Bernard? Yes, I know Bernard. A sneaky fellow. I gave him some good advice. He ignored it.'

'My uncle knows where you are going. He will be with you all the way and when you have the Calix he will take it, by force. It would be dangerous to resist. Better to leave now and abandon your search.'

I opened my mouth. Alastair put a restraining hand on my arm. To Carlo he said: 'You can tell your uncle we will not be put off and if you continue to threaten us I shall call the police.'

'I am not threatening you, Monsieur. I am trying to protect you. I have helped my uncle with his researches but now he has gone too far. I had no idea what he was planning. I do not want to be a part of it. I am going back, far from here.'

'Really? No family loyalties? And how will you leave?'

'The way I came. In my car.'

'The Cleo is your car?'

'I rented it.'

Alastair stared coldly. The young man didn't flinch.

'I don't believe you, Carlo. You want the Calix as much as we do.'

'The Calix is not worth the great risk my uncle is prepared to take. He plans an accident, with no witnesses.'

'How dramatic!'

The young man pursed his lips, shrugged and waved a hand in a dismissive gesture. 'You can believe me or not as you choose.'

I asked: 'Why should we believe you?'

'Because of how much I know. I know why you are in Vaison. I know who you are visiting in Malaucène. I know how you learned the secret of the Calix.'

'How?' I challenged.

'From what was written in the Canticum Canticorum. I have seen the Canticum. I have also read the journal of François de Castres. I know what he has written about the ring of Saint Jacques. I know what Leonard Bray has written about the ring in his new book and I know that you have been looking for the Sisters of Magdala and are now on your way to meet them. Do you think my uncle will permit you to meet them?'

I said: 'You're bluffing.'

'You think so, Madame? That is of no matter to me. I have given you some friendly advice. You would be wise to take it.'

'Is Labadie involved in this?' asked Alastair.

'Labadie is a fool. He trusts my uncle.'

'Why are you telling us this?'

He lowered his voice. 'Because, Monsieur, I fear the

consequences.'

He glanced behind him again. There was no mistaking his nervousness. Without another word he turned and walked towards the entrance. Then he seemed to change his mind, spoke briefly to a waiter, handed him a note and then followed him through the swing doors into the kitchen area.

How did he know so much? Above all, why was he telling us? I distrusted him. I suggested he was just acting as the good guy. 'Corsican families are very close. And vengeful. It would be a huge risk to betray Malvin. Carlo has been sent to frighten us.'

'Maybe,' said Alastair as we walked back to the car. 'To keep us away from the Sisters of Magdala, whoever or wherever they may be. They don't know any more than we do.'

'You think so?'

'Obviously. If they did they'd be there already.'

As soon as we were on the road to Carpentras the black Peugeot moved up like a faithful retriever at heel.

'You're right,' I said. 'They're following us. Just Malvin and Labadie. Can you shake them off?'

'Not at the moment. Too much traffic.'

I looked at the map. 'There's a small turning coming up on the left. In a couple of kilometres. It rejoins the main road further on. You could take that.'

'I'll try, but it'll be difficult against this traffic.'

He slowed as we approached the junction. There was a gap in the oncoming line of cars.

'No, you can't do it,' I warned him. 'They're coming much too fast.'

Ignoring me, Alastair suddenly said: 'Hold on!', switched on his headlights full beam, flicked the box into second gear and swung straight across the opposing traffic against a pandemonium of blaring horns, squealing brakes and angry shouts. Our tyres screamed as he made the right-angled turn and accelerated fiercely away from the outrage behind him.

'Madness!' I said when I got my breath back. 'We could have been killed.'

'Sorry,' was all he said.

In the mirror I could see the Peugeot still at the left-hand junction with a steady stream of vehicles preventing the same manoeuvre. It would be minutes before they could follow.

The narrow road we had taken was empty but he negotiated it like a rally driver. I was speechless. My fists were clenched. 'Sorry,' he said again. 'We had to get away.'

We rejoined the main road ten kilometres further on. There was no sign of the Peugeot.

'Lost them,' he said. 'They won't have any idea where we're going.'

'Do you?' I asked, through gritted teeth.

'A turning on the left, opposite the aqueduct.'

It was a modern villa behind a low wall. The front door was opened almost at once by a strikingly beautiful, dark-skinned young woman.

'Monsieur 'adley?' she asked.

'And Mademoiselle Sheridan.'

Could this be the mysterious Claudia? Evidently not, for without another word the young woman showed us into a room at the back of the house and asked us to wait. The room was mostly lined with bookshelves. There was a display cabinet full of striking Limoges pieces. The view from the window was of a small garden and terrace made brilliant with cannas and the marigolds beloved of the French.

I looked at book titles. Esoteric, serious, international. It was a library which supported Edouard's suggestion that Claudia was an academic. We waited for about ten minutes before a small, middle-aged woman came into the room. She wore a sleeveless dark brown dress with a flowing skirt just above her bare ankles and sandals. Her dark hair was cut into a deep fringe just above black eyebrows. Her eyes accentuated by make-up, high cheekbones, full lips, elaborate ear-rings and a jade necklace gave her something of an oriental look.

She wasted no time on preliminaries. 'I have spoken with your friends at Malaucène. You are mistaken, Monsieur. You will find nothing here.'

Alastair was equally direct. 'Madame Andrieu, the photograph you sent Edouard de Marcignac was not of the chalice you say was made for presentation by the Pope to the Abbazia di San Benedetto. It was a well-known piece sold at auction some years ago.'

She hesitated for only a moment. 'Really? I apologise. My assistant must have sent the wrong picture.'

'You have the right picture?'

'Not here.'

Unwilling to argue, Alastair switched to another challenge. 'You are an expert in Christian antiquities, Madame?'

'Not an expert, merely an amateur. An enthusiast for church silver.'

'Do you happen to know an Italian enthusiast called Respighi?'

She shrugged. 'Respighi? I know of a composer by that name. No one else.'

'Forgive these questions, Madame, but we have come a long way to discover what we can about the extraordinary legend of the chalice. I was, to say the least, amazed by what you reported from your visit to Rome. Were you totally satisfied by what you were told?'

She flushed at the implied accusation. Her voice was strained. 'I will not be interrogated. All I will say is that you are wasting your time. Go back to Gascony and forget about this silly game you are playing.'

Alastair flinched. 'One other question, Madame. What do you know of the Sisters of Magdala?'

She turned away for a moment as if distracted by something. When she spoke it was with a less admonitory voice. 'Monsieur, I can't help you. Please, I beg you to go away from here as soon as possible. You are on dangerous ground.'

'Dangerous?'

'I won't say any more. Just go. Please.'

She left the room as silently as she had entered. The young woman, who must have been waiting outside the door, showed us out.

'Why is she so scared?' I asked as we walked back to the car. 'And what did she mean by "dangerous ground"?'

'All I know,' said Alastair, 'is that she's desperate to prevent us from finding out.'

* * *

Dinner with Henri de Sault-Benoit-Roaix and his mother was subdued. The mood of the comtesse had changed since yesterday. Henri did most of the talking. Alastair kept the conversation away from the purpose of our visit. I was stifled by the formality. At the end of the meal, the comtesse rose from the table and escorted me to the drawing room, leaving Henri and Alastair to their cigars.

When we were shown our bedrooms I asked Alastair if he thought Claudia had telephoned the comtesse after our visit.

'It occurred to me.'

'What do you think of this? Henri's mother wants me to go with her to chapel very early tomorrow morning before breakfast. She pressed me hard. I've said I will.'

Alastair looked at me closely, waiting for an explanation. I blinked. 'I don't think we're going to an ordinary chapel. We had a peculiar kind of conversation. I felt I was having to pass some kind of examination. She asked what you and I are to each other, what is your profession and why you are so interested in heresies. I told her it was just part of an intriguing puzzle we'd been set by Edouard to amuse ourselves during our stay. She said it was not a subject for amusement. Then she asked if I'd been confirmed. I said I stopped going to church after my mother died. I can't think why I submitted to all this questioning except I had the feeling there was going to be some kind of pay-off I ought not reject. At the end she asked me - no, told me - I really must go with her. She goes every morning. She said it would be something I would never forget.'

'Where is this chapel?'

'Somewhere near. We can walk there. I've been instructed to wear a skirt, not trousers, long sleeves and to cover my head.'

'You'll go?'

'Why not if it pleases her? But she is very intense. She seems able to look right into me. That's unnerving. I'm on probation somehow. If I put a foot wrong before we get there, that'll be the end of whatever she's offering.'

'And what do you think that is?'

'I don't dare to guess. All I know is that it's a great privilege and I've passed the entrance exam. Heaven knows how because I don't know the rules!'

An early call had been arranged for me at five o'clock. It was still dark when I met the comtesse at the bottom of the staircase. She wore a long black cloak with the hood folded back over her shoulders and she held a black scarf.

'I shall have to blindfold you. This is an essential precaution when we admit strangers to the rites of our order. Had we not always taken such care, we could not have survived.'

I asked: 'Order? What then is your order, Madame?'

'You will be sworn to secrecy. We are the Sisters of Magdala. Our convent has kept the faith for more than seven hundred years. It is an order restricted to twelve members and six postulants bound by vows of loyalty and secrecy. We are outside the Catholic Church. They would regard us as heretics if they knew of us. I must warn you that before your blindfold is removed in the chapel, you will be required to take a sacred oath never to divulge our secrets. Are you prepared to accept the penalties you would incur by breaking such an oath? They are severe.'

Dangerous ground! I swallowed and said: 'Yes, I am.'

What penalties? It was all very theatrical but I was committed and couldn't back down now. The scarf was wrapped round my head over my eyes and tied securely behind. The comtesse grasped my hand firmly and led me from the warmth of the hall through a door into the cool early morning air. It was, as I had been told, a short journey. Very short. I counted six or seven hundred paces so I judged we were still within the precincts of the château. Then we crossed somewhere, a courtyard perhaps, in the open air before again being under a roof. I was led along passages, feeling the walls, and slowly down three separate flights of steps, being told the number of steps as I carefully put one foot in front of the other. The walls closed in so we could no longer walk side by side. The comtesse went a pace ahead, holding my hand all the time and telling me when we were about to turn this way or that. We passed through two creaking doors. If I tried to follow this route without a blindfold I would soon be lost. There was a pause, soft voices and another door was unbolted from the inside.

We had entered a resonant space. The chapel? I smelled wax polish and the heavy scent of candles. The comtesse let go of my hand. I stood still, taking slow, deep breaths. Someone approached and stopped nearby. A woman spoke to me in French.

'We welcome you as a friend. There is nothing to fear. First you must take the oath sworn by all strangers. It is simple but severe. You must swear to be bound by it. Please repeat after me: I swear that the holy rites I shall see and hear will be kept secret by me, forever.'

'The holy rites I shall see and hear will be kept secret by me forever.'

'On pain of God's wrath if I break my oath.'

I hesitated. The woman's voice insisted. 'Say it, please.'

'On pain of God's wrath if I break my oath.'

'I swear this in the name of Christ.'

'I swear this in the name of Christ.'

'May I be judged if I disobey.'

I hesitated again.

'Say it, please.'

'May I be judged if I disobey.'

'Come with me, sister.'

My hand was taken again and I was led forward several paces and turned to my left. The blindfold was untied and removed.

The scene was breathtaking. The chapel was about thirty metres square and lit by hundreds of candles. The vaulted roof was covered with mosaic tiles forming pictures in gold and red and blue. Looking down from the centre vault was the image of the Pantocrator, the creator of the universe and ruler of all things, as I had seen in Orthodox churches. The floor was marble. Nine chairs were drawn up on either side of an empty central space.

At the far end was a plain table. On it stood twelve white candles, a glass pichet of red wine and a basket containing a small, flat loaf of bread. Beyond this and extending several feet on either side was a simple screen of pure white marble carved in relief with a pietà of such extraordinary beauty that I caught my breath and almost cried out.

I blinked hard as everything else swam out of focus for the moment. The very simplicity of the pietà belied its artistry. It was unusually poignant - the dead Christ wrapped in his mother's arms, his face in peace, hers in pain, and slightly in the background another grieving woman who must surely be Mary of Magdala. The three figures were conjoined in a group that ached with sorrow.

The reredos was a masterpiece, a tragedy translated into stone. I gazed at it in awe. I didn't doubt this was the lost work of the master, Benedetto Antelami, brought to this place in or around the year 1218 when the custos was killed. It had been hidden here ever since. Were the Sisters of Magdala founded for the express purpose of venerating it? And what were the rites which I had sworn to keep secret forever?

I wondered if the chapel itself was of the same age as the reredos. It could be, with its Romanesque arches and carvings in limestone that still bore the marks of the masons' tools, and who had brought all this together, the precious reredos, the secret chapel and the women who tended it? The shock and elation of discovery and the heart-stopping beauty of the reredos were so overwhelming I had difficulty in holding back tears. The moment of joy was quickly deflated by the sudden realisation that this privilege was to be mine alone. My friends would never see the reredos.

Still with my eyes fixed on the pietà, I was guided slowly towards a chair that was placed next to that of the comtesse. The other chairs were occupied. All the members and postulants of the order were present, each robed in a cloak like the comtesse's and with their heads covered. They sat so still as to appear like effigies. The service began as all stood.

One woman led the worship from beside the altar. The Kyrie was sung in unison to a simple chant that reminded me of psalms I had once heard in Greece at Easter, though the women's voices gave a silkier texture to the phrases. Remembering what I'd told the comtesse about my lapsed church-going, I realised this was only a part-truth. Many times had I sat in the stalls of college chapels and cathedrals and listened to settings of the Anglican evening service. Listened, but not taken part. On travels abroad I invariably visited the most interesting churches, sometimes when a service was taking place. Memorably there had been Easter Day in Firenze, Christmas in Vienna, the great throng in Rome at Whitsun, the organ echoing round St Sulpice and St Eustache in Paris. Listening and watching. I was a voyeur and reviewer, not a worshipper except by proxy.

My mind was not taking in the service. Vaguely I recognised some of the Latin words of the Gloria and Credo. "Credo". I believe. What did I believe? Could I be like these women, dedicated to the maintenance of a mystery? What kind of women were they? The comtesse was one of them, an ordinary woman and mother, not a celibate. Other faces were indistinct beneath the cowls of their robes. Who were they? It occurred to me that one might be Claudia. Did the convent have dormitories and cells or did these worshippers come here each day before going about their daily business? Most people outside would still be abed. It was barely six o'clock. When the Mass was over, would the Sisters leave in secret, as they had come, and return to husbands and lovers?

The service proceeded to the Sanctus and Benedictus. Preparations were being made for the Eucharist. It was then I remembered the comtesse's response to Alastair's question about the cup of sanctity, abruptly stopping the conversation and leading us into the garden. Away from dangerous waters!

A tinkling bell was rung. The women got up from their knees and moved slowly in pairs towards the table. The comtesse whispered: 'You may come with me or not, as you wish.' I got up from my chair. How could I stay back now?

Two rows formed up in arcs before the table, the members in front, the postulants behind. The comtesse drew me to the rear.

Sentences and responses were chanted and all bowed their heads as the leader lifted the loaf of bread high in both hands and held it there as an offertory, speaking in Latin. No one moved. I felt a thrill of anticipation, of something extraordinary about to happen such as I had once experienced in a remote Greek church on Easter Eve when the great crowd standing silently in the town square waited for the stroke of midnight and the cry "Christos eneste!".

The loaf of bread was broken in two and passed to the women on each end of the row who broke it in half again and passed it to their neighbours. The piece placed in my hand was still warm. I copied the movements of the comtesse and placed it carefully in my mouth and swallowed it. Was this a terrible risk I was taking? What did I believe?

When all had eaten the bell was rung again. The first row knelt and bowed their heads, the others followed. The marble floor was hard on the knees. I was glad to be wearing a long skirt with soft folds. The leader stepped forward to the left of the table and reached beyond it to a corner of the reredos. Whatever it was that she touched, something moved with a slight grating sound. When she withdrew her hand she was holding a silver cup that glistened in the candlelight.

'I had to steady myself. So this was the great mystery of the reredos - a finely wrought chalice which must surely be the so-called Cup of Sanctity and at least the same age as Antelami's work!

The cup was brought to the table where it was filled with wine. It was then passed to the first woman in the front row who drank from it and passed it on. When it reached the end of the line it was passed to the postulants and then at last to the comtesse who drank and offered it to me saying: 'You must empty the cup.' As I drank my eyes lifted to the image of the dead Christ in his mother's arms. It was the first communion I had made since I was sixteen.

The empty cup was taken from me and passed back to the leader. All were kneeling with bowed heads. With the cup in both hands, the leader first polished the cup with a piece of cloth then moved very slowly back to the side of the reredos. A lock of my hair had fallen forward under my scarf and my eyes were watery, making it difficult to see. It was no matter. Whatever was done to activate the mechanism that opened and closed the hiding place, the secret was safe; the Cup of Sanctity would remain as secure as if I had never known of its existence.

A sentence was spoken in Latin and the grating sound was repeated, but that was not the end of the rite. All stood again and in single file approached the pietà where each of the worshippers knelt, leant forward and gently kissed the hand of the dead Christ. It was more than a token touching of the lips. It was a reverential act of love. When it was my turn I was conscious of being watched by eighteen pairs of eyes. The marble was smooth and warm. I dropped tears on it.

I forgot where I was until someone (the comtesse or one of the other women?) helped me to my feet and led me back to my chair. The rite was now complete. All turned in one movement towards the door. My eyes were bandaged again and a hand placed in mine. I heard the soft footsteps of the women leaving the chapel and only when all had gone was I led back along the route we had come.

When at last my blindfold was removed I found myself in the entrance hall of the château. A clock was striking the hour.

I had only a few seconds alone with Alastair before we were joined by Henri. All I had time to say, quite flatly, was that there was no longer any reason to prolong our stay at Malaucène. After breakfast I said: 'Let's get away as early as we can.'

'Away to where?'

'Back to Marcignac. Everything's all right. Tell you later.'

The comtesse didn't appear at breakfast but sent a message through her son thanking us for our visit and wishing us safe journey. Henri saw us off on the steps of the front entrance only an hour later. He asked us to convey his kind regards to his cousin and suggested that the games he devised for his guests were a little too devious.

There was no sign of the black Peugeot when Alastair turned out of the drive. I remarked on the absence of our followers. Alastair said: 'Henri fixed it.'

'What do you mean?'

'I told him the Peugeot had been tailing us and that the driver was someone the police might like to talk to. I think our friends will be delayed for quite a long time.'

I said nothing but set my seat to a reclining angle and lay back. We were well past Montpellier before I awoke and began to tell my story.

I had given much thought to what might be prohibited by my oath. Not the ritual of the Eucharist, that was traditional, not secret, but I must not, indeed could not reveal the whereabouts of the chapel. Nor the hiding place of the Calix. The Cup, I now knew, must have been venerated by the Sisters of Magdala or their predecessors for at least eight hundred years. Nor could I say anything about the twelve members and six postulants of the religious order, nor the solemn moment when the women silently approached the pietà and kissed the lifeless hand of the Christ. All this had been shown to me out of necessity, solely to convince me and my importunate friends to abandon our troublesome inquiries into the lost reredos of Benedetto Antelami and all that pertained to it.

39 - JULIA

They were burying the dead man where he had fallen. It was shocking, but I understood they had no choice. He was a big man and they had nothing with which to carry him. Besides, where could they take him? Two of them dug the grave and four lifted him into it, covering his body with a cloak. He almost slipped from their grasp as they lowered him into the dark earth fully clothed. His hat with the scallop-shell was placed in the grave. His scrip and staff they gave to one of their number, a man in the habit of a Cistercian monk. A small man whose face was wet with tears.

The weary-looking band of pilgrims stood round the grave. Led by a burly, heavily bearded man, they sang a psalm and intoned the Paternoster. Another of their number, also a Cistercian, sprinkled the grave with holy water and sent the soul of the dead man on its way with the solemn words of the Proficiscere. The small man stood on the edge of the grave weeping inconsolably as the earth was shovelled back into the grave. A wooden cross was placed at the head of the mound. The pilgrims stood there in silence for several minutes and then, with the rising sun at their backs, set out through the trees on the next part of their long journey. François stayed where he was.

I awoke feeling anxious and troubled. Slowly the real world came back into focus. I put a hand to my throat and felt the slender gold chain round my neck. The ring was safe.

The clock by the bedside told me it was not yet six. I got out of bed and drew back the curtains. The storm had gone.

There were things left unfinished. my father had written in his notebook of an "unquiet spirit". He was thinking of looking for a priest to conduct an exorcism. So unlike him. Normally he would have nothing to do with the Church.

Louise pointed out that he had been to the requiem for the murdered pilgrim.

I said: 'As a duty. He recorded it in his notebook.' I turned to the page I'd marked with a slip of paper. "Long and tedious service. Sententious waffle. Afterwards met an importunate fellow who wants to write a story for a London newspaper. Told him there is no story. Flea in his ear. Met Marcignac who suggested I should write something about the pilgrim. Afraid I was a bit curt. Got back home at five. Went to the barn. Called out to François. No answer. Locked him in."'

'Locked him in!' Louise exclaimed. 'What on earth does that mean?'

Edouard joined us. I asked if he knew anything about exorcisms.

'You're thinking of the barn?'

'François is still there, isn't he?'

'How do you mean?' Louise asked.

'Didn't you feel something the night we found the ring?'

'Imagination. We were all very tense.'

'François is a lost soul. We need to put him at rest.'

'An exorcism could do that?'

Edouard said: 'There's a Catholic rite. The priest who conducts it must be an official exorcist. A man chosen for his faith and humility. I was a witness on one occasion.'

'What happened?' I asked.

Edouard pursed his lips. 'Some years ago we had a young servant girl who was, I can only say, taken hold of by a foul-mouthed evil spirit. She was inhabited. There's no other word for it. The things she said and did. We had to help her. The priest was an imposing figure. He made solemn preparations. After the Litany and a psalm he wound his stole round the girl's neck. She was terrified. Then with his hand on her head he began the first part of the rite. There are three parts, all much the same. I remember that he called upon the vile spirit to get out and flee from this creature of God. He cried out that Jesus Christ who commanded the sea, the winds and the tempests commanded Satan to hear and fear. He chastised the evil spirit with terrible words and bade him flee whither he had come.'

Edouard went to a shelf, took down a slim volume and glanced at the title page. 'If you're interested, Julia, the whole rite is in this book. It was written ago by a Franciscan friar named Candidus Brognolus. The Alexicacon was published in Venice in 1668.'

He handed it to me. 'You're welcome to borrow it.'

'Thank you.' I hesitated. 'Tell me what happened to the girl.'

'There was a desperate struggle. I can still hear her unearthly screams, as if from another voice, not her own. Then she collapsed. The priest had great difficulty reviving her. When we tried to help he made us stand back. Exorcism is a dangerous business, Julia.'

Changing the subject coolly, he remarked that perhaps they would like to know he was thinking of making an offer to the abbey in Liguria for the Canticum.

'I can't think they will want to keep it, especially when I tell the abbot I will pay the price Malvin suggested. The money will be put to good use.'

He opened a drawer and took out a beautiful, leather-bound Bible. 'In English the Canticum Canticorum is known as "The Song of Solomon". At school we were told it was of no importance and because it seemed to be forbidden territory we read it avidly.'

He turned the pages and handed the Bible to me. 'This is in French. Your words will be better than mine. Please translate this passage for us.'

Hesitating for only a moment I began, with pauses as I chose the best words:

"How beautiful are your feet in their sandals! Your curving thighs are like jewels. Your navel is a round goblet that never lacks spiced wine. Your stomach is like a heap of wheat hemmed by lilies. Your breasts are like a pair of young fawns. You stand like a palm tree and your breasts are bunches of grapes. I shall go up into the palm tree and take hold of its branches and discover your breasts and your breath like the scent of apples and your mouth like the finest wine."

'Yes.'

Edouard took the book from me, turned back a page or two and asked me to continue.

'Really this is for a man to read, but I'll do my best. It goes on: "You have ravished my heart, my sister, with one of your eyes, with a single jewel from your necklace. How beautiful are your breasts, my sister, my bride! Your love is more fragrant than wine and your perfumes sweeter than any spice. Your lips drop the sweetness of a honeycomb. Honey and milk are upon your tongue and your dress has the scent of Lebanon. My sister, my bride is a garden that is locked, a spring that does not flow, a sealed fountain." And the girl replies: "Let the north wind and south wind blow upon my garden that its perfumes may flow out. Let my beloved come into his garden and taste its precious fruits!" And her lover says: "I have entered my garden, my sister, my bride, and have gathered my myrrh and spice. I have eaten from my honeycomb. I have drunk my wine with my milk." And then he says: "Beneath the apple tree I roused you where your mother bore you."'

There was a long silence before Edouard thanked me.

'It's a love poem of great sensuality. I shall take expert advice, but to my eye the Canticum is a manuscript of enormous importance. The treatment of the subject is astonishing, but we know medieval monks were not all saints. Some could be very worldly, as indeed were many priests, bishops and not a few popes in the Middle Ages. Maybe the illustrations shocked some of the brothers. But they have shown themselves to be very human. Who knows to what purpose or with what outcome? The book was probably hidden to prevent it being destroyed as sacrilegious.'

40 - NELL

No one spoke as I told of my stumbling, hand-held walk to the chapel; the soft voices welcoming me, the heart-stopping candlelit scene when my blindfold was removed, the terrible oath I had to swear to guard the secrets of the Sisters of Magdala. But there could be no prohibition on saying I had seen the reredos and the chalice that must be the Calix Sanctitatis. Why else had I been shown them except to bring an end to our troublesome search so we would go away and forget everything? As to the reredos, I had no doubt it was the work of a great artist. Its poignancy had moved me beyond words. 'And when the chalice materialised as if from nowhere I almost cried out. When I held it in my hands my eyes filled with tears so I could hardly see. All I can say is the cup is silver and simply fashioned. I am so sad that none of you will ever see it. I was allowed to go to the chapel only because I'm a woman. And because they dared to trust me. Somehow the Sisters have guarded their secret for centuries.'

Edouard thanked me solemnly. Everything, he said, tallied with the inscription in the Canticum, that Antelami's reredos was the guardian of the Calix Sanctitatis and, as had been written, that it was cared for by the Sisters of Magdala.

Julia remarked: 'It must have already been concealed in the reredos when it left the abbey, but who intervened to divert the cart to Malaucène? If the Sisters know what happened they will keep silent.'

'They had to stop us interfering,' I said. 'Claudia tried hard. Why? I am as sure as can be that, though the chapel was dark and the women never uncovered their heads, she was one of the postulants.'

Louise reminded us that Malvin knew about the existence of the Sisters of Magdala and the Calix.

'Malvin will never even get into the château, let alone the chapel,' said Alastair. 'Nell is right. She was admitted because we seemed to know too much. The comtesse took a risk that she would keep her oath of silence and somehow transfer it to us. And we shall keep the secret, shan't we? Who's heard of The Cup of Sanctity? It disappeared centuries ago. Its history is very obscure. So when we named it, the alarm bells rang. We told Henri we were on some kind of a treasure hunt. I'm sure his mother didn't believe us till we mentioned the Sisters of Magdala.'

Edouard nodded. 'Henri telephoned me soon after you arrived. He was astonished that I could send you half-way across France to play games. I assured him it was true.'

'Nevertheless just by being in the château we were a serious threat and in ignorance we would go rooting around, talking to others. The comtesse had to do something. So she decided to risk letting Nell into their mysteries so she could see that the cup is an object of great reverence and that it's kept where other hands will never find it.'

'The reredos too,' said Louise.

'I'm not sure the comtesse knows the story of Antelami's reredos. It's been there for centuries, an integral part of the chapel, the chalice with it. The abbey recorded that it belonged to the Sisters of Magdala who must therefore predate the cup's presentation by the Pope. An order founded, do you suppose, to protect the cup?'

It was plausible. A nice idea, as Edouard put it. There was another mystery. The letter from someone called Respighi. Julia suggested the name was yet another fiction by Claudia to deflect our search. 'She must have been getting a bit desperate. The more she tried to put us off, the more we seemed determined to go on.'

When we speculated on the fate of Malvin and the little bookbinder Edouard said: 'They're no longer our concern. The game is over. They've lost. You have won.'

The prize for each of us was our own choice of a silver spoon from Edouard's collection. He assured us they were all of fine quality and watched smilingly as, knowing little about English spoons, we chose with some hesitation. Julia chose one that was not hall-marked. 'Well done,' said Edouard. 'English, fourteenth century and very rare. Only two others are known.'

But all was not concluded. Julia was still talking about an exorcism and she was being pressed by Jane to sign the contract of sale and let work begin on the house. Could they meet on the site? It was a reasonable request. The terms of the sale had been agreed. Now that the festival was over, it was hard to find excuses for delay.

Julia asked Alastair if he would support her at the meeting. Louise suggested we should all go and invite her young American friend who knew quite a bit about medieval buildings and had a theory about the barn having an undercroft. She told us of Jake's early morning visit "looking for François" and his remark "I guess he's some place around here." Julia's father must have thought so.'

'I'll go with that,' I concurred.

'What do you mean?'

'I've felt it.'

'My father said "this place is haunted". Remember?' said Julia. 'And in the appendix to his manuscript he suggests that François is not at rest. Why would he have written that unless he had some kind of experience to support it?'

Louise said Edouard had agreed to ask Jake to join them for a picnic lunch.

41 - JULIA

Jane and her builder, a curly-haired Gascon with mahogany forearms and the muscles of a weight-lifter, arrived exactly on the hour. I ascribed this to Jane, a known stickler for punctuality, and wondered how long it would be before she had to surrender her fastidiousness to the more easy-going ways of the Gers. Still, that was her problem.

We walked all round the house before I produced the keys and let them in. Alastair kept a watchful eye on the inspection. The builder, who spoke good English, knew his job and had ready answers for all Jane's questions. There would be no problems. She could have a new oak staircase, a kitchen to her own design, two good bathrooms en suite, central heating. He would prepare an estimate.

Jake arrived in his bright red hire car. Louise and Nell followed. Jane went across and was introduced to Jake. She said she remembered him from the concert at Auch. 'That's smart of you,' he said. 'Well, you were taller than anyone else,' she said. The builder asked Jane if she had made up her mind about the work she wanted done. 'I don't have time. We'll have to come back,' she said. I could see Louise breathe a sigh of relief.

Nell came over. 'Where shall we have our picnic?'

'There's a shady bank right there by the barn,' Jake said and smiled at Louise who turned her back on him. Nell brought the picnic things. Alastair and I were introduced to Jake.

'So you've been here before,' said Alastair, offering a glass of wine. 'Louise says you have a feeling about this place. Is that a hunch, or more?'

'Much more. Come, I'll show you.'

He led Alastair and me to the far side of the barn where the land began to fall away towards the distant view. The unkempt ground was strewn with pieces of weathered stone that might have been left over from the original construction work. Jake pointed to the lower courses of the stonework.

'That's the oldest part of the barn,' he said. 'Medieval, eleventh or twelfth century. Everything above, the whole of the oak frame and roof, is much later. Fourteenth or fifteenth century, I guess. Look at this.'

He squatted close to the wall and described an arc with one hand about four feet above the ground. 'Sawn ashlar among the rubble. There was an opening here. A small door. It's been filled in and the level of the earth has built up over the years.'

Alastair squatted beside him and ran his hands over the stones as though trying to unlock their secrets. 'So you're saying the barn has been enlarged?'

'No.'

'No?'

'It was quite a different kind of building, a much smaller one.'

'Really? What kind of building do you suppose?'

'I don't need to suppose, I know.'

He grinned as he straightened up and looked Alastair in the face, waiting for the next question. His coolness was arrogant.

'Okay, how do you know?'

'I'll show you.'

He led the way back to the pile of ancient stones, turned over one or two and pointed to a piece of masonry that was broken in half. One of its faces was carved. The breakage had cut across what was quite unmistakably the weathered and lichen-covered image of a small scallop-shell.

'Your pilgrims' hostel,' he said with a casual wave.

We threw questions and suppositions at one another as we picnicked. I said I'd always thought it strange that the supposed hostel had never been recorded. Had it fallen down or been demolished? If so, why? Was this where François was taken ill?

Had he even died here? Cussac had threatened young Edouard with the ghost in the cellar but the house had no cellar. Pontet had said it was the barn that was haunted. Could there be a cellar beneath the barn?

Jake said the blocked up doorway showed that the original floor was lower but must have been raised on a platform of earth and rubble to take the huge weight of the superstructure. Helping himself to a slice of *jambon cru* to fill a baguette, he said: 'There's no evidence of anything below the floor from the inside.'

'You've been inside?' Edouard asked with a frown.

'Yeah. I helped myself to the key. Sorry. It's back where I found it.'

He bit fiercely into the sandwich. Apart from Louise, we all stared at him. I said 'Okay, Mister Marvel, what did you find?'

'Some of the floor is paved with flags, the rest with broad oak planks - the original boards, for sure. Hard as iron. The floor seems to be solid.'

'What if we unblocked the doorway?' asked Alastair.

'The whole wall could fall down.'

We were deferring to his expertise. I tested him. 'What would the hostel have been like?'

'A hostel some way from a church would have been very simple. Just one storey probably, with a vaulted roof and small windows. Simply a place to rest for the night in safety. Very basic. The bigger hostels along the route were attached to churches and had separate lodgings for men and women with places to bathe and feed and apothecaries to treat their ills.'

Alastair suggested we took another look inside.

'You won't find anything.'

'I've already found a couple of very interesting things.'

'I know,' said Jake dismissively. 'The bones of a severed hand and an ancient billhook.'

No one spoke for a moment. Jake finished his sandwich. 'There's one thing you could do,' he remarked casually. 'It would cost a bit. Archaeologists use radar to search for underground workings. GPR they call it. Ground penetrating radar. If there's anything under the barn, GPR will find it.'

Back in the chateau Edouard was examining the ring through an eye-glass. 'It seems hardly worn. It has the Christian symbol, most delicately done. I have never seen this on a ring of the period you claim for it. It is certainly a very early piece, perhaps as old as you want it to be, Julia, but there can be no proof that is from the first century AD.'

Almost reluctantly he handed it back to me. I fastened it to the chain and slipped it under my shirt. 'I don't need any proof. François suffered deeply on its account. He believed what he had been told, and I think he felt its power.'

Edouard smiled. 'The whole story is quite incredible. The cathedral authorities may find it so. If they should reject the ring, then I would be willing....'

I cut him short. 'They won't reject it.'

We returned to Jake's assertion that there was an earlier building under the barn. Edouard was less impressed by Jake's theories and knowledge of technology than by my determination not to give up until the matter was proved. He said he was willing to finance an investigation by ground penetrating radar.

'It seems you've been right about everything so far, young lady, so I will back you on this.'

'Not about everything,' I demurred. 'Just the few things that mattered.'

Time was running out. Patrice Roussillon had been pressing Nell to return to Paris, saying she would lose a big contract if she didn't get back to Paris for a briefing. Alastair had appointments in St Emilion. Neither could stay to watch the engineers as they started their investigations. The party that gathered outside the barn consisted of me, Louise, Jake (reluctantly included by Edouard because the GPR search was his initiative), Edouard himself and two engineers. The expert on radar was a thin, sandy-haired man with a long, drooping moustache which gave him a sad expression. He introduced himself as Yves Legrand from Bordeaux. His young assistant Didier was already unloading equipment from the back of a small van. There were two main items - a device with a computer screen, keyboard and printer, and another mounted on a trolley with antennae sticking out.

The floor of the barn had been completely cleared. All around were the rusted old machinery, tools, ladders, boxes and other objects that had cluttered the floor, together with the chest of drawers that had contained the skeletal hand and the billhook.

The equipment was moved into the barn. Powerful lights had been rigged up to illuminate the floor. Their concentrated brightness obscured everything above eye-level, so that the ancient structure seemed to have disappeared. Legrand sat on a folding chair in front of the screen and explained the process. He spoke rapidly in French. Edouard began to translate but was soon confused by the technicalities and yielded to Jake, who appeared to understand the system.

Didier began to wheel the trolley slowly to and fro across the floor, working to a pattern that covered the whole area. as Jake explained. 'The mobile instrument sends signals below ground and picks up echoes from these.'

'Like sonar searching for submarines,' I said.

'Exactly. The echoes show up as a trace on the screen there. Any voids below the floor or places where the ground has been disturbed and not properly consolidated will show up on the trace.'

We gathered round the screen which displayed patterns as the trolley moved on its course. Legrand pressed a button and the printer began to chatter. Paper spilled out in a continuous sheet which folded onto the floor.

Jake said: 'That's a permanent record of the trace on the screen. Legrand will interpret it for us.' He pointed. 'I can already see some irregular shapes. Voids, possibly.' He turned to Legrand. 'Il y a des vides là, monsieur, vous pensez?'

Legrand kept his eyes on the screen and shrugged. 'Peut-être.'

Getting tired of watching, we left Jake and went outside. Edouard asked Louise: 'Where did you say you met the young American?'

'At Auch, the night of the concert. He remembered me from London when James introduced him to me.'

'He's a je-sais-tout, don't you think? A bit of a know all.'

I defended him. 'We wouldn't be doing this if it weren't for him.'

'Well, let's see what happens,' said Edouard.

Jake came out to say the whole floor had been covered. We returned to the barn to find Legrand studying the print-out. Without a word he began to pace across the floor to the opposite end where he stopped close to the wall on the southern side, pointed with a sweep of one arm along an imaginary line and said:

'Voilà, mesdames et messieurs! La cave que vous cherchez. Autour d'ici. Assez grand, je crois.'

It took two days to organise the dig. Edouard wouldn't be hurried. The excavation had to be done with great care so as not to imperil the barn. To this end he had engaged a structural engineer and a local builder. While we waited for the work to begin Louise invited Jake to stay at Les Loriots, the house Edouard had lent her before their marriage. He was greeted boisterously by Balou and with a fierce handshake from Jean-Marc, the gardien. 'Nothing escapes him,' said Louise. 'He knows every inch of the land around.'

Jake asked if he knew where the pilgrim's remains had been discovered. Jean-Marc agreed to take him and me.

The way into the woods was closely hemmed by trees and thickets. Even in daylight it was a lonely and eerie place. There was no evidence of wildlife. The burly gardien progressed like an experienced tracker. It was hard to see how he knew when to change direction. Occasionally I spotted a slashed branch. Monsieur Bray had done this, Jean-Marc said.

He walked steadily ahead in silence, his eyes moving from side to side and his gun under his arm. At last we came to a track which Jean-Marc said was the work of les maladroits flics trampling the undergrowth with their grosses chaussures. The grave was at the end of this track. I'd been here before, of course. A barbed-wire fence had been erected around the spot and there was a small plaque announcing that this was the former resting place of an unknown pilgrim of the 11th or 12th century whose bones had been placed in the crypt of the church at Marcignac.

We stood side by side in silence.

'A lonely place for a grave,' Jake said at last.

I nodded. 'But where else could they have buried him? They'd been travelling for weeks. If one of them died on the road they would have no choice but to bury him on the spot and continue their journey. The pilgrims had to move on.'

'What about the marble with the inscription?'

'The monks at Flaran would have brought it here later.'

Jake suggested that Magnus could have been killed by brigands.

'My father didn't think so.'

'And you?'

'François was in a pitiful state, full of remorse. I'm sure he did it. I think his companions knew he did it.'

'He allowed the Jewel to be buried with Magnus.'

'He had to. He thought he could dig it up later. He stayed behind.'

'Intending to take the Jewel to the Abbey?'

'No.'

'Wouldn't he have wanted to go to the abbey and make a full confession and receive absolution?'

'He couldn't confess and keep the joyau, could he? The Journal was his confessional. It was also a coded message, hoping someone would find the Jewel and take it to the shrine so his mission could be accomplished.'

'And your father unlocked the code.'

I smiled. 'My father was a brilliant man.'

At dinner the following evening Edouard announced that work would start early the next morning. The print-out from the ground penetrating radar clearly showed a small area close to one wall of the barn where there may have been some infill and a much larger area of voids close to this.

Monsieur Clamaron, the structural engineer, said the area of possible infill would be the best place to start work with least risk to the building. He was worried that digging near the wall could destabilise it. The stonework was heavily eroded on the exposed west side, with wide gaps in the mortar. Despite its thickness a medieval wall would probably have only slight foundations and could be quite precarious.

Piece by piece, the workmen carefully lifted some of the stone flags and stacked them to one side. The earth was dry and fairly loose. The diggers worked with pick and shovel, keenly watched by the whole party. When their work yielded nothing but piles of dry earth, the watchers tended to drift away and wander around the neglected garden before being drawn back to the barn in case of missing the moment of discovery.

The excavation was moving dangerously close to the wall of the barn when one of the picks struck something sounding like rock. Clamaron immediately ordered work to be stopped. The rock might be part of the wall's foundation. They would have to work very carefully.

Tentatively the earth was scraped away with trowels to reveal a smooth slab of limestone. Further scraping proved this to be about forty centimetres thick - too heavy to lift by hand. Leverage raised it slightly so that it could be propped. Clamaron supervised the making of a steel cradle to fit round the slab. This was agonisingly slow. An A-frame was erected and anchored. The cable was fed over the frame and attached to a winch.

At last the motor was started and the winch slowly drew the cable over the A-frame, lifting the cradle containing the slab just clear of the ground. We edged forward. Clamaron yelled for the motor to be stopped. He waved everyone back, shouting 'Reculez-vous! Reculez-vous! Prenez garde!'

As we drew back the slab was slowly winched higher until it could be swung away and lowered to the ground. Its removal revealed a black hole. Clamaron called out in English: 'Please stay back, ladies and gentlemen. There is danger still.'

He shone a flashlight into the darkness, illuminating a steep flight of narrow stone steps. I caught my breath.

Edouard patted Jake on the back. 'Well done, young man! You were right.'

He smiled at Louise and added: 'And Jake shall have the honour of being the first to go below. That is fair, don't you think?'

Clamaron said the air below would be foul. Anyone going into the newly opened cave would need an oxygen pack. They would also need a helmet with a lamp. He would have to send to the pompiers for these. It would be a convenient time to stop for the repas.

Louise took Jake to one side in my hearing. Edouard's proposal, she said, was not an honour nor a reward for enterprise but a penalty. 'I know him. He's being naughty. He wants to punish you for your presumption. Everyone will understand if you say no thanks.'

Jake laughed at her. 'Turn it down? You've got to be joking! Any serious historian would kill to get a chance like this!'

I stared at the immense size of the slab. Its weight had just been demonstrated. Surely a cellar should have a hinged wooden door. The slab was designed to block the entrance to all comers. It would also seal the exit.

Louise had prepared a packed lunch which we ate while we waited for the pompiers. We sat in the shade on the bank Jake and I discussed our visit to the grave. I offered to lend him the Journal.

'François calls the ring the res sacra - the holy thing. He was obsessed with it, though he probably never saw it after he had set out on his pilgrimage.'

'He must have been a pretty cool kinda guy,' said Jake.

'Not cool, desperate. He wept for Magnus.'

'How do you know?'

I looked away. 'I just do.'

At last Clamaron came over to say that all was ready. Jake was rigged out with the oxygen pack and light. He was also given a small transceiver so he could call for any advice he might need. Before he stepped into the hole he made a great show of shaking hands all round and acting like he was boarding a space flight or embarking on some other great adventure. Then he put the oxygen mask over his face, donned the helmet and lowered himself into the hole.

It was a tight fit. A powerful beam of light powered by a generator probed the way below for him, casting shadows as he slowly wriggled down and disappeared from sight. Within a few seconds his voice came over the loudspeaker. He spoke in short, breathy statements as he was obviously finding his way.

'Ten steps. Quite steep.
'Cut from the solid rock.
'Floor's rock, too.
'Quite dry.

'Narrow opening.
'People were a tad smaller in those days.
'I'm inside now.
'Ceiling's higher here.
'I can almost stand up.
'Whoops! Not quite!

'Looking round.
'Rough walls on every side.
'A space here.
'About four paces across.
'Quite empty.
'Wonder what they did here.
'Could have been a sleeping place.

'Can't see all at once.
'Have to turn my head, direct the lamp.
'There's writing on the wall here.
'Latin. I'll spell it out.
'ME TAMEN URIT AMOR.
'Got that, Julia?

'Vaulted roof, cut from solid rock.

'Was this really a hostel?

'More like a dungeon.

'Amazing to think of it!

'All in good shape.

'No furniture.

'More writing.

'Kyrie Eleison.

'Christe Eleison.

'And a crude drawing.

'Man lying prostrate before an upright cross.

'No figure on the cross.

'Faces of hideous devils watching the man.

'Real scary.

'Looking round now.

'Door in one corner.

'Oak, maybe, with a simple latch.

'Latch works okay.

'This is very spooky.

'Hope the radio's working.

'Are you getting me?

'Switching to receive. Over!

I switched to transmit and said: 'Okay. No problem. Those words are from Virgil, Jake. From one of the Eclogues. It's about a shepherd who loves a beautiful boy. It means 'Love still fires me'. Are you okay, Jake? Over.'

Jake's voice again, very quiet now.

'Yeah, Okay.

'I'm going to open the door now.

'Hey! The light flickered then.

'Thought it was going out, for Pete's sake!

'Batteries extra!

'Hinges are stiff.

'Door very heavy.

'Have to push against the floor.
'But opening.
'Going through.

'Seems like a bigger space.
'That guy said the cellar was assez grand.
'He was right.
'It's huge. Extraordinaire.

'Following the wall to my left now.
'Lots of writing here. All in Latin.
'Drawings too, and candles everywhere.
'Should have brought a camera.

'End of this wall.
'Turning right.
'Tiny chinks of daylight above.
'Air-holes, I think.
'Shall I test for air.
'Better not.
'This place will stink.

'Muck on the floor.
'Now we've got bottles.
'Earthenware pots.
'A wine store, maybe.

'There's water here.
'Must be an inlet somewhere.
'And a drain.

'Wow! Something moved there in the corner.
'Yeah, there it is again.
'Something small.
'Got in through the drain, I guess.
'God, this is a spooky place!

'Horrible pictures.

'Filth and cobwebs.

'Rags on the floor and...

'Oh Christ, save us! No!

There was a long, long silence. I called out: 'Jake, what is it? Jake, over! Are you receiving me?'

It seemed minutes before he came on again. His voice was husky. 'Sorry, guys, I'm coming back.'

It seemed like an age before Clamaron grasped Jake's outstretched hand and hauled him up the last steps. Standing up with difficulty, Jake took off the helmet and mask and shook his tousled hair. I helped him take off the oxygen pack and transceiver. Without a word he walked some distance from the barn and sat slumped on the grass with his back against a tree.

'Are you all right?' asked Louise anxiously, going over to him.

I unscrewed the cap from a bottle of Evian and handed it to him. He drank a large draught.

'Yeah, I'm okay.'

His account of the cellar came out in bits, none too coherently, repeating more or less what he'd said over the radio, hesitating to come to the final point. No one prompted him.

At last he took another mouthful of water, rubbed a hand across his face and said: 'He's there. Yeah, he's there. My God, what a sight! A heap of bones and filth like rubbish swept into a corner. Curled up real small. I didn't know what it was until I saw his skull staring at me! The empty eye sockets and yellow teeth and one arm stretched out as though reaching for something, but without a hand. Christ, no hand! And a piece of rag round his arm. Stains on the floor. And writing everywhere. On the walls. On stained bits of paper. God knows how long it had taken him to die.'

His usual briskness and confident manner were gone. He was like a man in deep shock after a car smash. Edouard offered him whisky from a pocket-flask. While he was recovering attended by me, the others gathered into a quiet group, discussing what should now be done. Edouard said the authorities would have to be told.

Louise asked if this was really necessary. Would it not be better to say nothing and simply seal off the cellar with all its horrors? It had been like this for eight hundred years. Why disturb it now?

I was appalled at the suggestion. François de Castres had to be given a Christian burial with a Mass for the repose of his soul. We must take photographs before anything was disturbed. All the writing and pictures must be recorded for translation and study. Then there must some kind of service of exorcism in the undercroft, around the barn and the house. 'That is what my father would have wanted - to release François from all his agonies and for us to discover the truth of his last days.'

42 - JULIA

Confirmation of the awful truth came within two days when the photographs had been taken. There was now no doubt that François's terrible death was self-inflicted. And it was terrible indeed. First, before descending into the cellar, cutting off his hand with the billhook and casting it away. And then, horror of horrors, self-immurement. How it was done they could only imagine. By some means he had enabled the heavy slab of stone to be propped so it would fall into place behind him as he entered the dungeon where he starved to death on the twenty-seventh day.

The last, barely legible words on the papers that lay beside his remains were Domine adiuvandum me festina. I translated: 'O Lord, make haste to help me!'

Louise remembered a piece of scripture that had always horrified her when it was read in Chapel. "If thy hand or thy foot offend thee, cut them off, and cast them from thee."

'There's one thing I don't understand,' said Jake. 'Leonard Bray found a modern translation of the Journal. There must be other copies as well as the original manuscript. So why has nobody else gotten on to this story.'

'Someone did,' I said. 'A crook called Malvin, but he's in a police cell awaiting trial on serious charges. The other copies seem to have sunk without trace. The professor who made the translation obviously found the Journal hard to swallow. When he came to the account of the joyau, he wrote that the legend was no more to be believed than that the bones of the saint were carried on an unmanned ship from the Holy Land to Galicia. His scepticism would put off most readers.'

'Your father wasn't put off,' Jake remarked.

'The family name de Castres hooked him. He virtually told me so.'

Jake said: 'How did he know about the bottles in the cellar?'

'He guessed. Cellars are where you keep wine. The note he wrote - third bin, and all that - was just a way of telling me to look for a cellar, that's all.'

'Unless he had some kind of....'

'Visitation?' I interposed.

'You said it. Who knows? And what about that bit of Virgil?'

'It's a poem about the shepherd Corydon who passionately loves a boy called Alexis but is scorned. I wonder how François knew Virgil?'

The news of the skeleton under the barn had probably been leaked by one of the contractor's men. Among the first of the media on the scene was the English journalist who had unsuccessfully tried to interview my father after the requiem mass at Marcignac. His newspaper had sent him from London to follow up the story. He asked me what had prompted me to use radar to search beneath the barn. He was persistent, saying I must have known there was something to find before going to such lengths, and suggesting that my father had led me to this discovery. What was known about this second skeleton? Could it be the remains of another pilgrim? How long might he have been there? How had he died?

I was as patient as I could be, honest in my answers but giving nothing away. I wasn't prepared to speculate, nor to be quoted. The bones would have to be carbon-dated before any conclusions could be drawn. The radar examination was made to confirm archaeological evidence that the barn once had an undercroft. What we had found was a great shock. All I could say about the dead man was that he had suffered a terrible end.

The journalist was far from content. He gave me his card and asked me to keep in touch. His newspaper might pay the costs of further investigations in return for an exclusive story.

There was also a local reporter from the SudOuest and an over-zealous French television crew who finally provoked me into asking the police to eject them. The police were already on site to follow up my report of the gruesome findings in the cellar. Two officers went down below with Jake to inspect and remove the grisly remains.

The slow wheels of officialdom would now begin to turn. An inquest, forensic tests. Only then could there be a Christian burial and a requiem mass.

Louise was delighted to hear from Nell. She showed me her letter.

Darling Lou,

I am still wondering at it all. Alastair and I talked endlessly about it last night at a super little restaurant he knows hidden away in a back street of the 5th. He came to Paris specially to see me! We talked about us too. I do like him, really, though I'm not sure about anything long term. I shall be going back to London next week and A. is taking me to see his father.

I can't get François out of my mind. Will Julia go ahead with an exorcism? I think she has to. That place is seriously spooky. When Jane hears about what's been going on she'll back out of the deal, won't she?

All that apart, it was marvellous to spend so much time with you. The house is lovely, even without the orioles. I've done some sketches which I'll send you when I get time to pack them properly. Pastels, but keep them far away from the Degas, please! I'm just a midget compared with that man.

Patrice was quite gracious when he said goodbye. He's come to accept that I'm not available. Besides, he's playing around with one of his clients. He may offer me more work in a month or two. If so, I shall be happy to come back. As you once memorably said to me, this is an embraceable city - if you take it on its own terms.

What about you, Lou? Are you truly happy? You ought to be. Edouard is a remarkable man and I've no doubt he loves you for what you are. Be good. I'd forget Jake if I were you.

Much love, Nell.

Nell said nothing to me about Jake but she was right about Jane backing out. I said 'I knew she could never live here with the barn next door and the constant reminder of what happened to François.'

'Not only Jane. When the story gets around it could be quite difficult for you to find a buyer.'

'I've already found one,' I said with a little smile.

Louise looked at me questioningly and then smiled too, knowing the answer. I nodded. 'Edouard has made me a good offer. He wants to bring the house back into the estate. He'll restore it and says I can use it whenever I want to come back. He says it's important for me to keep contact with the place where my father wrote his last book and where I found the Jewel. He's so thoughtful, Louise. You have a good husband."

* * *

With the help of Ferran, the sacristain at Marcignac, I found an elderly priest willing to undertake a form of exorcism on the site at Le Belvédère. Father Paul lived in a distant parish but, after listening to my detailed account of the life and death of François de Castres, agreed to drive over the following evening after Mass. He stipulated that no one was to attend except those present at the time of the discovery of human remains.

It was dusk when a much battered 2CV stumbled down the rutted track and shuddered to a halt outside the barn where Edouard, Louise, Jake and I were waiting. From it emerged a slight, stooping figure in a black, wide-skirted soutane. With his back to us, he reached inside to collect a small attaché case, a white surplice, a violet stole and a black biretta. He stepped back from the car, slipped the lace-trimmed surplice over his head, straightened it fastidiously and covered his thin grey hair with the biretta. He picked up the case and folded the stole over one arm before closing the door of the car and turning to face the welcoming party.

I introduced myself and the others. Father Paul's handshake was delicate, his fingers long and slender like a musician's, but any suggestion of softness was offset by piercing black eyes which glittered like beads of jet in his pale face. He immediately asked to be shown the barn.

Jake brought a lantern, opened one of the doors and led the way. The junk that had been removed to make way for the radar investigation had been piled neatly in one corner, leaving most of the floor unencumbered beneath the barn's massive oak frame. The lantern made but a slight pool of light in the dark interior. The priest stood in silence near the entrance, screwing up his eyes as if trying to fathom the distance. I took the lantern and bade him follow me carefully to the black hole where, I said, the steps led to the cellar and the human remains that had been discovered.

Father Paul said it was not necessary to go below. He removed his biretta, kissed the stole and put it round his neck. From his attaché case he took out a small crucifix and a phial of holy water, placing these on a convenient cross beam nearby. Holding his missal and another small book, he bowed reverently towards the crucifix and turned to face his tiny congregation.

'I shall use a modified form of the Rituale Romanum prescribed by Pope Paul the Fifth in the early seventeenth century for the exorcism of evil spirits. From what you tell me, this place is haunted by the spirit of a priest who has long since departed. You believe he bore the guilt of a mortal sin and died unshriven. You have told me how he expressed remorse in his journal and called upon God for mercy and comfort. If he never made confession to a priest, he would not have received absolution and therefore died in fear of damnation for grave sins unconfessed and not absolved. However you have told me how in his journal he published a form of confession, though without naming the greatest sin of which you believe him to have been guilty. God will judge him. It is for us to pity him and pray for him and, I hope, to release him from this place where his restless spirit still resides. Evil spirits may haunt him. I shall therefore use the Latin commands that have long been understood by evil entities who work to confound God's purpose. I ask you to turn your minds to this unhappy spirit and to pray continuously, each in your own way.'

We stood solemnly around the dark hole in the floor. After a long moment of silence, the act of exorcism began, just as Edouard had said it would, with sentences and responses from the Litany. Apart from the opening Kyrie Eleison, only he and I were familiar with the words. Father Paul then read, in Latin, from Psalm 54 - Cum clamarem ad Dominum, exaudivit vocem meam, ab his qui approprinquant mihi.

I whispered a resumé to Jake. 'When I call upon the Lord, he will hear my appeal for help against those who attack me.'

Father Paul then implored God's grace against the wicked dragon and cautioned all evil spirits to give some sign of the hour of their going out. The Gospel was the first chapter of St John prescribed to be read at Christmas, with its powerful declaration - In principio verbum erat - "In the beginning was the Word". The priest then protected himself by the sign of the cross. Slowly and firmly, stretching out his right arm with his index and longest fingers pointing imperiously he turned to all four quarters and uttered the first commanding and awesome words, threatening any evil entity that might be present. I whispered a translation as best I could for the benefit of Jake and Louise, helped by having read the book Edouard lent me. The archaic language would not have been easy for the other two.

'I exorcise you, most vile spirit, the very embodiment of our enemy, the entire spectre, the whole legion, in the name of Jesus Christ, to get out and flee from this place. He himself commands you, who has ordered those cast down from the heights of heaven to the depths of the earth. He commands you, he who commanded the sea, the winds and the tempests.

'Depart therefore in the name of the Father, and of the Son, and of the Holy Ghost. Give place to the Holy Ghost by the sign of the Cross of Jesus Christ our Lord, who with the Father and the same Holy Ghost lives and reigns one God, forever and ever, world without end.'

All spontaneously responded 'Amen'.

Turning again to the north, south, west and east and making the sign of the cross each time, Father Paul bade all evil that might be present in that place to yield, not to him as a man but to a minister of Christ.

'For his power urges you, who subjugated you to his cross. Tremble at his arm, who led the souls to light after the lamentation of hell had been subdued. May the body of man be a terror to you.'

He made the sign of the cross on his chest. 'Let the image of God be terrible to you.'

He made another sign on his forehead. 'Resist not and do not delay to flee from this place and though you know me to be a sinner, do not hold me in contempt. God the Father commands you. God the Son commands you. God the Holy Spirit commands you. The sacred cross commands you.'

'Go out! Give place to Christ! I adjure you in the name of the immaculate lamb who trod upon the asp and the basilisk, who trampled the lion and the dragon, to depart. Yield to God! Give place to the Holy Ghost!'

After a moment of complete stillness, he took up the phial of holy water and sprinkled it, first into the depths of the cellar, and then pacing all around with Jake beside him bearing the lantern and us following. He continued the while, with powerful adjurations, to command all evil spirits. I felt that any still at large must now be cowering in fear and awe of this god-given authority. I could almost imagine them, dark and awful, crawling away to whatever ghastly mire they inhabited - subjected, scourged and contemptuously dismissed by the almost palpable power that emanated from the slender fingers of this man of God.

I turned my mind, as Father Paul had instructed, to François: to his cries for help; to his great burden of guilt; to his love for Magnus that sinfully exceeded his love for God and brought him to a pitch of uncontrolled violence and so murder; to his theft of the ring and his futile belief in its healing powers; to his desperate act of self-punishment by the terrible amputation of his hand and his immurement in the undercroft, to suffer a long and lonely death haunted by demons. I prayed for him, that he would be released from his burden of guilt and find peace, repeating the words used by Ferran as he stood by the sarcophagus - "Qu'il repose en paix!"

'Requiescat in pace!' said Father Paul in concert with my thoughts, as he asked us to pray for the soul of "our brother in Christ".

Returning to the sombre hole that led to the cellar, the priest knelt and began the words of the Paternoster in French. Edouard followed and the others also knelt and picked up the words. Father Paul blessed himself, got to his feet, removed his stole and kissed it. He replaced the crucifix, the phial and his books in his small case and, without a word, left the barn. The exorcism was over.

Outside an enormous moon was rising above the horizon. No one spoke. The only sound was of a nightingale somewhere in the woods.

* * *

We turned off the Pilgrims' Road at Lavacolla. This seemed an appropriate place to rest, as I told Nell and Louise, as it was the last stop made by medieval pilgrims on the Camino de Santiago and so should be ours also. Here, as they approached the city dedicated to Saint James the Great, Saint Jacques or Sant' Iago, the weary but excited pilgrims would have gone out of their way to gain the first, distant view of the shrine by climbing Monte del Gozo. If they were riding, they would have dismounted at this point and made their way to the shrine on foot - barefoot, if they were specially penitential.

All that could now be seen from Lavacolla was the twentieth century's sprawling contribution to the scene. When we moved off again and came nearer to the city, modern developments all but concealed the great cathedral on the hill except for its three ornate towers with their steeples, cupolas, finials and crosses.

Finding somewhere to park the car seemed so mundane. How much better it would have been, said Nell, to walk barefoot along a cobbled road into the plaza del Obradoiro in ignorance of what to expect and there to be humbled and uplifted by the immensity and richness of Diego Gelmirez's extravagant architecture.

Louise had suggested we should stay the night next to the cathedral in the Hostál de los Reyes Catolicos, once a pilgrims' hostel, now a very luxurious parador. I overruled her. Though we had not travelled the Camino Santiago on foot, we were, I said, simple pilgrims, as François had set out to be. Five-star comfort would be quite inappropriate, so without consultation I had booked three rooms in a modest hotel in the Rua San Francisco, a mere two minutes walk from the plaza.

After checking in and leaving our bags we made our way to the huge square and stood near the entrance of the great Hostál, gazing at the flamboyant west front of the cathedral - a riot of baroque ornament with St James at the top of a central arch in the habit of a pilgrim. Two kings could be seen kneeling at his feet with a carving of the star that led the shepherds to his supposed burial place in a Galician field. The lintel of this arch was inscribed with the figures 1188, the year of its completion.

We drank water from bottles carried in our packs and watched groups of people making their way across the enormous plaza to the cathedral. Some were obvious tourists, others wearing the scallop-shell emblem that proclaimed them as pilgrims lined up below the stone staircase to the west entrance. They were of all ages and wore motley clothes, walking boots or trainers. After many weeks - months even - they had reached the end of an arduous road that began, for some, on the right bank in Paris, for some at the abbey in Vézelay, for others in Le Puy or Arles. Some would have come from beyond France.

It was more than an hour before the time appointed for my meeting with the unnamed cathedral functionary who was to receive me.

'What if he rejects it? asked Louise.

'He won't. Not out of hand,' said Nell. 'He'll want to hear Julia's account. He will take time. He will ask pointed questions.'

'A Spanish Inquisition?'

'A serious interrogation.'

Nell said: 'I would have thought that, even though they cannot prove the authenticity of the ring, they will want to add it to their other sacred treasures. Here it will be safe for all time. Isn't that what matters?'

I sat silently, nervously fingering the chain that hung inside the neck of my long-sleeved shirt. It was no longer a matter for discussion. My thoughts were with my father, wishing he could be here, feeling his presence somehow. The ring of St James would not be rejected, I was sure. Nell was right and whether or not the cathedral authorities approved it, all that mattered was that the ring should be kept here forever, for this was where it would already be were it not for the temptations and agonies of my kinsman François de Castres.

It was fifteen minutes to the appointed time. We got up and walked side by side across the wide expanse to climb the well-worn staircase to the door through which all pilgrims enter, prepared to marvel at what we knew lay beyond.